Issued to the Bride: One Airman

Cora Seton

Author's Note

Issued to the Bride One Airman is the second volume in the Brides of Chance Creek series, set in the fictional town of Chance Creek, Montana. To find out more about Brian, Cass, Connor, Sadie, Jack, Logan and Hunter, look for the rest of the books in the series, including:

Issued to the Bride One Navy SEAL
Issued to the Bride One Marine
Issued to the Bride One Sniper
Issued to the Bride One Soldier

Also, don't miss Cora Seton's other Chance Creek series, the Cowboys of Chance Creek, the Heroes of Chance Creek, and the SEALs of Chance Creek

The Cowboys of Chance Creek Series:

The Cowboy Inherits a Bride (Volume 0)
The Cowboy's E-Mail Order Bride (Volume 1)
The Cowboy Wins a Bride (Volume 2)
The Cowboy Imports a Bride (Volume 3)
The Cowgirl Ropes a Billionaire (Volume 4)
The Sheriff Catches a Bride (Volume 5)
The Cowboy Lassos a Bride (Volume 6)

The Cowboy Rescues a Bride (Volume 7)
The Cowboy Earns a Bride (Volume 8)
The Cowboy's Christmas Bride (Volume 9)

The Heroes of Chance Creek Series:

The Navy SEAL's E-Mail Order Bride (Volume 1)
The Soldier's E-Mail Order Bride (Volume 2)
The Marine's E-Mail Order Bride (Volume 3)
The Navy SEAL's Christmas Bride (Volume 4)
The Airman's E-Mail Order Bride (Volume 5)

The SEALs of Chance Creek Series:

A SEAL's Oath

A SEAL's Vow

A SEAL's Pledge

A SEAL's Consent

A SEAL's Purpose

A SEAL's Resolve

A SEAL's Devotion

A SEAL's Desire

A SEAL's Struggle

A SEAL's Triumph

Visit Cora's website at www.coraseton.com
Find Cora on Facebook at facebook.com/CoraSeton
Sign up for my newsletter HERE.
www.coraseton.com/sign-up-for-my-newsletter

Prologue

GENERAL AUGUSTUS REED knew better than most the way courage and cowardice raged a constant battle in a man's soul. All his life he'd felt confident courage won out as far as he was concerned.

Not today.

As he sat back in his wooden chair in his office at USSOCOM at MacDill Air Force Base in Tampa, Florida, his gaze rested on his cell phone. Soon enough he'd have to make a call he dreaded.

His daughter, Cass was getting married in a few hours.

And he wasn't there to walk her down the aisle.

There were all kinds of reasons why not. Reasons that involved meetings, tasks, duty—hell, even national security—but he could have overcome them if he'd really tried.

He hadn't tried at all.

He'd never once gone back to Two Willows after his wife, Amelia, died. That was more than anyone could expect him to do.

Even if it meant the gulf between him and his girls

had widened into an abyss.

At least he'd done one thing right, the General assured himself. Amelia had left him instructions to send Cass a man—a good man. He'd sent her a Navy SEAL.

Brian Lake.

Now Cass was marrying him. That filled him with a small sense of accomplishment. It was as if he'd managed to build a slender bridge to Two Willows, the ranch where his daughters lived. That bridge wouldn't hold his weight yet.

But maybe someday it would.

He opened the bottom left-hand drawer of his desk and surveyed the small stack of envelopes that remained there. His wife's legacy to him. Drawing out the top one, he smoothed his hand over Amelia's neat script. Cass had sent the box of letters shortly after her mother's death—when it became clear to both of them the General wasn't coming home.

He opened the letter Amelia had dated for today.

Dear Augustus,

I wish I could be there to see Cass walk down the aisle—and you with her. I know you are as handsome as ever, and Cass will enter her married life with her father's support and comfort through one of the most important days of her life.

The General stiffened.

Swallowed.

He'd let Amelia down—again.

But she didn't understand; his wasn't a job he could

turn his back on easily. Trouble could crop up anywhere in the world at any moment—it was a far different time—

The General blew out an angry breath. Did he think he could fool himself with his own lies?

Truth was he couldn't face the ranch. Couldn't walk the land she'd walked all her life. Two Willows was Griffith land—not Reed ground. Every inch of that property reminded him of his wife.

He wasn't ready to go back to it.

Not yet.

He returned to the piece of paper in his hand. Up until Amelia's death, the General had been able to wave away her hunches and suspicions as mere women's intuition. But nothing could explain these letters. Letters she'd written before her stroke. Years of letters carefully dated—each of them prescient in ways the General could hardly believe.

Augustus—enough bullshit. I know you're not at Two Willows for Cass's wedding. I've tried to ignore these feelings—this intuition—through all the letters I've written you so far, because I cannot believe a man brave enough to face death a thousand times over during his career has succumbed to a fear so irrational.

The General stared at the page. Read those sentences again. This was an Amelia he'd never seen before—or read before. She… knew?

Knew how badly he'd failed her?

Augustus, treading on Two Willows land won't

make me any more dead, just as sitting there in your office won't make me any more alive. You are a man of science—of knowledge. You know this. What are you doing in Florida when Cass is marrying the man she loves?

The General couldn't have been more shocked if Amelia had walked through the door and bashed him with her pocketbook, which he'd figured she'd like to have done once or twice when she was alive.

She never had, though. Had never raised her voice to him—not like this.

Now her exasperation spilled right off the page.

What's done is done. But it's time to pull yourself together and get it right. It's Sadie's turn. Do you have a man for her?

He did. Thank God. It was a small straw, but the General grasped it with all his might. Connor O'Riley was about to leave for Two Willows. He should arrive before the reception was over.

Send him. And while you're waiting for the magic to happen between them, start putting your affairs in order and get ready to go home. It's been far too long, Augustus. You know that.

Your loving wife,
Amelia

He did know that. And Amelia was right; he should go home. It was time—long past time, if he was honest with himself.

But that didn't make it easier.

"General?" The door opened and Corporal Myers stuck his head in. "General, things just went all to hell in—"

"Thank God!" The General surged to his feet, startling the corporal but ready for action. For decisions. For the kind of work that would keep him up day and night for weeks handling an international crisis.

He'd head to Two Willows when it was over.

If something else hadn't gone wrong in the world that he needed to fix.

Chapter One

PARARESCUEMAN CONNOR O'RILEY was standing in the large square office he'd shared at USSO-COM these past three months, when Logan Hughes walked in whistling, sat down at his desk and thunked a tall takeout cup of coffee near the monitor of his computer. A barrel of a man from Idaho, with biceps as big as cantaloupes, the marine was always cheerful, and Connor had grown to enjoy his sense of humor.

"Hello, baby girl!" Logan kissed the palm of his hand and slapped it against the photograph of a dark-haired young woman with blue eyes that hung on the wall nearby. Then he pulled a breakfast sandwich out of a paper bag and began to eat.

"Don't let the General see you do that," Connor said automatically. The photograph was of the General's daughter—Lena Reed—and the General didn't stand for any nonsense where his family was concerned.

"Don't let him see me eat?" Logan asked in mock confusion.

"For fuck's sake," Jack Sanders said from across the room. "Do you two have to do the same routine every.

Single. Damn. Morning?" Jack was a member of the Special Forces whose far more serious disposition was always at odds with Logan's lighthearted joking.

"Nope. This is the last time," Connor said. It was true—he was due on a plane in just over two hours. He'd land in Montana before the day was done, and soon he'd see Lena Reed in person. But he wasn't traveling to the General's ranch to visit Lena. Sadie Reed was his mark.

He glanced at the photograph that hung over his desk, near enough to slap a kiss on like Logan had Lena's. He'd been staring at Sadie Reed for nearly three months, trying to come to terms with the strange twist his life had taken.

Soon she'd be his wife.

Of course, she didn't know that yet.

"Thank God," Jack said. "Because I don't think I could stand it anymore."

"Just because O'Riley's leaving doesn't mean I plan to stop." Logan took another large bite of his sandwich. He chewed and swallowed. "Lena and me have gotten to be old friends." He patted the photograph.

Connor rolled his eyes. The General had done a fine job pairing his oldest daughter, Cass, with Brian Lake, a Navy SEAL who'd been here for the first month of their joint time at USSOCOM. Despite the fact he'd never had any intention of marrying, Connor thought he, himself, had a fair chance with Sadie, who seemed a practical—and pretty—young woman with a penchant for gardening. But he had no idea what the General had been thinking when he picked Logan for any of his girls—or Jack, or Hunter Powell, the Navy SEAL sniper who rounded out the "task force," either. Logan's brashness would clash with Lena's reputed temper.

As for the pairing of the youngest Reed daughter, Jo, with the battle-hardened Hunter? How could the General have made such a mismatch? At thirty-four, Hunter was the oldest of them. Jo, with her elfin, mischievous face, was only twenty-one. The two would have nothing in common.

But by far the worst of the pairings had to be Jack and Alice Reed. If he hadn't known Jack was with the Special Forces, he would have pegged him as CIA. A slipperier man he'd never come across, and he'd seen the soldier eye Alice's photograph with similar doubt. Alice was beautiful, Connor would grant her that, but it was a beauty as otherworldly as the premonitions Brian said she had. According to the SEAL, Alice was as fey as an Irish pixie, and Connor, who'd grown up on tales of the wee folk, knew well enough not to mess with them.

How on earth was a girl like Alice going to fall in love with a just-the-facts, cagey man like Jack?

And what was the world coming to when an airman like himself had to be this concerned with the love lives of the men around him?

It was all the General's fault, of course.

But no—that wasn't true, was it?

It was all his own fault. And love was what had gotten him into this mess in the first place. The irony of that hadn't been lost on him.

Connor had given up on love a long time ago. He'd wrung it out of his system as just another lie that people believed because it made them feel better. He'd seen the way love could get two people in its grip, bring them together and then tear them apart. His own parents' divorce had put an ocean and most of a continent between him and the mother and brother he'd loved. It had ripped him from the country he'd called his home for his first ten years. It had taken his magical, safe childhood and crushed it under the heel of the rancor and discord that had divided his family ever since.

Connor liked women, and dated frequently, but he'd never—not once—risked losing his heart. Not to Lila, who he'd met on leave, nor to Bridget, who he'd met through a dating app, nor to the other women he'd flirted with online and met up with in person when the timing worked out.

So he still couldn't explain why he'd lost his head during his last mission.

As a pararescueman, he'd made many jumps into difficult circumstances, and he'd seen things that would leave most men curled into a fetal position for days. But the last jump he'd made into Syria had touched him in ways nothing had before or since. Not because of the injuries sustained by the pilot he'd been sent to rescue; the pilot had survived, and that was what counted.

But because during that short and successful mission, for the first time in his life he'd witnessed true love—and true selflessness.

And had been thoroughly humbled by both.

He'd gone beyond the bounds of his mandate to rescue two innocent bystanders in that godforsaken war. He'd thought he'd done what was right.

Too bad the Air Force disagreed.

So here he was at USSOCOM as one of the General's misfits. Part of the Joint Special Task Force for Inter-Branch Communication Clarity—a bullshit title for a team that didn't even exist. All Connor and the rest of the men who had landed here three months ago had done was kill time with busywork that accomplished nothing.

They weren't here to do anything but wait their turn to serve the General's real purpose for them. One by one he'd ship them off to Two Willows. One by one he'd marry them off to his daughters. Bit by bit the man would reclaim control of his ranch after a feud with his girls that had lasted for years.

And by following the General's orders and playing his part in the ruse, Connor would clear his record of the big black stain that threatened to dog him through the rest of his life. In the process he'd become part owner in a jewel of a ranch in Chance Creek, Montana. He'd get a new start. Another chance.

A wife.

At first Connor had been as horrified as the other men at the predicament he found himself in, but as the weeks had passed and he'd followed Brian's progress from intruder, to fiancé, to Cass's soon-to-be husband at Two Willows, he'd come to see his fate might not be so bad.

Connor missed ranching. It was in his blood, after all. He'd ridden as soon as he could walk, first at his mother's family's small holding in Ireland, and then—after his parents' divorce—on the huge Texas spread where his father worked as overseer. Connor had always wanted his own place. Always thought it was out of reach.

But it wasn't anymore.

The only catch was he had to pledge his heart to Sadie Reed, whose enigmatic face had stared out of the frame hanging by his desk for the last three months. Sadie, who by all accounts was as tied to her Montana ranch as he'd thought he was tied to Ireland as a child. She had tended its extensive gardens—and its hedge maze—since she was young, and she ran a farm stand and sold herbal cures to her neighbors, according to Brian.

He remembered the helicopter ride back from Syria. Remembered Halil's words in the midst of all the chaos and noise. *Find a wife. Make her your everything.* Advice from a stranger, in a war zone, on the other side of the world.

Exactly what he'd always sworn to himself he'd never do.

Exactly what he had to do now.

It was going to be all right, he told himself. Despite his past, he could make a commitment and stick to it.

Because from everything Brian had told them, Two Willows was as special a place as his mother's small holding, *Ard na Greine*, in Ireland, and he could see for himself Sadie was a special woman. If he had to marry—and he had to, not just for his own sake, but for the sake of every man in this room—he could do a lot worse.

If Sadie would have him.

Logan finished his sandwich, balled up the wrapper and pitched it into the trash can across the room, pulling Connor from his thoughts.

"Ready to catch yourself a wife, O'Riley?" he asked.

"Ready as I'll ever be." Connor wondered who'd take over his line tomorrow in their daily routine. Jack? Probably not. Hunter?

Nah.

"See you on the other side," he told them, all too used to these kinds of unanswered questions. Someday maybe they'd all be together again on the ranch.

But only if he succeeded at his mission.

And married Sadie Reed.

HER GARDEN WAS dying.

On the morning of Cass's wedding, Sadie stood among the rows of plants, her practiced eye noting the yellow and brown shadings among the verdant green. She'd learned the art of tending the three acres that formed the kitchen garden, and the hedge maze that took up an additional acre, at her mother's knee, parroting the Latin names and uses of each plant as her mother imparted the information she'd learned from her mother before her. She still ran the farm stand her mother had run, and her mother before her. It sat at the end of the lane, and worked on the honor system, with prices clearly marked and a tin for her customers to leave their money in.

Sadie couldn't remember a time when she hadn't spent her days here, or in the maze, or in the long, large greenhouse where she started delicate seedlings, grew plants used to a milder climate and prepared the herbs that went into her remedies.

Only once had she let the wider world interfere with her duties, and that had ended disastrously in a shoot-out that almost took her sisters' lives just a few weeks ago. Mark Pendergrass was gone—wounded, soon to go on trial and hopefully be locked up for a long time. Sadie was glad. She didn't know how he'd managed to steal her heart. Had no idea how she'd missed all the signs that he was nothing but trouble—that he'd been using her all along to get to her ranch.

Mark and his friends had wanted to use Two Willows as a home base for their large drug distribution network. Cass's fiancé, Brian, had helped to drive them out. Cass had fought for the ranch, too. So had Lena.

Sadie had done nothing. And her shame at the part she'd played in nearly losing her family's home still made her heart ache every time she thought of it.

Now the very land was punishing her.

How else to explain the damage in her garden? Sadie had nourished each and every one of these plants from tiny seedlings she'd cared for in the greenhouse. She'd transplanted them with one eye on the phase of the moon and the other on the weather. She'd fed them, watered them, cared for them. Even sung to them from time to time.

Why were they dying?

Because of her betrayal?

Sadie knelt beside a tomato plant that had only recently grown as tall as her thigh and bushed out well beyond the cylindrical cage that gave support to its stem, but now had shrunk in on itself, its foliage a sickly yellow-green that made Sadie wince. Its fruit was withering on their stems, the thin, wrinkly skin of the tomatoes auguring tasteless sponginess rather than firm, mouthwatering bursts of flavor.

Why? Why was this happening?

Because she'd turned her back on her garden? Neglected it in favor of following Mark Pendergrass around on his errands, waiting on him hand and foot, hoping for a morsel of his attention?

She was lucky she hadn't received any, she knew now. Lucky she hadn't even tempted the man. He'd squired her around in public like they were a couple— sometimes. The rest of the time he'd ignored her unless he needed her for something. He'd kissed her a couple of times. Groped her once or twice. That was the extent of his attentions, something that had shamed her at the time. She'd felt he treated her like some childish virgin, which she wasn't, even if she hadn't had a string of boyfriends. Now his neglect left her thanking her lucky stars.

To have slept with the man who'd tried to kill her

sisters—

That would be too much to bear.

"I'm done with men," she told the tomato. "Forever."

The tomato didn't listen. It didn't speak to her, either, even when she touched its leaves. Even when she dug her fingers into the dirt at its roots. Not a word.

Not that tomatoes spoke with words.

Sadie had always felt the plants communicated with her in the same way the future communicated with her sister Alice. "It's like I can hear—or see—or something," Alice always said when people questioned her about her hunches. "Like I have access to information other people don't."

That's what it felt like to Sadie in her garden. When she was near a plant she simply knew what it needed, as if it had told her in words.

At least, that was how it had always been—until the day of the shoot-out.

Since then it had all shut down. She couldn't hear or see or feel anything—about the tomatoes, the carrots, the herbs, the berries out back of the greenhouse, or the hedge that formed the maze, either. The whole ranch had gone silent. A door had shut on her, cutting off the most important part of her existence—her connection with the growing things.

Her connection with her mother.

Sadie knew what it meant. The ranch didn't want her here anymore. Everyone had told her Mark wasn't the one for her. Even the plants had shrunk away from him whenever he came near. She'd known he was trouble. She'd known everything she was doing with him was wrong.

She'd done it anyway.

Now she had to pay.

The price was steep—steeper than she'd ever thought possible. Because while Sadie had foreseen a day when Mark would lose interest in her, and she'd always known it was possible she might be caught helping him in his illicit activities—and suffer the consequences of being found guilty, including the censure of her sisters—she'd never once dreamed that the ranch itself would turn on her and kick her out.

"I'm done with men," she told the garden again. "I'm done, I swear. I'll devote my life to you. I'll never look at another man for as long as I live."

A half-ripe tomato fell with a plop off the shriveled plant into the dirt.

Her remorse wasn't good enough. Her broken heart wasn't enough.

"I don't want you to die," she whispered to the plants surrounding her. She'd lost too much that she loved already. More than eleven years had passed since her mother died. All that time she'd kept her promise to Amelia. She'd kept the garden flourishing, nurtured her sisters, and their neighbors, too. She'd done everything she could to keep her mother's spirit alive in the growing things at Two Willows.

But that was over. If it was a choice between her happiness and the health of Two Willows, the ranch had to come first.

The signs were clear.

She had to leave.

For good.

WHEN CONNOR KNOCKED on Two Willows's front door, he could tell Brian and Cass's reception was in full swing at the back of the house, but he'd been raised right, and he wouldn't walk into a wedding uninvited. He shoved his hands in his pockets, and took a deep breath to settle his nerves. Soon he'd meet Sadie—the woman he was supposed to marry.

Things like this didn't happen to a man every day.

In truth, he didn't know what to make of Sadie. She wasn't his type. The women he dated were bold, fun-loving—as apt to pick him up in a bar as he was to pick up them. Women who knew exactly what they want-ed—and saw what they wanted in him.

Connor had never felt any impetus to settle down before. Why would he? He knew what marriage was—a temporary pretense masked as something permanent. A vehicle for promises men and women couldn't keep.

His parents' marriage had torn two families apart. Forged on a holiday when his mother and father had met in Paris, their long-distance relationship couldn't stand up to the realities of living together when his father had left Texas and moved to Ireland to be with his new wife.

Connor supposed he should give his dad credit for lasting thirteen years in a country where the ranches were called farms, and the largest of them were a fraction of the size of the Texas holdings he'd grown up around. Not that his father ever owned the land he worked there. He'd been a foreman all his days, and hoped Connor would follow in his footsteps.

But Connor wanted his own land. That was why he'd joined up in the first place. He'd planned to scrimp and save until he could buy some—but land was expensive.

Which was why he was here.

Part of the reason, anyway.

Sighing in exasperation, not wanting to remember the other half of the equation that had brought him to this Montana ranch, he pounded on the door with his fist. Couldn't anyone hear him?

It would be good to see Brian again. The Navy SEAL had—

The door swung open and Connor forgot everything but the woman standing in front of him.

Sadie Reed. Dressed in a spring-green bridesmaid gown, her hair piled on top of her head. She looked thinner than she had in the photo back at USSOCOM. He saw a wariness in her eyes he hadn't noticed before. She looked older than her twenty-two years somehow, but at the same time she had an innocence about her he found unnerving. She was... stunning. Something shifted in Connor's heart, exposing a chink in the armor he'd surrounded it with. He'd always prided himself on his ability to remain detached. Without warning, that detachment gave way to a desire to connect. He nearly reached out and touched Sadie—until he saw her eyes widen and he snatched his hand back. Desperate to fill the awkward silence between them, Connor did what he always did when the situation got tense.

Fell back on the Irish accent he could still produce at will. He hammed it up to show he wasn't taking any of this seriously—least of all the heritage he'd left behind.

"Well, hello there, lassie," he said heartily, as Irish as the green hills of County Galway. "You must be Sadie Reed. I'm Connor O'Riley. The General sent me."

THE WORDS OF greeting Sadie had prepared when she heard the knock on the front door died on her lips when she took in the handsome features of the man before her. He was tall, broad-shouldered, lean with muscle, with hair so dark brown it was almost black and piercing blue eyes that danced with mischief. But it was his outrageously fake Irish accent that left her speechless. No one quite so unusual had ever washed up on her doorstep before.

"That's right. I'm Sadie." She made no move to ask him in, despite his mention of her father. The General had sent Brian, after all—the man Cass had married just an hour ago. And even if that had turned out for the best, Sadie was still wary of anyone who had the General's approval.

She let the silence stretch out—a tactic she'd learned from the General himself. People liked to fill silences. Maybe this Connor O'Riley would spill the beans about why he was really here.

"The General says it's time," Connor said finally when it became clear she didn't mean to speak. He stepped forward, edging his way into the house.

Sadie took in the rucksack he carried. Her suspicions grew. Did he mean to stay?

"Time for what?" She shifted and blocked his way so he couldn't pass the lintel of the door. Up close, she had to crane her neck to see his face. Connor was no shrinking violet. His biceps, covered with a blazer appropriate for the occasion, strained his sleeves and she didn't think her two hands could encompass his muscles if he flexed his arm. His thighs nicely filled out the black jeans he wore with the jacket.

Those were cowboy boots under his jeans, she realized. Was this man at home on a ranch?

Why did that thought light a curl of interest low in her belly? His raffish good looks weren't enough to fool her.

"Time to start building," Connor said.

Sadie had to admit he was easy on the eyes. She felt drawn to him despite herself. Wanted to know more about him.

Which meant she was a hopeless case.

Tangling with Mark Pendergrass should have taught her that no man was worth falling for. He'd chewed her up and spit her out—humiliating her in the process. Even now she felt vulnerable—naked almost—dressed in this bridesmaid gown, a pretty picture for a man's enjoyment. Connor looked like he was enjoying the sight of her all too much.

She couldn't wait to change back into her jeans.

"Building what?" she asked in exasperation. "You aren't making any sense."

"Building your legacy." Connor eased forward until he had room to set his rucksack down. Sadie eased back. What else could she do faced with this monster of a man?

"My... legacy?" What was he talking about? The only legacy she had was the pain and shame of her own behavior these past few months. She'd fallen for a man who cooked meth—whose business it was to profit off the suffering and addiction of others. A criminal and the kind of person she'd been raised to despise.

She'd spent months dancing to his tune like a puppet.

A senseless, stupid puppet.

She wasn't going to be fooled again. Not by any man.

Not by this... joker.

"Your mother made Two Willows's gardens what they are today. She caused the greenhouse to be raised and planted the maze around the standing stone."

Connor had dropped the exaggerated Irish brogue, leaving her wondering if he was Irish at all. He could be as American as she was.

"Now it's your turn," he went on. "You want to put your mark on this ranch, don't you? What do you want me to help you build?"

The ground shifted beneath Sadie's feet and suddenly she wondered if it was her mother, not the General, who'd sent this man.

An image filled her mind—a walled garden—a place to withdraw from the world when it made no sense, when only growing things and the birds that visited could soothe the soul. She saw herself standing at a doorway looking in through a circular portal formed by a curved gate and the arch above it. A magical entrance to a magical place she could retreat to when the world got too much.

Connor's eyes flashed, as if he'd caught a glimpse of the vision she'd seen.

"Whatever you can think of, I can build," he told her, leaning closer. "Like I said, the General sent me. Today we celebrate your sister's wedding. Tomorrow we get to work."

SHE WAS HOOKED. Just like that.

Connor saw the light go on in Sadie's eyes and knew she'd thought about her legacy—surprising in one so young.

But as quickly as that light turned on, it blinked off again. Her wariness was back.

"I don't need anyone's help to build a legacy," she said as if it was the most ridiculous idea in the world. "My legacy is my healing. I help people every day. At least—"

She trailed off. Connor took another step forward. Sadie stepped back. He was almost far enough inside the house to shut the door behind him, and somehow

Connor knew it was imperative he be able to shut it. She could still drive him away. And he'd be damned if he'd leave now that he'd met Sadie.

"I need to pay my respects to Cass. The General gave me something for her."

Sadie bit her lip. He could almost see her mind racing to solve this dilemma. She wanted to block him from her home, but already he was in the door, with a present in his hand for her sister—from her father. How could she kick him out?

Connor took advantage of her hesitation, stepped forward and shut the door behind him.

There.

Home free.

Thank God. Connor knew he'd do whatever it took to actually make this his home.

"Five minutes. Then you need to hightail it out of here and back to the General. We let in one of his goons; we don't need any more. And I don't need your help building a legacy."

"Sure you do." He reverted to the brogue. "Every lovely lass needs a legacy."

Ignoring her protests, he dropped his rucksack and strode through the house, intent on finding the party, but he faltered when he reached the large, old-fashioned kitchen. He'd heard from Brian that this room had taken the most damage during the shoot-out that occurred when drug dealers came after Cass and Lena a few weeks ago, but it was one thing to hear about it and another altogether to see it with his own eyes.

He knew there hadn't been time between the shoot-out and the wedding to renovate the house, which is partly why the wedding was being held outdoors. Brian had ripped out the damaged lath and plaster walls, leaving the studs still visible.

The windows had been replaced, and he could tell the back door was new. But what kept his gaze frozen in place was the heavy, old-fashioned table that stood in the center of the large room.

Bullets had scored several deep grooves in the wood. Connor leaned over and ran his hand across one of them. Did the General know how close his daughters had come to disaster? If so, why wasn't he here, himself?

He looked up to find Sadie watching him.

She shrugged. "I wasn't here," she said. "Not until the end." Her shuttered expression hinted at pain as she made her way to the back door. "Cass is outside."

He figured he'd save his questions for another time. He knew Sadie's boyfriend—ex-boyfriend—had been one of the men who shot up the house that night. Mark Pendergrass was still getting over significant injuries while awaiting trial. Just the thought of him made Connor's hands ball into fists.

"I'll be glad to have another man around the place I can trust," Brian had told him on the phone several days ago. Connor knew he was afraid of reprisals. When he and the Reed women had blown up the trailer where the dealers had stashed their drugs on Two Willows' land, they'd put a crimp into a large operation.

Outside, the reception was in full swing. Guests ate barbecued chicken and steak and any number of other dishes laid out buffet style on tables on the lawn. Someone handed Sadie a glass of champagne. Connor accepted one, too. Sadie led him to where Cass stood talking to a small knot of guests. Brian stood by her side.

"Connor!" Brian spotted him, broke away from the guests and came to greet him, engulfing him in a quick, manly hug accompanied by several slaps on the back.

"Brian—looking good."

"Meet Cass."

Brian made the introductions and Connor shook her hand. "Glad to meet you," he said honestly. "Brian's a lucky man."

"I'm glad to meet you, too," Cass said, smiling. Connor could see why Brian had fallen for his bride. There was something open and honest about Cass's expression, and Connor knew she was optimistic and hardworking from everything Brian had told him.

"He's got something for you," Sadie told her sister, nodding toward Connor. "Something from the General."

Cass's eyes widened. "From the General?"

"I was just with him, ma'am," Connor said. "Flew in to Chance Creek today. Hope you don't mind; the General sent me to stay awhile." He passed her the small wrapped gift the General had handed to him.

"He did?" She glanced at Brian for an explanation. Brian just shrugged.

"I'm here to help Sadie—with her legacy."

"Legacy?" Cass repeated, much as Sadie had earlier. Now she looked to her sister, but Sadie simply lifted a shoulder.

"According to him, I'm supposed to plant another maze."

"Not another maze," Connor corrected. "Something that calls to you. Something that's all your own."

"What kind of a plant would that be?" Cass looked confused.

"No—not a plant; a legacy. It could be anything." Connor warmed to his theme. He'd been the one who'd proposed the idea to the General when he'd learned the history of the maze and standing stone from Brian. Two Willows was a special place, and he knew from his childhood special places needed to be tended and expanded in ways that connected people to them. A standing stone was something that drew people to a certain place in a landscape. A maze was another. Sadie needed to come up with a third. "Anything I can plant or build."

"We could use a better clothesline," Cass said.

Sadie rolled her eyes. "A clothesline isn't a legacy," she said before Connor could say so. "He means something like... like... a walled garden."

Connor's instincts sprang to life. Sadie did get it— and she did have dreams he could translate into reality. He'd build her something that made her as interested in him as he was in her at this moment.

"That's it exactly. A walled garden—with benches

and pathways and a fountain—"

"It was just an example," Sadie said sharply. "It's not something I actually want."

She might as well have doused him with cold water.

"Well, whatever you do want, I'll build it," he reiterated. It took a lot more than a surly lass to throw him off the scent of his mission.

"That sounds lovely." Cass's lips twitched in a way that told Connor she saw right through him, right through this whole situation.

"That sounds like the General interfering again," Sadie said.

HER LEGACY. SHE didn't need a legacy, Sadie thought as she watched Cass unwrap the General's gift—a beautiful necklace that made both of them go silent. It was a locket like the one he'd given their mother long ago. Sadie remembered Amelia wearing it all the time when she was young, but the necklace had gone missing only weeks before her death. She wondered if the General knew that?

Forcing those old memories away, she kept her mind on her own problems. The legacy she'd lost. No one had noticed so far—not Cass, not any of her sisters—but soon everyone would realize something had gone horribly wrong with her. Her glance strayed to her extensive garden, the greenhouse beyond it—and the maze. From here the rows and squares of vegetables and herbs still looked lush and well-tended. But her sharp, practiced eyes could pick out the first signs of trouble.

Spots on otherwise emerald-green leaves. Brown edges. Drooping stems. Infestations of hungry insects.

All through the garden, nature was playing havoc with her plants.

And it scared Sadie. Scared her more than anything else had since the day her mother died, and even on that occasion her intuition with the plants had been strengthened by the sudden shock—not wiped out by it.

But now she felt like she was working blindfolded when she went out to the garden. Worse, like her plants didn't recognize her. Like she was anyone who'd stumbled into their rows rather than the one person who had a special connection to them.

Not to mention she couldn't create her cures, which were her real legacy. Without that connection to her plants she couldn't compound her tinctures and tonics and salves.

What had happened to her?

A man's loud laugh made Sadie jerk around to search the crowd, her heart in her throat.

Was that Mark?

No—of course not. Thank God.

Sadie got herself under control. Mark was in the hospital... under guard. She was safe from him.

She wasn't safe from her memories, though.

She still couldn't believe she'd been so stupid to let Mark use her like she had. She'd been a fool to think such a handsome man was interested in her—or that he'd been worth the time of day.

Mark was a criminal. A callous, miserable loser. Someone who designed drugs to hook their users and siphon off all their money until he'd wrung every last penny from them. Once the scales had fallen from her eyes, Sadie had become aware for the first time in her life of the way that drugs pervaded her little town. People were using them to escape from their problems—to have a little fun. But by using them they were letting trouble into their lives.

Letting Mark into their lives, with his greedy hands outstretched demanding more money—and more and more.

Thank God she hadn't fallen down that trap. She'd tried pot once—didn't like it. Had told Mark so, and he'd backed off. Of course, he hadn't been after *her* money; he'd only wanted her land, and the ability to use her ranch as a cover.

She scanned the happy crowd around her again. Wondered who among them were hiding secret addictions. She hoped not many; she wished happiness to all of them. Wanted it for herself.

It was funny about the pot—it hadn't slipped her into that comfortable state she'd heard about—that Mark had told her she'd like. Instead, the herb had whispered to her of its true meaning, and in her mind's eye she'd seen the religious rites once practiced with it, the way a certain set of peoples had once understood it as a pathway to the divine.

Now it had been overbred, planted far beyond its natural borders, hyped up and hopped up and changed to be more potent—to be used, rather than honored.

Nature knows, she remembered her mother saying once. *It knows our intentions—and it gives us what we deserve.*

Plants could heal—and harm. Like people.

Connor cleared his throat and Sadie shifted her attention back to the interloper. What were his intentions? They weren't as simple as he was making them out to be. He wasn't here to build her legacy. He would be just one more obstacle between her and the healing knowledge that had once existed within her—that she had taken for granted like Alice's foresight and Lena's resolve to run the ranch. The healing knowledge that had disappeared with her ability to tend plants, since the two were inextricably entwined.

"I'm here to help you," Connor said in a low tone, as if it were just the two of them standing here.

"I don't think that's true," she told him. She figured he was a message from her father. That he was disappointed in her behavior and that from now on he'd keep a close watch on her via this enormous airman he'd sent.

But she'd already received another message from the plants—the land—she loved so much.

They didn't want her here anymore.

It was time to leave.

COULD THIS BE his home? Connor wondered as he took in the large white house, the back porch, the neat, orderly rows of Sadie's garden and the rutted dirt track that led to the barns and outbuildings in the distance.

"Come grab some food from the buffet," Cass said, sending a signal to her sister with her furrowed brow.

Sadie didn't seem to notice. Her gaze was on her gardens, her mind obviously somewhere else.

"Sadie? You coming?" he asked.

"What? Oh—okay." She followed along and Connor resisted the urge to take her hand to guide her through the crowd. She was so slim and girlish in her bridesmaid gown, he instinctively wanted to protect her. He knew that was partly why the General had sent him; trouble could return to Two Willows, and the General wanted men on the ranch who knew how to handle it when it did. He knew he couldn't send them all at once, though. They were infiltrating Two Willows one at a time.

Now Connor understood the pressure Brian must have felt when he'd first arrived.

What if the plan didn't work? What if Sadie didn't find him attractive, or interesting—what if she didn't care about men at all?

Sadie sent him a sideways look that traveled over his body and up to his face. When her gaze met his she blinked and colored a little.

A grin tugged at Connor's lips.

She cared about men.

And maybe found him just a little attractive, after all.

He definitely found her attractive. He was glad last night he'd sent texts to Lila, Bridget and a couple of other women he still chatted with online and told them goodbye. He wanted to begin a new life here at Two

Willows, with Sadie Reed.

He'd wondered if he was ready for it, but now that he was here, the whole thing seemed like a brilliant idea.

At the buffet, he handed Sadie a plate and went along the length of the tables, offering her portions of dishes he thought might interest her. To his surprise, Sadie meekly allowed him to serve her, murmuring her preferences as they went. In the end, both their plates were stacked high with food when they went to find a table.

But the tables were mostly full.

He was about to admit defeat and suggest they divide up when Sadie said, "Let's eat on the porch." She led the way up to a grouping of wicker furniture and indicated he should take a seat. He hoped the settee would hold up when he sat down. Not that he was overweight—far from it. But the wicker looked like it had been out here a long time.

Sadie took a seat on one of the chairs opposite him. "Are you from Ireland?" she asked conversationally, as if he were any old guest at the wedding.

"Yes. Originally," he admitted.

"So that accent isn't entirely fake."

"No. Not entirely." He was a little abashed. Women usually found his accent charming, but when he turned it on, it was an obvious ploy, and Sadie had seen right through it.

"You must have moved here young."

"Ten." He took a bite of potato salad, chewed and swallowed. "Lived in Texas until I joined up."

"Texas? Some of those spreads down there put Two Willows to shame."

Connor thought about the huge spread he'd grown up on. Big enough to be its own state, they used to joke—not even trying to cover their pride. But that spread hadn't belonged to him or his father, and the sun beat down hard on that flat Texas land. It had its own beauty, but not like Two Willows. "Not much can hold up to this." He waved his fork at the house and the land around them.

"Two Willows is pretty special," Sadie agreed quietly.

They ate in silence a minute, and Connor wondered what was bothering her. His presence? The shoot-out that had taken place here only weeks before?

He found it hard to make the kind of small talk that might set her at ease. He was too aware that this was the woman he was to marry. Back at USSOCOM, she'd merely been a two-dimensional facsimile of a woman he'd constructed in his mind from her photographs and the information Brian had told him. Here she was in the flesh. A young woman with serious blue eyes, a way of looking at him like she was searching his face for clues about what lay beneath.

Connor thought she was the type of woman who looked beyond surface features to the depths of people—and problems—for what lay at their heart. He was uncomfortably aware that such scrutiny could unearth things about him he didn't want her to know.

What would Sadie think of his shallow existence—

the way he'd held back from forming deep attachments to other people? What would she think if she knew that the few minutes he'd spent with Halil left him feeling he understood the Syrian man better than those he'd served with?

He'd spent far too many years hiding in plain sight. No one knew him. Definitely not the women he'd date previously.

But Sadie would have to as his wife.

"Brian told me about the maze," he said finally when he'd cleaned his plate.

"Do you want to see it?" Sadie set down her plate on the table, although she'd only picked at her food.

"Sure." His casual shrug hid his true feelings. Ever since Brian had first mentioned the maze, Connor had known it had significance for him.

"The land holds its own secrets," he remembered his granny saying when he was young. "Even when men think they're putting their stamp on it, often they're following the land's own will." They'd been standing before a Neolithic dolmen in County Donegal at the time, Connor staring at the massive stones, wondering how his forbears had moved them. It was one thing to get the enormous uprights into position, but what about the capstone? It wasn't like they'd had cranes to lift it into place.

His grandmother had been right; he'd been busy thinking about the men who'd built it, but the real question was why? Why there? Why like that?

Could the land really call men to do its bidding?

He scanned the ranch around him again. Two Willows had secrets. He could feel them whispering in the soft breeze playing with Sadie's hair as they made their way down from the porch, through the gathered guests, across her garden to the tall hedges that formed the maze.

"Shall I lead?"

Connor hesitated. He'd have liked to take his time and explore the maze on his own, finding his way into the heart of it. But on the other hand, he was here to woo Sadie.

He nodded. "This time. Next time I'll try it on my own."

She entered the green passage, striding quickly enough Connor knew he would struggle to retrace their steps. He'd get the chance to learn his own way through its passages later, though. He reckoned this was the first of many times he'd trace his way through the maze.

When they reached its heart, he wasn't disappointed. There stood a tall, rectangular stone, rough-hewn and ancient looking, as if it had been here since the dawn of time. It couldn't be that old, of course. Maybe a hundred years—a hundred fifty at most. But he felt a kinship between it and the ones he'd seen back in Ireland.

It had presence, and Connor stepped close, wanting to get a better look.

Sadie pressed a hand on the stone, as if greeting an old friend. She was silent a moment.

Listening.

Tenderness flooded Connor's heart; she reminded him a little of women he'd known back in Ireland. Kind, warm women with an extra bit of knowing he'd always wanted to have, too. How many times had he seen his grandmother get that distant look? He wondered what the stone was telling Sadie.

A shaft of sunshine loaned it a golden hue. Connor couldn't help himself; he placed both palms on the stone's warm flanks. Its rough texture under his hands made him fully aware he was really here in Montana. Here at Two Willows. Getting ready to convince Sadie to marry him.

Was this madness? He glanced at the serious woman watching him soundlessly. Sadie had reacted to his arrival with little more than a cool detachment. She wasn't interested in him. For all he knew she wasn't interested in marriage. He could be on a fool's errand.

But standing next to her, both of them touching the stone—acknowledging silently its power—he thought not. They were similar in this at least; they respected the landscape that defined them.

It was funny; he'd thought this mission would require him to overcome his own reluctance to settle down and share his heart with a woman. But only an hour in, Connor found himself wanting to try. Something about Sadie tugged at his heart in a way he hadn't experienced before. Her sense of place, maybe. Her sense of mission.

Sadie knew what she wanted. Knew where she was meant to be. Connor had never felt that way since he left Ireland.

But if he was falling for her, he wouldn't have to overcome his own inclinations to marry Sadie; he'd have to overcome hers. Sadie's indifference to him could prove the impediment that made him fail at carrying out the task the General had given him.

Connor didn't like failure. He wasn't used to it. Hell, even when he'd been kicked to USSOCOM, he hadn't failed. On the contrary, his demotion came because he'd succeeded in saving Halil and his wife.

Is love worth fighting for? he asked the stone silently— as if it could answer.

Too late, he remembered Brian claimed it could.

Connor jerked back his hands, took in Sadie's surprised expression as she stepped back, too, and searched for an explanation he could give her.

Before he could think of anything to say, the breeze played up, tossing Sadie's hair into her eyes. It tossed something else past him—a ripple of color that landed in the hedge behind Sadie.

"What's that?" He leaned past Sadie, just as she turned to investigate, too. Both of them reached for it at the same time, and their fingers touched before Sadie snatched her hand away and Connor lifted a faded hair ribbon from the greenery.

It was striped red, white and blue, but instead of reminding him of the American flag, it called to Connor's mind the stripes of the French one. His parents had met in France—in Paris. They'd fallen in love there. Married there. Then traveled to Ireland to settle with his mother's family.

When he held the ribbon up, Sadie shook her head. "I've never seen it before."

On an impulse he caught her wrist and tied the ribbon around it. "Now you won't forget the day you met me," he said lightly. He knew he'd never forget the day he met her. Sadie was something else. Different from the other women he'd known. He wanted to touch her again. Wanted more.

Before she could pull away, he bent down and kissed her.

As BOTH SHE and Connor reached for the ribbon, just for a moment—for one split second—Sadie felt her awareness sharpen. There was the hedge, thirsty, the needled tips of its branches feeling the blight of too much sun and not enough water—an imbalance that went too far beyond the normal long, hot Montana summer days for the hedge to withstand. Sadie sucked in a breath, grateful beyond measure for the return of that knowledge before she yanked her hand away, and Connor pulled the ribbon free of the branch where it had landed.

In that instant, the awareness disappeared. The world went mute again, and Sadie stared in shock at the man beside her as he held up the ribbon for her to inspect.

"I've never seen it before," she managed to say, her mind still reeling. The fingers of her free hand ran lightly over the needles of the hedge again, but she felt nothing. Heard nothing. It was as if a wall had dropped down between her and the natural world.

Then Connor bent to tie the ribbon around her wrist. When his hands touched her skin, her awareness crackled on again, then off. On and off, until Sadie wanted to scream.

What did it mean?

"Now you won't forget the day you met me," he said lightly. And before she could pull away, he bent down and kissed her.

The world exploded in sensation. The thirsty hedge, the parched grass beneath her feet, the sere breeze that caressed her face. The acres of kitchen garden behind the walls of the maze, each plant crying out for its own mixture of water and nutrients.

Connor pulled away. With him went her awareness again. Sadie grabbed hold of one of the branches of the thick hedge to steady herself, but felt nothing. No sense of thirst, of too much sun, of dwindling reserves of water in the ground deep below her.

Nothing at all.

Swallowing, Sadie looked at Connor. Really looked at him. His strong features were framed by dark hair. Wide blue eyes watched her, but she couldn't tell what he was thinking. Had he felt it, too?

No.

No one else ever did.

So how had he—

"I have to go," she blurted and spun around.

"Sadie—"

"Cass needs me." She lifted the hem of her brides-maid gown.

And ran.

Chapter Two

I T TOOK HIM nearly a half-hour to find his way out of
the maze, and by that time Connor was ready to
barrel straight through its evergreen walls. He needed to
find Sadie again. Talk to her.

But he figured if he damaged the maze, it would set
Sadie against him forever. Besides, his Gran would rise
from her grave and read him the riot act if he desecrated
something as special as the maze out of sheer impa-
tience.

Chasing Sadie now wouldn't score him any points,
anyway. His kiss had surprised her. Hell, it had surprised
him.

But she'd reacted to it.

When his mouth had brushed her cheek, she'd jolted like a live wire conducting a current. He wasn't sure
if it was attraction—or fear—that had made her suck in
her breath, but she couldn't say she was immune to his
touch, for better or for worse.

He decided to look for Brian, but before he'd taken
three steps out of the maze toward Sadie's garden, his
phone buzzed in his pocket and he pulled it out and saw

his father was calling.

"Dad, what's up?" he said when he'd accepted the call.

"Not much. You in Montana?"

"That's right." Connor hadn't exactly come clean about the trouble he'd gotten himself into, or about the nature of this mission. Instead he'd classified it as a leave, and told his father he had come to help out a friend.

His father hadn't been entirely pleased. Sean O'Riley might share his ex-wife's Irish ancestry, but he was a Texan through and through, as his forefathers had been for over a hundred years. He couldn't understand why anyone would want to live anywhere else than Texas, which made it hard for Connor to admit he was trying to make Montana his home.

"Should have come here. Haven't seen you in a while."

"You could always visit me." Connor said the words out of habit. His father rarely left the spread he oversaw, and never for as frivolous a reason as a visit to his son.

"Heard from your mother lately?"

"You could call her yourself, you know." How many times had they had this exchange? For a couple divorced for twenty years, they were awfully nosy about each other's business.

"Answer the question."

"I hear from her every week. You know that." Whether by phone, text, email or video chat, Keira O'Riley never failed to reach out to him. She'd always wanted him to be clear that she loved him despite the distance between them.

Despite the fact she'd let his father take him to America.

"How about Dalton?"

"Nah." His brother was a whole other matter. Dalton had stayed in Ireland when the family split, and while Connor told himself it wasn't Dalton's fault their mother had kept him there any more than it was his fault his father had taken him to Texas, he hadn't been able to keep from resenting his brother for getting his mother's full attention. And he had the feeling Dalton felt the same about him and his father.

Not for the first time he wondered what his parents had been thinking when they each took a child from their marriage. Had they thought it was somehow fair? Had they known even when Dalton was twelve and Connor ten that Connor would thrive on a huge spread and Dalton would suit the smaller Irish ranch?

And what about the part of Connor that longed for those green, green hills? Was there a similar part to his brother that craved the wide open, sunny skies of Texas?

He'd never know. They didn't speak of things like that, when they spoke at all.

"All seems well, Dad," he finally said with an equal amount of pity and irritation. Sean O'Riley had hied himself home to Texas after thirteen years in Ireland, swearing he couldn't stand another misty morning on a ranch no bigger than a thimble, but he'd never found himself another woman.

Connor thought he missed his wife.

"Good, good." His dad paused for so long Connor thought he might have hung up. "Might take you up on that."

"Up on what?" Connor paced the long rows of Sadie's garden, turned onto a main path and headed back toward the party. He spotted Brian near the back porch steps talking to a knot of well-wishers. The evening was mellowing out as the sun went down, and the murmur of voices and the lilt of dance music made Connor want to belong here.

"On visiting. I'm taking a vacation in a few weeks."

Connor stopped in his tracks. "A vacation?" He didn't think he'd ever heard the word on his father's lips. "A vacation?"

"That's right." Sean sounded testy. "A man can take a break now and then. 'Specially one who's worked as hard as I have."

"Of course." Connor rushed to appease his father. It was just he couldn't remember an instance when Sean had taken more than an hour or two off work to fish in the pond, let alone travel to another state for a real vacation. His trip to Paris as a young man when he'd met Connor's mother was the single instance of that kind of thing. "I'm sure we can put you up."

If he was still at Two Willows. If Sadie hadn't run him off by then.

"When were you thinking?" he asked.

"Three weeks from today," his father said, as if

planning vacations was as normal as drinking a beer. "I plan to stay awhile, too."

"O-okay." Hell, he'd better work fast to have things in order by then. "Any reason in particular for taking a vacation now?"

Another long pause had him pacing toward the party again. Something was up with his Dad. He wished he knew what.

"Henry put his foot down. Said I'd better be gone for a month. I ain't staying away for a month, though. Three weeks tops."

Connor nearly laughed in relief. Henry Butler owned Valhalla, the enormous spread Sean oversaw. The man had urged Connor's dad for years to take regular breaks. "No health issues, then?"

"Health issues? You think I've gone soft?"

"No, Dad." He was glad to hear his father was in good health. Sean was nearing sixty. It was time for him to slow down. Ranch work was hard on a man—it wore you down over the years. "I look forward to your visit."

After a few more minutes of small talk about cattle, drought, the price of grain and the relative sizes of Valhalla and Two Willows, Connor signed off the call and pocketed his phone, just as he reached Brian.

"Here he is now," Brian said, moving aside so Connor could join the conversation between him, his new bride and her sisters, all congregated around her in their bridesmaid gowns. "Connor will take care of Two Willows while I'm gone."

The dark-haired woman to Cass's right scoffed

openly. "We don't need help caring for Two Willows. Sadie will take on Cass's jobs, and I'll run the cattle operation—like always," she asserted.

Lena Reed. Connor bit back a smile. He'd already heard from Brian she was a firebrand and fiercely protective of her role as overseer of the ranch. The General had a bad habit of sending men to take the position from her and she'd dug her heels in good this time; she wouldn't hand it over again.

Brian didn't seem to care. "We agree on practically everything," he'd said once in a video chat with the men left behind at USSOCOM. "She's lived here all her life. She knows this ranch like the back of her hand. Why butt heads when she's right?"

Connor figured they'd come up with a kind of partnership when all the men had arrived on the ranch. They'd either divvy up responsibilities or make decisions by democratic means. He had no problem with Lena having her say.

"I won't interfere," he told her. "I'm here to help Sadie."

Lena raised an eyebrow. "Help her with what?"

"Make her mark on the property." He explained the concept of the legacy the General had sent him to build.

"You're so lucky," Jo said to Sadie.

Alice kept her gaze on Connor, though. "That won't be easy," she said finally.

"Is that one of your predictions?" Connor challenged her. Brian had told him about them.

She nodded. "It is."

When she didn't back down, Cass said, "What will you build, Sadie?"

Brian was looking at his wife fondly. Cass was obviously be the peacemaker in the family, Connor thought.

Sadie shrugged. "I haven't decided yet." Without another word she left the group, ran lightly up the steps to the back porch and disappeared inside the house.

"Connor, can I have a word?" Without waiting for Connor to answer, Brian guided him away from the others to an unused table far from the dancing. "Cass and I will head out for our honeymoon in an hour or so. I wish you'd been here longer so I could show you the ropes."

"I'll figure things out." Brian had been sending him notes about the ranch and the General's daughters every day for the past few weeks. He was about to set out with Cass on a road trip down to the Grand Canyon, among other places. Connor wondered again if the General should have sent all the rest of the men at once, but he guessed that wouldn't have worked very well, given Sadie's cold reception of him. The women might have ganged up and kicked them all to the curb.

"Just because we ran off the men trying to get a hold of this ranch doesn't mean we're out of danger here." Brian leaned forward. "I figure this is bigger than just a handful of small-town operators, you know? Someone's bound to come sniffing around sooner or later to find out what happened. And they'll probably want revenge. The General should have sent the others with you."

"I've got it handled," Connor said. He figured it'd take time for their enemies to regroup. The main players were injured—on their way to jail.

"Cass and I should have booked a shorter trip. I just felt—"

"Cass needed a break. A month away. I know, you've told me." A half-dozen times. "She's been through a lot. You two need a chance to be together without all this. I'll handle it. Don't worry."

Brian sighed. "That's just it; I've already gotten used to worrying about Two Willows—and Cass's sisters. You know they all can't leave the ranch—"

"At one time. I know." Brian had made it clear how much the tradition meant to Cass and her sisters. A Reed had to be on the ranch at all times to guarantee the General's safety. Their mother had come up with the superstitious compact with the land, and the girls treated it like a sacred prophecy. The General's daughters might hold a grudge a mile long against their father, but they'd protect him until the end.

"Really. I've got this. Sadie and I will finish up the repairs to the house, too," he said to Brian. "Enjoy your honeymoon."

"Make Sadie fall for you. None of us get this ranch unless all of us succeed," Brian reminded him.

"I know. I won't screw up."

He hoped he sounded a whole lot surer of that than he felt.

"THERE YOU ARE, Sadie. We should talk," Cass said

when she entered the kitchen. She looked up, spotted Alice sitting cross-legged atop the refrigerator and sighed. "Alice, not in your bridesmaid gown."

Sadie suppressed a smile. The top of the fridge was Alice's favorite perch, bridesmaid gown or no. They'd been chatting amicably about the wedding and their guests—but not about Connor, which Sadie appreciated. She had a feeling Alice knew something had happened between them. She got hunches about things all the time. Sadie touched the ribbon on her wrist, not sure why she hadn't pulled it off and thrown it away.

"It's perfectly clean up here." But Alice climbed down gracefully. "I'll keep our guests happy while you two talk."

Sadie watched her leave with misgivings. She'd been worried for days Cass would spot the signs of trouble in her garden and confront her. Or maybe her sister meant to talk about Connor.

Sadie didn't want to think about him.

"I updated the manual Mom left me," Cass told her, leading the way up to the bedroom she now shared with Brian and picking up a three-ring binder from her desk. She hugged it to her chest for a moment. "It means a lot to me," she admitted. "It's hard to let it go."

"It's only for a month," Sadie reminded her, but she understood. Right now, a month seemed like far too long to be without her sister. Somehow she'd have to get the garden to hobble along until Cass returned and she could make her escape. She prayed no one noticed the problems until then. Her sisters had been so kind, even when it became clear how she'd betrayed them by dating such a monster—letting him get so close to them. But if they realized how she was struggling to do the tasks she'd always done so easily, they might think about the matter more closely.

They might realize how much she was to blame.

"You need to be the one who stays," Cass said, handing her the binder.

Sadie took it, her mouth dropping open. Had Cass read her mind?

"I mean, you can leave for errands of course, things like that, but for the most part, it has to be you." Cass must have noticed her confusion. "That's what Mom said to me when she died. 'Let it mostly be you.' To stay on the ranch. That's part of the job. Part of what I do here."

Sadie understood in a flash. "For the General."

Cass nodded. "For Mom," she added. "One of us always has to be here. Let it mostly be you," she repeated, and Sadie knew that those words must have run through her sister's mind a dozen times a day since their mother died. "While I'm gone," Cass amended. "Once I'm back it'll be me again. But out of all of us you're the most connected to Two Willows physically. It makes sense for it to be you."

"Okay." But the word felt like dust in Sadie's mouth. Didn't Cass see she wasn't connected to Two Willows at all anymore?

Except when Connor touched her.

"Is something wrong?" Cass touched her arm. "Are

you still worried about Mark? He's gone, honey. He can't hurt you now. And even if he could, Connor's here. He's Brian's friend. He'll protect you. Brian told me all about him earlier. They served together back at USSOCOM."

"It isn't that." But of course it was, in a way. Mark might not be here, but he could still hurt her. He was hurting her with every breath she took. She'd chosen him over the land. Over her sisters.

Now the land wouldn't forgive her.

"You'll feel better in time," Cass promised her. "I know it doesn't feel like it now, but it will happen, believe me. When I learned who Bob really was, it hurt so bad I didn't think I could ever love again. But now I have Brian. You'll find someone, too—I know you will."

Sadie wanted to tell her she was wrong, but this was Cass's wedding day, and she couldn't allow even a hint of her own pain and confusion to mar it. "Of course," she made herself say. "I know that."

"You'll be so busy doing my jobs and your own you won't have time to think about anything for the next month anyway," Cass told her and patted the binder. "Think of Connor as a guardian angel, standing in for Brian while we're gone. The days will pass in a flash and I'll be back. By then you won't give two hoots what Mark did."

"He nearly killed you," Sadie blurted. "You think I can forget that?" She cursed herself for letting the words spill from her mouth.

Cass softened. "Of course not. But you can't hold on to that. You have to move forward. Find your own happiness. None of us can change the past."

Sadie nodded. "Have fun on your honeymoon. You deserve to have a good time."

"Have fun building your legacy. Make it something really special—something worthy of Two Willows." Cass kissed her on the top of her head. "Come on, we'd better get back to our guests."

Sadie followed her downstairs, blinking back tears. How could she build something worthy of Two Willows when she wasn't worthy of it? Connor would have to accomplish that on his own.

As if her thoughts had summoned him, the man himself appeared at the back door when they reached it. She let Cass go first and watched her sister head straight for her new husband.

"Dance with me," Connor said.

And the moment he took her hand, the world came alive again.

AS DUSK EASED into nighttime, Sadie danced with him, drank with him, toasted the happy couple with him and introduced him to the men and women who came to make his acquaintance, but the whole time Connor felt as if the beautiful young woman by his side was somewhere else.

It was as if she was listening for something only she could hear. He thought she'd beg off after their first dance, but to his surprise she allowed him to ask for another, and then another. Even when they moved away from the dance floor, Connor was all too aware of the way she kept brushing his hand with hers, touching his sleeve, bumping her elbow against his. With any other woman, Connor would have thought she was flirting—taking the opportunity to touch him and send a signal of her interest.

Sadie didn't seem the slightest bit interested in him, however. Certainly not in what he said. He had to repeat himself more than once throughout the evening to get her attention.

When the happy couple left, and the other guests slipped away into the night shouting their goodbyes, all the remaining Reed women began to clear the dishes from the outside tables. Connor pitched in, but soon Alice's yawns became enormous, and Lena and Jo were visibly drooping.

"You three go to bed," Sadie ordered, suddenly present after hours of distraction.

"We need to help," Alice protested.

"You've been run off your feet helping to put on this wedding," Sadie told her. "And you two need to be up before dawn to do your chores," she said to Lena and Jo. "You'll have to fend for yourself for breakfast, but there are plenty of leftovers. I'll get the rest of this cleaned up. Go on," she continued when her sisters balked. "Up to bed; all of you." She turned to Connor. "You, too. You can have the guest room. For now."

"I'm not sleepy." He turned back to folding up the rented chairs they'd used for the reception, brooking no argument. Lena, Alice and Jo trailed away inside and went to bed.

Under a full moon and the fairy lights that had been strung around for the wedding, they continued to work. Sadie moved in and out of the house, packing up food and bringing in the dishes and silverware. Connor stacked the chairs and folded up the tables as she cleared them. When they were done, they moved inside where Sadie washed the dishes and he dried them. Not knowing where everything went and what was borrowed and what came from Two Willows, he stacked the dry dishes on the long, scarred kitchen table, his gaze taking in the bullet trails again.

One of those bullets could have ended Cass's life. Is that what Brian thought every time he saw them?

Connor didn't think he could stand the thought of Sadie in danger. Now that he knew her—and thought of her as his future wife—he wanted to protect her from anything that might hurt her.

They worked in silence for a long time, but when Sadie had drained the sink and rubbed the counter with a damp cloth for the last time, she came to take the broom out of his hand to put it away. Once again, she brushed her fingers over his, an act that sent his senses tingling.

Once again, she ignored him, that faraway look on her face.

Connor took her hand, determined to get to the bottom of her behavior. He set the broom against a wall, tugged her outside, down the steps and into her garden, where they both looked up at the large, full moon already dropping toward the west.

"My gran would say it's a night for pixies," he told her in a low voice, still holding on to her.

There was his Irish accent—not the fake brogue he'd tried on her earlier, but the real deal. The one that shone through his slight Texas twang when he thought of home.

"She'd be right; the whole world is awake for this moon." Sadie chuckled, but she shivered, too. She tried to pull free of his grip, but he kept hold of her, unwilling to let go.

"My gran was a little like Alice," he went on conversationally. "She saw things ahead of time. On a night like this I'd catch her listening."

"I bet she was always listening." Sadie clamped her mouth shut. Connor turned to her.

"You hear it, too? Like Alice?" Brian hadn't told him that.

"Not like Alice," she said quickly.

"But you hear something?" He could believe it. On this night, under this moon, standing on a property as special as the one he'd left behind when he was ten— with a woman as beautiful as Sadie, he could believe it.

She shrugged and tugged her hand free. When she wrapped her arms over her chest as if cold, Connor decided he'd pushed her hard enough for one night.

"It was a fine reception," he declared to set them back on common ground.

"It was. I think they'll be happy. Don't you?"

"I do." He'd read the love in Brian's and Cass's eyes and he wondered if his parents had ever looked at each other that way.

"Why did your family move to Texas?"

He gave her an abbreviated story of his parents' meeting in Paris, falling in love, their quick marriage and the way they'd settled in Ireland until his father couldn't stand it anymore. "He never loved it like the rest of us did. He was a Texan through and through."

"But he lost his wife and one of his sons when he left."

"That's true." Connor shifted closer to her. He couldn't help it. "And if you're asking if it was worth it, I don't know the answer to that. Seems to me he's always been lonely."

"He never remarried?"

"No. Neither did she."

"Maybe they'll find their way back to each other."

"After all this time?" It seemed more unlikely than the pixies his gran would claim were watching him even now.

"You're right; that's silly. Things don't work like that in the real world."

He couldn't stand to hear the pain in her voice. Was she mourning the man who'd played her to get to her ranch? He hoped not.

"So what'll it be, lass?" he asked, slipping into his thick Irish accent again as he reached for her hand. "What kind of legacy will you build with me?"

HE WAS TOUCHING her again. And she was feeling it again. All evening she'd experimented with the phenomenon. After a lifetime of living with a connection to the natural world, now she could only dial into it through the conduit of Connor.

She'd tried to see if it would work with other people. She'd touched her sisters, their guests. Brian. Not one of them had sparked the awareness; only Connor did.

She'd have to keep him here.

No.

Sadie wrenched herself away from the idea. That wasn't what the ranch was trying to tell her, even if she wanted to believe it—and after hours of being close to the handsome airman, she did want to believe it. It was telling her she had to leave, and that her place on the ranch would be filled by Connor. He felt things, too— he had the ability she'd lost.

Why else would he be here—now? Why else would his touches turn her senses back on? Fate was showing her she'd been replaced.

She could barely admit to herself that when Connor had arrived, a little part of her had hoped he was there for her the way Brian had seemed to come for Cass. She'd hoped Fate had placed him in her way—as ludicrous as that was after the disaster of her relationship with Mark.

She didn't deserve a second chance, certainly not with a man as special as Connor. It wasn't just the way he brought back the connection to nature, either. Every time she touched him—

Sadie didn't know how to put it into words. A fire lit deep inside her. A wanting so fierce it unnerved her. Connor seemed to be kind, attentive, thoughtful, strong—everything Mark wasn't. Everything she'd always wanted in a man.

But she wasn't allowed to want anything.

She definitely wasn't allowed to want Connor. The man had to stay here. He had to tend Two Willows. She had to keep away from him—

Sadie shook her head again. No, she couldn't stay away. She had to *teach* him.

She straightened, the thought taking hold of her. That's why Fate had placed him here when she had to stay for another month; their time at Two Willows would overlap so that she could show him all he needed to know about the garden, the greenhouse, the maze, the produce stand and the cures she created and sold. He'd have the internal knowledge he needed, of course, but she could help with all the practical aspects. She'd work with him on the legacy project and use that as an excuse to tell him everything she could about her home.

By the time she had to go, he'd be all set to keep Two Willows safe and sound.

The thought tore at her, but Sadie made herself face it. The important part was the ranch—not her. If she could leave it in Connor's hands she could be—not happy, maybe, but content.

That was the best she could hope for.

"Sadie?" he said again, pulling her from her

thoughts. "What kind of legacy will we build together?"

"A garden, of course," she said slowly. It had to be a garden; how else to give her the chance to tell him what he needed to know?

"You already have gardens."

"A walled garden." She wanted to cringe with the irony of it. A walled garden. A garden with walls meant to keep her out. Banishment from Two Willows would be so—

He didn't remind her she'd said she wasn't interested in such a thing just a few hours earlier. "A walled garden," he repeated instead. "I like it. A safe place. A retreat."

She didn't know whether to laugh or cry. This ranch used to be her haven. Not anymore. But that was all right. There was a big world outside Two Willows, she reminded herself. A world she'd dreamed of as a girl. She could go anywhere. Be anyone when she left. And that's what she'd do—keep moving. She'd see everything.

And in time, she'd heal.

"That shouldn't take too long," he mused. "Although the rock work—"

"We have a month," she told him.

Connor frowned, and his grip on her hand tightened. "Why a month?"

"Because when Cass gets home, I'm leaving."

Chapter Three

"L EAVING?" CONNOR'S HAND tightened involun-
tarily around hers, but he let go when she tried to
tug away. "What do you mean you're leaving?"

She didn't answer for a moment, and Connor could
swear she used the time to compose a lie. "I want to
travel. To see the world. Do you think one lousy ranch
could hold me forever?"

He couldn't have been more surprised if she'd
slapped him. One lousy ranch? He looked at her more
closely. Her features were tight, but not with anger.
With something else.

Anguish?

"I think you love your home," he said honestly.

Sadie flinched, and he remembered all the photos
the General had placed around the office back at
USSOCOM. It had taken him and the others weeks to
realize what they were.

Intel.

He'd learned a lot about Sadie from those photos,
and the gist of it was she loved Two Willows. Had a
connection with her gardens that went far beyond the

proud grower of a few fruits and vegetables.

"Of course I love it, but that doesn't mean I never want to go anywhere else. Plenty of people leave home."

"I know. I'm one of them." That didn't make the ache for the land he'd loved in Ireland any easier to bear. "Where are you off to then?" he asked as lightly as he could under the circumstances. Sadie couldn't leave; he was supposed to marry her. It was the only way to clear his military record—and the only way to keep the General from selling the ranch out from under all of them. But he couldn't tell her that. Brian had managed to marry Cass without ever spilling the beans on the issue. Now he said he was on his wife's side and wouldn't stand for interference with the ranch, but none of their names were on the deed. Only the General's was.

"India," she said after only a moment's hesitation. "I've always wanted to see India."

Connor had the feeling she'd only thought of the place in the last half-second. "I know someone in India," he said before thinking better of it.

Sadie narrowed her eyes. "A woman?"

"No—yes," he admitted, thinking better of lying. "An old friend. She runs a guest house there. It keeps her busy."

"See? Plenty of people like to travel."

He wanted to deny it. Wanted to tell her she couldn't go, but that wouldn't work. She'd only become more determined to leave.

"You can't go until we build the walled garden."

"Then we'd better build it fast. We have one month," she reiterated. "I'd like to leave sooner."

Sooner? Connor panicked. "How about this, lass? If you stay the full month, I'll buy your ticket to India and I'll set you up with my friend. With a job," he rushed to add when she turned on him a look that could strip paint from the walls. "She's always looking for help with the guest house. You'll need work if you want to pay for your travel."

At first he thought she'd say no, but after a long moment, Sadie nodded. "One month," she repeated.

"One month," he affirmed, already regretting his rashness. He needed more than a month to convince her to be his. He'd put himself into an impossible position. But he'd read the determination in Sadie's eyes. If he'd tried for longer, he would have lost her then and there.

Better start working on his goal, he told himself as he bent to kiss her again.

Sadie slipped away from him. "See you in the morning."

All he could do was watch her go.

THAT KISS IN the maze. How could one brush of his mouth over her cheek make her insides molten and turn up the volume on her connection to the world? It had been magic—no other word would do.

And the memories of Connor's touch made it hard to fall asleep.

Tossing and turning in her bedroom, Sadie knew the

man was probably sound asleep just a few steps away in the guest room down the hall. Good thing Brian had already moved his things into Cass's room.

Or maybe Connor wasn't sleeping. Maybe he was thinking of all the things he'd like to do to her.

Things she'd like him to do.

Sadie turned over and buried her face in her pillow. That was the worst of it. After being burned by Mark— nearly losing her sisters and her home—how could she even think about another man touching her? It was as if her body had severed its connection with her mind— her soul. She had promised herself never to be led astray by another man, and here Connor was tempting her to let go all of her good intentions and—

Stay.

God, she wanted to stay, Sadie admitted to herself. India sounded exciting and exotic—even dangerous in a titillating way as a destination for a woman traveling on her own. But Sadie wasn't exciting, exotic or dangerous. She'd always been connected to this ranch in a way that didn't feel like it was hemming her in—it felt like it was lifting her up.

This was her land.

Or it had been.

Now she wasn't sure of anything.

Sadie turned over onto her back. She wasn't sure of anything except the desire that raged inside her for another of Connor's kisses. Another of his touches on her wrist.

And other places.

Another flash of knowing that the land used to give her as a matter of course.

When she woke again, a shaft of sunlight spilled into the room through a gap in the curtains and Sadie blinked, trying to remember why a twist of anticipation curled through the dread she'd come to expect each morning.

Connor.

Connor O'Riley was here to build her legacy project.

And even if she wanted to leave, she would have to stay until Cass came home, which meant four weeks of accidental touches that would put her in contact with this land—her world—again.

Four weeks of not-so-accidental touches while she made the most of the opportunity to get her gardens back on track.

Four weeks of kisses—

No. That's where she had to draw the line.

Because after four weeks were up, she had to leave Two Willows, and she wouldn't be fit company for a man like Connor—or anyone else.

One thing at a time, she decided. It was Sunday, which meant Ellie Donaldson would be by for her herbal tonic. She came twice a month, and the woman was far too discerning for Sadie to fool if she'd just rolled out of bed when she came by. Time for a shower, breakfast and her usual morning rounds of the garden before heading to the greenhouse. Thank goodness she still had a bottle of the tonic from a previous batch she'd made before the shoot-out.

Without Cass to oversee breakfast, the kitchen looked like a small tornado had whipped through it, since everyone else had served themselves, but no one had thought to clean up afterward. With a sigh, Sadie first ran out to get her farm stand set up for the day, then came back and managed to feed herself several slices of toast and an apple while washing up. When she'd drained the sink, put away the clean dishes, wiped down the table and counters, and swept the floor, she was an hour past her usual time getting out to tend the garden, and she hurried outside to make up lost time.

Once she reached the garden, however, she wished she had lingered inside longer. Never in her years of care had it looked so dismal. Up until now she'd convinced herself that no one but her would notice the spots, dried leaves and drooping fruit, but she couldn't hide this anymore.

This was a disaster.

Sadie made herself walk every row and note every symptom of disease and failure in the plants. She told herself she'd come up with a plan of action. Most gardeners couldn't feel the needs of their plants, after all. There were rules to follow when you were flying blind. She'd simply have to learn them.

But I have learned them, a little voice said. *I know the rules. I'm following them.*

And her plants were still dying.

Tamping down her rising panic, Sadie moved on to the greenhouse and let herself into the humid building, hoping against hope to find an improvement here.

She was disappointed.

Her seedlings were leggy, drooping, sad little affairs that weren't likely to last until they were supposed to be transplanted. That meant her succession planting would be thrown off, and there'd begin to be holes in the supply of vegetables and fruit that helped keep food on the table—and in the farm stand.

When she went to the cabinets that held her pre-made herbal remedies, things were even worse than she remembered. There was only a single bottle of Ellie's tonic left.

Which meant when it was gone, Ellie's arthritis would come back. Seeing as she made her living with her sewing needle, that wasn't good.

With a glance at the old clock hanging on the wall, Sadie pulled out the ingredients to make up a new batch, but she knew the effort would be useless. Without the extra sense she'd always relied on, she couldn't balance them to make the perfect formula. Every root and leaf was different; what made her remedies effective was the way she could concoct the perfect mix.

But not anymore.

"Good morning," Ellie called when she pushed the door open a few minutes later. "How is my favorite girl?"

Sadie's heart warmed, even though she knew every young woman in Chance Creek was Ellie's *favorite girl*. Just for a moment she let herself bask in the positive glow of the older woman's attention. Whenever Ellie stopped by, Sadie thought of her mother. She'd been eleven when Amelia had passed away. Right at the age when a girl needed her mom the most. Cass had done everything she could to step into Amelia's shoes, and they'd always had guardians, but none of them had come close to Amelia.

Sadie missed her mother with an ache that never faded.

"I'm fine," she made herself say, although she was far from it.

"Tired, I'd say." Ellie patted her arm. "After a wedding it's to be expected. The rental company was picking up their things when I pulled up. Don't worry; looks like Lena is taking care of it."

Sadie sighed in relief. One chore she didn't have to do.

"Your sister looked beautiful yesterday in your mother's gown," Ellie went on. "I remember Amelia wearing it like it was yesterday. She bought it from me, you know; one of my earliest customers."

"I know." Most women in town went to Ellie's Bridals for their gowns, and had since she set up shop back in her twenties. Alice had altered the dress to fit Cass, and all of them had agreed she'd been stunning in it.

"You'll look beautiful in it, too, when it's your turn." Ellie beamed at her.

Pain blossomed behind Sadie's rib cage. Her heart squeezed with the knowledge she'd never have a turn. Not after what she'd done.

"Thanks."

Ellie cocked her head. "Your time will come," she said gently. "I bet there's a man just waiting for you."

Choking on the woman's kind sentiment, Sadie hurried to the table where she'd left the tonic. "I'll write you a receipt."

"Not yet." Ellie hurried after her. "There's something else I hope you can help me with." She hesitated. "You won't tell anyone."

"Of course not." But Sadie's heart quailed. She couldn't help Ellie with anything else—not without the mixture already prepared.

"It's… tiredness. I'm tired all the time. I don't know what's wrong with me." Ellie's distress was palpable.

Sadie took a calming breath. "Why don't you sit down and tell me about it." She guided Ellie to a café-style table and chairs in the corner.

Ellie did. "It's nothing specific. In a way, it's everything. I just can't do what I used to do. Or if I do it, I'm tired later on. My muscles ache. I fall asleep as soon as I sit down at night."

"What about Caitlyn? Isn't she helping you at the shop?"

"Oh, she's a big help, but she's got her children, and I don't want to ask her to—"

"Ellie, you're going to have to ask her to do things for you." She took the older woman's hand. "I can give you something to help with your energy, and you should go have a checkup to rule out the possibility there's something going on I'm not qualified to diagnose. But the thing is—" There was no easy way to say it so she blurted it out. "You're getting older. You aren't always going to be able to do the things you used to do."

"Well, that—sucks, as the younger generation likes to say." Ellie braced her hands on her knees, thought a moment and nodded. "Of course, you're right. I will go to the doctor to be on the safe side, and I'll take whatever you've got, too, but I guess it's time to have a talk with Caitlyn."

"How do you think that will go?" Like all healers, Sadie knew the most important part of the cure was listening.

"Oh, she'll be thrilled." Ellie laughed. "She's always telling me I'm not letting her work to her full potential. Pretty soon she'll take over and it'll be Caitlyn's Bridals." Ellie's face fell. She blinked rapidly. "Oh, there I go. Look at me, making a fuss."

Sadie squeezed her hand. "Ellie, when things change, we grieve. That's the way it is." She was grieving, too. Every day on the ranch was one closer to when she'd leave and she didn't know how she'd bear up under the exile. She could well understand how Ellie felt. "Talk to Caitlyn. Tell her what you're feeling so she knows. She won't want to trample on what's important to you. She's excited about her career, that's all."

"You're right." Ellie dabbed at her eyes with a hemmed handkerchief she'd pulled from her pocket. "She's a good girl."

"And you're a wonderful aunt."

Ellie sighed. "I try to be." She pulled out her wallet as Sadie went to find the tincture for energy she always had on hand. As she paid what she owed, Ellie smiled. "I'll go home, grab the bull by the horns and sort out a new way for us to work together. Maybe it's time to put her name on the sign along with mine. We can run the shop fifty-fifty for a while."

"That sounds like a wonderful idea." Sadie wished she had as much gumption when it came to facing her own future.

"I don't know what I'd do without you, dear," Ellie said. "I'm glad you're one thing that will never change around here."

"YOU CAN'T LET her leave," Logan said when Connor made a video call to the other men at USSOCOM.

"Obviously." Connor knew that much. What he didn't know was how to convince Sadie to stay. He'd tossed and turned half the night, trying to sort out the problem. It hadn't helped his phone kept buzzing. Lila was in a chatty mood—and even Bridget had texted him once or twice. Neither seemed to believe he was well on his way to matrimony, and he was beginning to doubt it, too. Sadie seemed determined to leave.

"Did she say why she was going?" Hunter asked.

Connor gave his attention to this much savvier question. "She said she's been stuck here on the ranch too long. She wants to see the world; India in particular. The thing is, I don't buy it. There's something else going on I can't figure out." He didn't tell them about her surreptitious touches the previous night. He figured that would quickly mire them in the kind of locker room talk he didn't want anywhere near his Sadie.

Connor repressed a chuckle. *His* Sadie. She was far from that, and he'd have to solve this mystery and convince her he was a man worth loving if he wanted her to be his.

Was he worth loving?

For the first time in his life Connor took stock of himself.

Hell.

"What is it?" Logan demanded.

"He just said he can't figure it out," Jack told him.

Their argument gave him a chance to recover his bearings, staggered as he was by his assessment of himself. Why *would* Sadie fall in love with him? What had he ever done except work and fool around with women when the opportunity arose? He supposed his commitment to the Air Force was a point in his favor, but he had little else to show for his years on earth. Few good friends. No sense of what he wanted from his future.

He'd have to work on that.

"Is it about the General?" Hunter asked. "Seems to me there's still a lot of bad blood between him and his daughters. He didn't even go to Cass's wedding. That has to have made them mad."

"Maybe." Connor wasn't sure, but it could explain why Sadie wanted to leave. "I keep thinking it's got to do with Mark Pendergrass."

That shut them all up. "He's in no fit state to come sniffing around there again, is he?" Hunter asked.

"No. I don't think we have to worry about that. I think it's more of a *once burned, twice shy* type of thing."

"Which means you've got to go easy when you pursue her. Be persistent—you don't have much time. But be careful, too. You can't ride roughshod over her the way Pendergrass did," Hunter said.

"She'll be embarrassed about that," Jack said suddenly. "Making a mistake about who you think someone is—that kind of thing smarts."

Connor blinked. That was the first personal comment he'd ever heard the man make. Had Jack made a mistake about someone once? he wondered.

"Build up her confidence," Hunter said. "Hard work helps."

Connor knew what he was thinking. "You want me to get her to help me build the garden."

"Building a wall that big? That's hard work," Hunter said with the emphasis of a man who'd done the job before. "Lots of heavy lifting."

Connor knew that. He'd already booked a backhoe to help dig the footer for the big stone wall. He was going to do this right. But Hunter wasn't kidding—it would take a lot of sweat and labor to build the thing.

"I'll give that a try."

"Eyes on the prize," Logan said and the others signed off.

As if he could look away from Sadie, Connor thought. His gaze was drawn to her wherever he found her. Leaving the house a moment later, he spotted her instantly in her garden. When he caught up to her she was rubbing a tomato leaf between her finger and thumb. She held it up to her nose and frowned.

"Trouble?" he asked.

She nodded. "The tomatoes don't seem to be happy."

"Some years are better than others, aren't they?" He knew all about it from the cook on the ranch where he'd grown up. Some years they'd have more tomatoes than they could count. Other years the yield crashed.

When he looked up she had a strange expression on her face. "I... guess so," she said. Then she reached out and touched him.

Her sudden gesture caught him off guard, but her look of intense concentration surprised him even more. She closed her eyes for a moment, and when she opened them, she nodded. "Okay. Okay—I can do that."

"Do... what?"

She pulled her hand back as quickly as she'd reached out. He realized the ribbon he'd wrapped around her wrist the day before was gone. He wondered if she'd saved it or thrown it away. "Think of each year as different," she answered in a rush. "Like you said. Some years aren't going to work as well." But even as she spoke she was surveying the row of tomato plants, all of them looking the worse for wear, and he could tell she wasn't satisfied.

"I want to start on the walled garden as soon as possible. I've got a backhoe coming this week," he went on, as she took a few steps, bent down and stuck her hand in the dirt near the roots of another tomato plant. "Which means we need to measure it out today. Got a few minutes?"

"Sure," she said distractedly. "I'll join you there in a jiffy."

When he realized he'd been dismissed, Connor cocked his head. "Where do you want the thing?" he asked a little more testily than he'd meant to.

"Over there." She gestured to an open space set back farther than the greenhouse but off to one side. She bent back over the tomato plant and Connor sighed, but trudged away.

When he reached the area she'd indicated, he began to pace out a rectangle. Given Sadie's distraction, he wasn't sure if she actually would join him, but about ten minutes later she did, and immediately began to criticize his plan.

"It's facing the wrong way. You've made the long wall run north-south rather than east-west."

Rather than being angry at her criticism, Connor was gratified. She was interested enough to have an opinion. That was something.

He showed her the sticks he'd collected to use to indicate the corners. "Why don't you mark the dimensions you like and then we can adjust them as we measure again?"

At first he thought she'd go for it, but then her shoulders slumped. "It's useless, you know. I won't even get to plant it. I told you—I'm leaving as soon as Cass comes home."

"Then Cass will use it," he told her, keeping his tone neutral. "And Jo and Alice and maybe even Lena. And so will their daughters. And their daughters. You're not the only green thumb in history, you know."

She jolted as if he'd slapped her. "I know that," she snapped.

"That's what a legacy is, right? Something you build for the benefit of those who come after you."

She sucked in a breath. "So what you're saying is to stop being so selfish and start thinking about everyone else."

"Your words, not mine." He wasn't being kind and he knew it. The guys back at USSOCOM would have something to say. But he figured he needed to jolt her out of the funk she'd fallen into and find out what was behind her desire to leave.

"You're right," she said, surprising him all over again. "I am being selfish. I'll help you build the garden. For the good of everyone else."

It was a victory, but not a very satisfying one, Connor thought. "For your good, too," he said. "Even if you don't stay to use it, by the time you're done, you'll know how to build a wall. That'll come in handy anywhere. Even India."

What the hell was he saying? Sadie already knew how to build walls. She'd built one so high between them he didn't know how he'd breach it.

Someone needed to teach that woman about doors, he thought as he wedged a stick into the dirt and followed Sadie as she paced out the perimeter of the garden.

WORM CASTING TEA. She'd gone too heavy on it the last time, and proved the old adage you can have too much of a good thing. Her tomatoes wanted her to dial it back, but they craved the calcium from crushed egg-shells Sadie had neglected to give them recently. It was so simple even a new gardener should have been able to figure it out, but learning it directly from the plants was so much easier than guessing.

If only she could figure out why her connection only worked when Connor was touching her.

And why, if he felt that connection, he wasn't saying anything. Surely he must see the damage to her garden—so why didn't he talk about it?

Did he want her to ask for his help? Was that it? Did he need her to grovel?

Sadie's back straightened, but she realized she'd beg if it meant saving the garden.

First, though, she'd try to learn more. If Connor did share her ability to connect with the growing things around her, he was a master at hiding it. Why?

She'd always kept her abilities a secret so as not to be labeled. She'd heard the way people talked about her older sister Alice since she was very young. "She's different," they would whisper when they thought Alice was out of earshot. Sadie had instinctively known how that hurt her sister.

She hadn't wanted any part of it.

Was it the same for Connor? He was a warrior—not

afraid of anyone.

Still, even warriors had feelings, she supposed.

She tried to focus on the work at hand, but thinking about the walled garden she'd never get to plant made her even more confused. Would Connor stay and plant it?

Would Cass try her hand at keeping it up?

The gardens were already large enough they took most of Sadie's time. Cass could never tend them with all her other duties. Alice had no interest in gardening, and Jo and Lena were far too busy with the cattle to take it on.

"This is pointless," Sadie said again, coming to a halt.

Connor bumped into her, then steadied her with a warm hand. "Legacy," he said quietly, even as the whole world around them came alive to Sadie in a symphony of information.

Keep touching me, she willed at Connor. She needed this connection; the three-dimensional world she'd always inhabited before the shoot-out at the house.

As if he'd heard her, Connor stooped to place the rest of the stakes on the ground and set his other hand on her hip. "Sadie Reed, I'm going to kiss you," he announced. He didn't leave her much time to react before his mouth brushed hers softly, brushed it again, and then he tugged her close and kissed her for real.

Instantly, sensations overwhelmed her. Connor's touch electrified her—his kisses turned her insides warm and fluid, leaving her pressed against him, her arms reaching of their own accord to wrap around his neck. She felt the pleased, verdant expectancy beneath her feet—as if the very dirt they trod on yearned to be coaxed to bloom and thrive once the garden was built. Images filled her mind of green bowers, vined walls, shrubs and flowering trees, roses winding over an arbor, delphiniums, asters, peonies—

The swirl of flowers and plants spun in her thoughts as Connor's kiss deepened. That he seemed unaware of the frenzy of life working beneath their feet, waiting to grow—to blossom—became a thread of doubt that tangled through everything else.

Connor had to tend this garden when she left—

A landslide of images cascaded through her mind, as if the land itself was reacting to her thoughts. The garden's green abundance turned to dust in her mind, and Sadie gasped. She pulled away from Connor, broke the connection, and the roar of life that had tumbled through her just moments ago disappeared altogether, leaving her stumbling in its sudden absence.

"Sadie?"

She held out a hand to stop his pursuit. "I don't—I don't understand—" She stopped short when she saw he looked as blank and shocked as she felt.

"You have to stay," he said suddenly, his light Irish accent clear again. "I need you here. Not just because of the legacy. But because of you. When I touch you, something happens—" He shook his head. "I can't explain it."

Neither could she. Were they talking about the same

thing?

"It's like part of me—part of me that had died—comes to life," he went on, and Sadie's heart beat hard. "I didn't think it would feel like this."

He visibly got control of himself, and looked up at the sun high in the sky. The warrior in him was back, all the raw, anguished truth of his feelings corralled behind walls so thick she'd never penetrate them.

She craved the man who felt things—and tried to express them.

But she couldn't have him.

Because she couldn't stay.

"We better get back to work and get this measured out," Connor said curtly.

Sadie stared after him as he scooped the stakes from the ground and kept walking. He was right. No matter what else happened, they had to finish the garden within a month. No time to sit here staring at the dirt.

Even if a tiny blue flower now winked at her from the prints of Connor's boots in the dirt where he'd stood just a moment ago.

Chapter Four

"WHAT ARE YOU doing in Montana when you should be in Ireland?" Connor's mother asked for the third time.

He stood on the back porch, having stepped outside so the phone conversation wouldn't wake up anyone else so early in the morning. A week had passed since the wedding—a week since he'd left Florida and his career as a pararescueman behind—but Connor still woke before dawn like clockwork. He'd spent his days shadowing Sadie as much as possible, and either helping Lena with the cattle or dry walling the living room and kitchen when he could tell Sadie needed time alone. He hadn't made much progress with her—or the garden, but the kitchen and living room were ready to paint now. After he and Sadie had finished with the garden measurements, he'd called in an order for the granite stones, which should arrive any day now. The foundation was dug and the footer installed. The walls of the garden would be tall enough that they needed a concrete base reinforced with rebar.

When his phone had buzzed, he'd just been finishing up his breakfast and he grabbed it, expecting it to be Lila again. Bridget's texts had tailed off, but the more he explained to Lila he was off limits, the more she messaged him. His mother had probably thought to leave a message, but now that she had him on the line, she wouldn't quit.

"I'll come as soon as I can, but I've got a job to do here," he said again.

"Well, I don't understand what Montana can hold when you could be home with us. You are out of the military, aren't you?"

"Not quite." But he would be soon enough, something he found difficult to contemplate. "You could always visit me here, you know." He'd said the words automatically, but his mother paused long enough to get his attention.

"What is your father doing these days?" She asked the question casually, but Connor wasn't fooled, and in light of the similar conversation he'd had with his father just a few days ago, his patience gave way.

"You could ask him, you know. The two of you should be able to have a conversation."

"If your father wants to talk to me he knows how to reach me; I've never left *my* home."

"But you expected him to abandon his without a backward look." Connor had no idea why they were hashing over this old ground.

"He was the one who said he'd move to Ireland. I never changed my mind; he did."

Connor hated the old pain in her voice. "Well, the

two of you will have to come to some sort of under-standing, because I expect you to be civil at my wedding." He meant it in a general way—something in the future to aspire to.

But his mother took it specifically. "Wedding? Connor, are you getting married? When? Soon? Who is she—you never mentioned a thing! Oh, of course I'll come to Montana for your wedding. You couldn't keep me away!"

Connor hadn't heard her so excited in years, and even as he opened his mouth to disabuse her of the notion he had set a date, a new thought came to him.

What if he gave his mother the wedding she want-ed? What if he lured her here to Montana? His father, too. After all, he was supposed to marry Sadie—sooner or later.

What would happen then?

He stepped back inside and glanced at the calendar on the wall. Thought about the plans he'd made for his fathers' visit. Picked a date five weeks out and named it. That gave him three weeks to build the garden and woo Sadie before his father arrived. Cass and Brian were due back then, too. They'd have two weeks to plan the wedding if she said yes. Since his father planned to spend three weeks at the ranch, maybe his mother should, too.

And if Sadie said no, he'd still stick around in Chance Creek long enough to let his parents spend some time together.

Could he heal the rift between his folks?

Even if all they did was talk civilly after all this time it would be worth it.

And maybe—just maybe, if she actually did agree to marry him—their wedding could heal the rift between Sadie and her father, too. The General hadn't come to Cass's wedding, but anything was possible. He might come this time.

"Come early and stay for a while. How about three weeks? Can you swing that?" he asked his mother.

"Of course!"

"THE MOST IMPORTANT thing to remember is you have to listen," Amelia was saying as Sadie woke up, took in the familiar surroundings of her room and realized she'd been dreaming—and she was alone. A moment ago she'd sat in the dirt between two rows of bush beans, Amelia cross-legged in the dirt across from her. Her mother had pointed to the brown spots spoiling the lush green foliage. "Listen to the plants, the ground, the air, the rain. All of it has something to tell you, but only if you take the time to listen."

Was that the problem? Sadie sat up, pushed the covers to the side and got out of bed. The wide floorboards were cool under her feet but she could tell already the day would be warm. When she reached the window, she pulled back the white lacy curtains and spotted Connor out in the rectangle where the garden's footer had been laid. He was looking from corner to corner, obviously building an image of the garden in his mind. He'd said the granite would be here soon. She liked the idea that it had been quarried in Silver Falls like the standing stone must have been.

Soon there'd be a beautiful walled garden on the ground Connor paced.

That wouldn't be hers, she reminded herself.

Still, she said she'd help, so she should dress, get her breakfast and get out there.

But something caught her eye.

Sadie moved closer to the window. She could just see the top of the tall green hedge that formed the maze. And it was—

Brown.

Fear, plain and simple, pierced through her. If the hedge died—

If it died—

What did that mean?

An image slipped into her mind from some long-forgotten memory. Her mother standing in the garden on a blustery day, one hand holding her wide-brimmed hat on her head. "It'll be there long past you and me," she was saying to someone. "That maze holds the heart of the ranch. It's part of Two Willows now."

The vision left as quickly as it had come, and Sadie understood it must have happened when she was very young. Back when the garden was her playground. When she'd learned the lore of the dirt and plants at her mother's side.

If the hedge died—would her memories of her mother die, too?

"Sadie?"

She turned with a start when Jo opened her door a few inches. "Yes?"

"I just wondered—Cass used to get the groceries—we're out of bananas…" Jo trailed off sheepishly. "I can run to town."

"No, I'll do it. Add anything you like to the list and tell everyone else to, as well." Cass's jobs were her jobs, after all.

And if that meant she didn't have time to go inspect the maze, well—so much the better, since she had no idea if she could save it.

Hours later, Sadie still hadn't made it out to the garden, to the maze or to help Connor. Cass did so many more tasks than she'd even realized, and catching up with them had taken all morning and well into the afternoon. She'd never dreamed they created so many loads of laundry, or that the house got so dirty so quickly. First Amelia, then Cass, had always collared her and assigned her tasks as needed, but she'd never been the one in charge of the whole show, and there was a lot to do.

By the time she'd run her errands in town, driven home again, switched the loads of laundry and cleaned the first floor of the house, it was time to prepare lunch.

Now she understood why Cass snapped at them sometimes at the dinner table. No sooner did you clean up from one meal than it was time to make the next one.

The only bright spot of the day was the kiss Connor snagged when he'd passed her in the hall mid-morning.

Just for a second, her whole body tuned into the ranch, but then he was gone and the feeling was gone, too, leaving her frustrated and more than a little confused. She still didn't understand what to make of what happened when they touched, and when she finally opened the back door to head to the greenhouse, she decided she'd have to do more experimenting.

HUNCHES HAD SAVED his life more than once, and when a red Ford truck pulled around the house and parked near the carriage house late that morning, Connor straightened from the piles of stone he'd been inspecting and strode toward it, just as Jo clattered down the steps from the back porch and went to meet the man who climbed out of the driver's side.

He'd been excited about the delivery of the stones since it meant he could finally begin the real work of building the walled garden, but as he watched Jo and the stranger talk, his hackles rose. The man kept stepping closer to Jo, and while she kept stepping back, her body language confused Connor. It was as if she was leaning toward the man at the same time she was moving away.

The man looked up from his conversation with Jo, spotted Connor, tipped his hat to Jo, climbed back into his truck and took off.

"Who was that?" Connor asked when he finally reached Jo.

"Said his name's Grant Kimble. I've never met him before, but he's heard of me."

"How?"

Jo looked at him askance. "Probably from someone in town. Everyone knows I breed puppies. That's what he was after." She hugged her arms over her chest and Connor noticed her gaze slid back toward the direction the truck had gone around the house.

"You sold him one?"

"Of course not. My puppies are booked up years in advance."

He'd underestimated Sadie's younger sister, Connor realized. She was a businesswoman and she hadn't been swayed by the man's attentions.

"Want to see them?" Jo asked suddenly.

"Sure."

She led him around the side of the carriage house to a door he hadn't noticed before. Inside was a clean, bright room that had been walled off from the rest of the carriage house. A litter of black-and-white McNab puppies greeted him with wobbly legs and wagging tails while their mother got to her feet and came to check him out. She was obviously comfortable with Jo, and soon she'd sniffed him up and down, decided he was all right and allowed him to kneel down near the puppies and play with them.

"Haven't had a dog in years," he told Sadie. It was wonderful to be the object of the attention of so many happy puppies. Connor felt himself relax in a way he hadn't in ages.

Puppy therapy. It should be a thing, he decided as he let them lick and sniff and climb all over him.

She studied him. "You can have one," she said after

a minute. "I don't see any harm in you."

Connor chuckled, wondering what she meant by that remark. "There's a man or two out there who'd tell you different. Anyway, didn't you just say your puppies were spoken for?"

She smiled. "I like that. Your accent."

Connor hadn't realized he'd slipped into it. Not the showy brogue he used when he was making fun of his origins or wanted to deflect someone's attention. And not the slight Texas twang he'd learned from his father. Only when he was truly comfortable did he slip into the true accent of his youth—a light Irish burr.

"Is Ireland beautiful?" she asked.

"It is."

"You don't want to go back?"

He'd yearned for it for years as a teen, but Connor realized that old pain wasn't nearly as sharp anymore. "I like to visit, but I'm an American now."

"What about Texas?"

"Texas is too matter-of-fact for my taste. Nothing like Ireland."

"You miss the magic," she said flatly and caught him off guard.

"I guess that's true."

"Plenty of magic here," she said with a sudden smile that transformed her face. Jo was as much a beauty as her older sisters, but she was still maturing into it, Connor realized. "Is that why you left the Air Force?" she went on. "Not magic enough?"

He chuckled. "No, not much magic in the Air

Force, you're right about that, but that wasn't the reason I left. Chalk it up to a little misunderstanding."

"Who misunderstood? You—or the muckity-mucks at the top of the food chain?"

"Let's just say I still think I'm right."

Jo nodded. "This one's yours," she said, handing him a squirming puppy. "Max. He'll be here for you when he's ready. You can visit him whenever you like—just come and get the key when you need it. And don't let anyone else in here."

"I won't. Thank you." Connor understood the trust she'd placed in him, and for the first time since he'd arrived at Two Willows he felt a thread of hope. If Jo could see the good in him, couldn't Sadie be persuaded of it? He bent closer to Max, letting the puppy check him out, warming to the little critter instantly, and decided to leave that question for later. First things first. Brian had trusted him to watch over Two Willows, and that man in the truck—Grant—had rubbed him the wrong way. He'd seemed cocky, the way he'd tried to change Jo's mind. And he especially didn't like that the man had left as soon as he spotted Connor. An honest man would have stuck around and shook his hand.

Time to head to town, he thought. He'd talk to Cab Johnson, the sheriff, whom Brian had told him all about. See if the man knew anything about Grant.

But first he'd have some fun with Max.

An hour later, he sat in a booth at Linda's Diner, a cup of coffee in front of him, and watched the sheriff demolish a slice of cherry pie.

"Grant Kimble, huh? Never heard of him," Cab said when he'd swallowed his bite.

"Do a lot of strangers come through Chance Creek?" Connor took a sip of his coffee. Strong. Just the way he liked it. He thought about having a burger, too, but decided he'd wait to eat until he was back at Two Willows with Sadie.

"Some, but a man looking to buy a dog? That kind of thing runs through the grapevine. Jo doesn't advertise online. She's strictly a word-of-mouth businesswoman. People wait for years for her puppies."

Connor leaned back, nodding. And yet she'd handed him one as if it was nothing, watching over him with satisfaction as he and Max had gotten to know each other. Connor looked forward to when Max was old enough to roam the ranch with him. A dog seemed the perfect addition to his life here at Two Willows.

"Mae?" Cab called the waitress over. "You heard of a Grant Kimble? Man looking to buy a dog?"

The attractive brunette nodded. "Was in here the other day asking questions. I heard Tom Mackenzie suggest he take a chance with Jo Reed down at Two Willows." She turned to Connor. "That's where you're staying, right? Did you see the man?"

"That I did, lass," he answered, slipping into the overblown brogue that seemed to win him favor with the ladies. He supposed it was a habit he needed to change. Linda's Diner wasn't a pickup bar, and he wasn't in the market for a girlfriend anymore. Still, he knew from experience it would help get him what he wanted. He'd always been able to flirt his way to the information he needed. The ability had come in handy throughout his life—including during his time as a pararescueman. "It's like a secret weapon," one of the men on his team had once said.

Right on cue, interest lit the woman's eyes. As he described the man who'd stopped to talk to Jo, she nodded.

"That's him." She lingered at their table. "Another piece of pie, Sheriff? Something for you?" she asked Connor, sending him a glance that told him she wanted to further the conversation.

"Well, now, there might be something I want," Connor said, leaning forward as if they were the only two people in the room.

Mae smiled. "Spell it out for me and I'll write it down." She held up her order pad and pen, leaning forward, too, as if to give him a better look at her ample cleavage.

"All we need is the bill," Cab said flatly, a hard edge to his voice that shattered the mood.

Connor sat back, jolted and a little embarrassed by Cab's words. They felt like a rebuke, but all he'd been trying to do was elicit more information from a possible informant who should know a lot about what went on in this town.

Without another word, Mae tallied up the bill and handed it to Cab. "Come back anytime," she said to both of them, but a quirk of her eyebrow told Connor it was him she wanted to see again.

When Connor turned back to the sheriff, the man was regarding him with something far too close to contempt for comfort.

"Didn't peg you for trouble," he said.

"I was just trying to—"

Cab held up a hand to stop him. "This is a small town. People watch each other and people talk. The General sent you here to help Sadie Reed, so don't tell me you were just trying to…" He trailed off and waved a hand.

"I could have found out more. Where he came from. Why he's in town."

"Maybe, but the General asked me to keep an eye on his girls and I let that slide once. I'm not letting it slide again. If you're not serious about Sadie, you back off, do your job and get out of Chance Creek. If you are serious, walk a straight line. Got it?"

"Yeah, I got it." As much as the rebuke smarted, Cab was probably right. Connor didn't care enough about Grant Kimball to risk his relationship with Sadie over the man. He could have asked his questions straight up, anyway. Mae seemed happy to tell them anything she knew. So why fall back on the old accent trick?

Habit, he guessed. A habit he'd have to break before it caused trouble between him and Sadie.

He wanted her. Not because of his mission. Not because of the ranch.

He wanted her for the way the whole world seemed to come alive when they touched.

The way she cared so desperately for her ranch.

The way she watched him so hungrily when she thought he wasn't looking.

"I got it," he said again.

"Good."

"YOU'RE IN A good mood," Sadie said sourly when Lena popped into the house for a late lunch. No one had shown up on time for the meal, and the way they were each filing in at their own schedule meant a chore that should have taken an hour to prepare and clean up had already stretched out to two hours. Connor hadn't shown up for lunch at all; he was still in town and she wondered what had delayed him.

"Of course I'm in a good mood. I've got the whole ranch to myself. Not a single man has interfered with me today."

"Brian's coming back, you know." She hoped Connor was, too. For the garden's sake, she told herself quickly. No other reason. She pulled out the soup she'd just put away and ladled some into a pot to reheat. Another dish to wash.

"I can handle him. But for now I'm going to pretend he doesn't exist. No man does. I'm blissfully on my own, running my cattle the way they were meant to be run. You make sure you keep your man in check. He takes one step too close to my cattle and I'll give him what for."

"Connor's not *my man*," Sadie told her tartly, pulling out the chopped salad she'd made, too. Once again she'd be late getting out to the garden. She was getting so far behind, her customers had taken to coming to the back door with their requests for vegetables. She was behind making her cures and tonics, too. Not that there was much she could do about that. She had a long afternoon ahead of her if she wanted to catch up.

"Are you sure? Looks like your man from where I'm standing. He follows you all over the place. He's building you a garden."

"That's why the General sent him; to build something that will last—like the maze. And to keep him out of trouble, I think. Jo says he got himself into a mess back in the Air Force."

"Just like Brian did in the Navy, huh?" Lena thought about that, taking a seat and serving herself some of the salad. "Since when is the General the patron saint of lost causes?"

"I don't know. I think it's his job to funnel them out of the military without making a fuss."

"As long as they don't stay here. Apart from Brian. He's all right," Lena conceded. "But you move Connor along when he's done. We don't want to give the General ideas, right?"

"Right," Sadie answered faintly. Her heart had sunk into her stomach when Lena said to move him along. If Connor left, she wouldn't be able to hear what the garden needed. She'd been using surreptitious touches to find out what her plants wanted to keep them happy, trying to heal the garden as much as possible before she left. Connor was supposed to take over for her—

But Sadie had to admit to herself she didn't know what was supposed to happen. For all Connor helped her tap into the knowledge she needed, he never showed any interest in actually gardening.

What if he wouldn't—or couldn't—take her place?

Chapter Five

WHEN CONNOR GOT back to Two Willows, Sadie was washing lunch dishes in the kitchen and from the way she was banging them around as she did the chore, she wasn't happy. He'd missed lunch, he realized. He'd stayed too long chatting with Cab, forgetting that if they didn't all eat around the same time at the ranch, it made more work for Sadie. He'd have to make amends.

It didn't help that Cab's words kept ringing in his head, or that he felt guilty for his casual flirtation with Mae. He'd never thought about the careless way he flirted with women when it helped him reach some goal. Trotting out his accent was something he did in his line of work—another tool in his toolkit.

He'd have to keep that particular weapon in its holster.

"I could use some help out back this afternoon," he said cautiously.

"I've got plenty to do already."

"Look, I'm sorry I was late for lunch. Don't suppose there's a sandwich for me in that fridge."

"If there is, you'll have to make it. And then you'll have to clean up after yourself; I've done enough of that today already."

She was pissed. Connor wondered if something had happened while he'd been gone. "Has someone come to bother Jo again?"

"Bother Jo? Why would you ask that?" She spun around from where she'd been drying silverware and putting it away in a drawer. "Who's been bothering Jo?"

"Bothering is probably too strong a word," he amended. "A man was here this morning. Looking to buy a puppy. I didn't like the look of him." Especially because it had been obvious the man was flirting with her, and Jo needed to hang on until Hunter got here.

"She doesn't have any puppies to give away like that anyway," Sadie said, turning back to her task. "She has a waiting list a mile long."

Connor didn't tell her he'd managed to jump to the head of that list.

"I'll just grab something—"

"I waited," she blurted out. "For you. To have lunch. Until it was damn clear you weren't coming."

"You waited?" He hadn't expected that. "Sadie—"

"Forget it. I've got to get to work."

Connor decided he'd have to forego lunch or lose his chance with Sadie today. She was acting as if he'd stood her up for a date—and maybe he had in a way. With a last, longing look at the refrigerator, he followed her outside and into her garden, where she began to walk up and down the rows, examining the plants carefully.

She'd waited for him. And he'd let her down. He didn't want to do that. He wanted Sadie to feel like she could depend on him.

"About the walled garden," he tried again. "I think we should begin to think about what to plant there. You'll want to order any trees ahead of time—" He cut off when she turned a scathing look in his direction.

"Trees? I'm not planting trees. I'm not planting anything. I told you I intend to travel as soon as Cass gets back." She straightened, shaded her eyes and sighed. "Damn it," she muttered, and before he could answer, she strode off toward the carriage house where an old silver truck had pulled in.

Connor made to follow her, but felt a light touch on his arm, and looked up to find Alice standing next to him. He'd seen her at meals, of course, and around the house, but this was the first time she'd made an effort to seek him out. "Give her a minute," she said. "Something's going to happen." Like Sadie, she was dressed in jeans and a plain shirt. Her hair was done in a loose braid that fell halfway done her back.

Connor bit back an expletive—if something was going to happen, he needed to be with Sadie, but Alice's grip on his arm tightened. "She's in no danger."

Connor relaxed a little when a middle-aged woman climbed out of the vehicle and made her way to meet Sadie. The two of them talked, the woman gesticulating and placing a hand on her forehead. Sadie listened patiently and nodded at first, but then shook her head.

Connor expected the conversation to end, but the woman wasn't put off that easily. In fact, the more Sadie shook her head, the more her visitor talked. Alice folded her arms over her chest as she watched her sister. Finally the stranger threw up her hands and climbed back into the truck.

"I'm sorry," he heard Sadie call after her, but the way the woman backed out, spun the wheel and roared off told Connor she wasn't satisfied with the exchange.

"I've never seen her do that before," Alice said in a soft voice.

"Do what?"

"Turn away a customer. Something's wrong." She closed her eyes as if she was listening to something far off. "It's like...the tie that binds Sadie to Two Willows is disintegrating. She's trying to leave." Alice opened her eyes, her lips parted in shock. "Did you know that?"

"She told me she wants to," he admitted. "When Cass gets home."

"You have to stop her." Alice got that far-off look again, but a moment later, she shook her head. "I can't see what will happen, but I know she's not supposed to leave—not for good."

"She's a grown woman. She can do whatever she wants." Connor shrugged, although the gesture cost him. He didn't want to lose Sadie either, but he didn't know how to tell Alice that.

Alice stared at him. "She can't leave," she said again. "That's perfectly clear. We Reed women have to stay."

"Only one of you at any given time." Brian had explained the women's superstition, and with his Irish background, Connor had been prepared to go along with the whimsical fancy of it, but this was taking it too far.

"For short periods that works, but that isn't what we're talking about. We're talking about Sadie leaving—for good. She can't do that."

Alice had gone so pale Connor placed a hand on her elbow to steady her. "Look, I don't want that—"

Alice jerked, swallowed, swayed—and grabbed hold of him for support. Just as quickly she wrenched away from him again and scrambled back a few feet.

"Alice?"

She held out a hand to stop him when he tried to approach. He could almost see the thoughts running through her mind. "You—" She straightened, and the shock on her face faded. Her color returned. When she smiled, he thought he saw triumph mixed with her relief. "You're—" She didn't finish her sentence. Just lifted a hand to cover her mouth and turned to look at Sadie, who was still staring in the direction of the departed truck. Connor got the sense she was holding back laughter. Alice dropped her hand and waved toward her sister. "Go be with her. Sadie needs you." She shook her head, becoming serious again. "We all need you."

Just like that, she left him standing in the garden, more baffled than before.

SHE'D NEVER TURNED someone away before, and it felt

worse than Sadie had imagined. Nora Ingram's head-
aches were exactly the kind of thing her herbal cures
could treat, but she didn't have the correct tonic on
hand, so now the woman would probably take some
over-the-counter pain medicine that might wreak havoc
with her digestive system over time.

Sadie realized she'd taken her skills for granted all
these years in a way that made it doubly bitter to lose
them. Why hadn't she expressed her gratitude more
often? She was selfish. Self-centered—

In disgust, she turned back toward the garden, but
nearly stumbled over the uneven ground when she
found Connor striding toward her. Was that the answer?
Was she meant to help Connor step into her shoes?

And if so, why didn't he show some interest in gardening—?

Sadie's shoulders sagged. He had, hadn't he? And
she'd cut him off. But he'd been talking about trees and
decorative plants, not healing ones.

What am I supposed to do? She sent her petition up to
the sky, not knowing who she was asking. What would
her mother have done in this position?

The answer came clearly.

Listen.

She needed to stop thinking so hard; stop trying so
hard. She needed to pay attention.

The garden will tell you.

It was as if her mother had spoken aloud.

Of course.

Sadie squared her shoulders and went back to meet

Connor. For the next several hours she obediently did as he asked, listening to his plan for how to build the wall now that the footer was in and the stone delivered. Discussing which ornamental trees and dwarf fruit trees might thrive within its walls when they were done. Debating if the warm, inner, south-facing walls could support something that usually only grew several states south of here.

Despite herself, Sadie warmed to the task, and the walled garden began to take shape in her mind. "We could espalier a peach tree against the south-facing wall," she told him. Peaches would be delightful if they could pull it off.

"I think it would need more shelter," he said, and explained his own ideas. He might not be a gardener, Sadie thought, but he was an enthusiast.

He could be trained.

Was that what she was meant to do? Train Connor to take her place? Train him, and then stay on as his assistant—

No. She'd have to be truly tone-deaf if she thought that was the answer. It was clear she needed to leave, but she had three weeks to teach Connor to listen to the plants and grow to love them.

Spending time with Connor was no hardship, either. He was funny, for one thing. Nice to look at. He asked her question after question to coax a detailed plan for the walled garden from her. She couldn't remember anyone taking such an interest in the growing things at Two Willows since her mother had passed away.

Of course, she touched Connor every chance she got—to get information about the soil, nutrients and growing conditions for the plants that would someday grow here.

And because she felt so alive when she did.

Back in the house later that afternoon, Sadie found herself humming as she did Cass's chores. She ran down into the basement, pulled out a load of sheets and towels and folded them neatly on a table placed there for the purpose. Upstairs again, she delivered fresh towels and sheets to each room. Her sisters could remake their own beds, but she'd do up Connor's out of courtesy since he was a guest.

The buzz of a cell phone had her patting her pocket as she entered the guest bedroom, but it wasn't hers. She caught sight of Connor's sitting near the edge of his desk. She went to push it to a safer position and couldn't help seeing the messages that lit up his screen. There were three of them.

I'm in the tub. Remembering Milan. Lila

Come on, handsome. Are you really going to blow me off? Bridget

So excited about your wedding. Just found my mother-of-the-groom dress! Mom

The sheets and towels slid from Sadie's hands.

Connor was already involved with two other women.

And he was marrying one of them.

WHEN CONNOR ROUNDED the door into his bedroom and found Sadie there ahead of him, his first impulse was to take her in his arms and kiss her.

And he followed it.

He knew he was taking a chance, but after the wonderful afternoon they'd spent together, he figured his odds for success were much higher than they'd ever been previously.

So when Sadie answered with an uppercut that would have split his lip if he hadn't automatically blocked it, he couldn't have been more surprised.

"Who's Lila?"

Too late he spotted his phone on the desk. Even as he watched it lit up with a new message. Lila—and even Bridget—wouldn't leave him alone. And there was always the chance some other woman he'd dated could text him out of the blue. He could only imagine what Sadie had seen. It had never meant anything. He'd stopped answering when he'd come to Two Willows and met Sadie. He'd lost interest in flirting with anyone else. That didn't stop the messages, though. If anything, they'd picked up.

"She's no one," Connor told Sadie. "Just a girl."

"Just a girl? Does she know about Bridget?"

Connor stifled a curse. This was worse than he'd expected. "She doesn't need to know about Bridget. Bridget's nobody—"

"Right. So which one is your fiancée?" Sadie looked mad enough to spit—or to hit him again.

Connor couldn't keep up. "Fiancée?"

"Fiancée! As in, your future wife?" Sadie glared at him. "The one whose wedding your mother can't wait to attend?"

"Oh!" Clarity crashed over him. His fiancée. Right. He supposed he couldn't tell Sadie he was staring at her right now. He might not be the smoothest of men, but he was smart enough to know this wasn't the way a lass would like her proposal to play out. "Let me explain."

"When a man starts with *let me explain*, it's hopeless." Sadie tried to push past him, but Connor caught her, and as always when they touched Sadie sucked in a breath. He affected her; he knew that. He couldn't let her run out of the room thinking he was the bastard she thought he was right now.

But how to explain it all. He was who he was because of how he'd grown up, but he didn't want to dwell on that. He wanted to change.

"My mother and father are still in love," he blurted.

Sadie stopped struggling. "What does that have to do with—"

"They're still in love. At least, I think they are. Neither one has moved on. Both keep asking about each other," Connor said, hoping like hell he could make her understand. "I'm tricking them."

She watched him warily. "How?"

"If they think I'm getting married, they'll both come to Montana. Short of my funeral, it's the only way they'll agree to be in the same place at the same time. They'll have to talk to each other face to face."

"You think that will make them patch things up?

After what—twenty years?"

When she put it like that, it became clear how ludicrous the idea was. "No." He ran a hand through his hair. "Yes. I don't know. I have to try. I told them both I was marrying in five weeks."

"Won't they be furious when they find out you lied to them? Or are they used to that?" Anger tightened her features. "How about Lila and Bridget? Are they used to that, too?"

"They both know the drill." Fuck. Had he really just said that?

"So you're a cheat as well as a liar. I should have known. All men are." Sadie kicked the pile of towels on the floor and sent them flying before she shouldered past him and out the door.

DINNER TASTED ABOUT as good as she felt that night. She'd burnt the fried chicken. Poured too much milk into the potatoes before she mashed them. She swore the lettuce in the salad had wilted in her hands as she prepared it. Her sisters picked at their food, then escaped from the kitchen one by one. Sadie refused to acknowledge Connor manfully cleaning his plate.

"We need to talk," he said after the meal when they were alone.

"We don't need to do anything. You need to head back to Texas—or Ireland—anywhere but here!"

She pushed back from the table and stood up. As she began to collect the dirty dishes and scrape the leavings into the trash, Connor stood up, too, and crossed the room to touch her.

She batted him away, and a wet chunk of mashed potato flew from the fork she held and stuck to his shirt.

"None of those women mean a thing to—"

Sadie had heard enough. All she could remember was Mark dancing with Tracy Jones at the Boot. Flirting with her. Going home with her. Leaving Sadie there to find her own way back to Two Willows. She'd never told her sisters about all the ways Mark had humiliated her. She hoped they didn't know. Doubted it; this was a small town and people talked.

She wasn't going to let this… man… come and do it to her again.

"Sadie, I mean it. You're different. You're special—"

You're special. Hadn't Mark said the same thing when he was wooing her?

She had to stop Connor. Stop those sweet words that had fooled her once and couldn't fool her again.

"Come on, honey. Give me a chance to—"

In a fury, she scooped the pile of potatoes Lena had left on her plate and threw them at Connor. "Get away from me!"

The white mess stuck to his chin and the stubble of his beard. His expression darkened, but Sadie didn't care. She grabbed a chicken bone from Jo's plate and tossed it at him. It bounced off his head.

She was done with men. Done with them.

"Sadie!"

Past caring. Past listening. No one cheated on her.

No one—

She lifted the salad bowl, still more than half full, and flung its contents at the airman—

But she lost her grip and the bowl followed.

Connor caught it in one hand. Thumped it down on the table in a shower of lettuce, carrots and cucumber.

Came after her.

Sadie shrieked, but Connor hooked her with an arm around her waist and dragged her close. "Stop throwing things at me, woman."

"Don't you *woman* me—"

Connor cut off her words with a kiss that electrified Sadie down to the tips of her toes, even if it did taste like mashed potatoes. The world, muted since they'd left the garden, came to life in vibrant sound and color. "I need you," Connor said and kissed her again.

Shocked all over again at the buzz of the connection between them, Sadie couldn't pull back. She wanted more—needed more—needed to get that connection back for good. She lifted her arms and twined them around his neck, the taste of salad dressing and mashed potatoes on her lips.

She was hungry for him, she admitted to herself. Or maybe just hungry, she thought with a desperate inner laugh. She kept kissing him, even though she knew she should pull back. Should still be furious with him. She should have run.

"Sadie, you're amazing," Connor whispered.

Some instinct told her he was speaking from his heart. Still, how could she trust him after what she'd seen? Men played with women. Used them.

So even if she felt more alive in Connor's arms than she had in months—years—she couldn't give in to it.

"No!" Sadie came to her senses and tore herself from his grasp. "No—I won't play this game." This was a man who juggled women like bowling pins, who thought it perfectly acceptable to play them off each other. A man who'd make up a wedding to trick his parents. Or who maybe really was getting married, and only lying to fool her.

She'd been a fool for far too long.

This had to stop now.

"Don't ever touch me again," she hissed at Connor and walked out the back door to deal with the farm stand.

Let someone else clean up the mess.

Chapter Six

"LIKE YOU'VE NEVER screwed up," Connor said to Logan several days later when he'd locked himself into the guest room and set up the video call to the men back at USSOCOM. He'd hoped that in the interim he'd be able to make things up to Sadie, but she'd turned a cold shoulder to him he couldn't seem to get past. The garden wall was progressing slowly, since he was doing all the work himself, but at least he'd finished painting the living room and kitchen—switching to the inside work when his back told him it was time to stop hefting stones into place. Sadie had been peevish through the whole process—especially with how it had made it harder for her to handle meals—but Connor thought the results looked good. The only bright spots in his days were spending time with Max, who seemed to grow every time he turned around. The puppy was always cheerful and overjoyed to seem him—unlike some people.

"I've screwed up," Logan admitted, "But not like you are now. You mess this up for yourself and you'll screw all of us over, O'Riley. The General should have sent me next. I'd get the job done."

"You think so? Lena will kick your ass to kingdom come the first time you open your mouth."

"She'll take one look at this fine example of Grade A American beef and fall all over herself trying to get a bite of it."

"You are so delusional—"

"Cut the crap," Hunter said, his thick Southern drawl like a honeyed whip. "Both of you need to get your heads on straight."

"I'm not the only one who can blow this." Connor turned on him, still stung by Logan's attack. "You're as liable as either of us to screw it up when it's your turn."

"I won't screw it up." But Hunter glanced away at something off-screen, and for the first time Connor wondered if the SEAL could carry it off.

"You sure about that? You've never said one thing about Jo." He couldn't blame the man. Hunter was the oldest of them. Why had the General paired him with twenty-one-year-old Jo, his youngest daughter?

"What do you want me to say?" Hunter drawled. "A man doesn't talk dirt about his future wife."

"Is she your future wife?" Connor pressed. Because if Hunter knew already it wouldn't work, they needed to have that conversation. None of them would end up with a ranch if they all didn't follow through. And what about their records? He needed his name cleared—

"I said I'd marry her, and I will."

Now Logan and Jack were staring at him, too. "It ain't that easy," Logan said. "You have to persuade her to marry you. And you're one ugly son-of-a-bitch, so if your crappy attitude is the cherry on top, this ain't going to work."

Connor suppressed a grin at the spark of anger in Hunter's eyes. The man liked to act like nothing fazed him, but that *ugly* crack had hit the mark. So the man was vain. Interesting. Connor had no doubt Hunter got his fair share of female attention, even if he spoke little and laughed even less.

"What about you?" Logan turned on Jack.

"I'm here, aren't I?"

"That doesn't answer the question."

"What was the question again?"

"Are you going to marry Alice?"

"You just told Hunter that wasn't the question."

"No, I didn't."

"You don't listen very well, do you? You don't even listen to yourself."

Connor sat back as the conversation between the two men settled into the kind of bickering that usually drove him nuts. Today he'd noticed something new.

Jack hadn't answered the question.

He never did.

Why was that? Connor knew better than to jump in and demand he do so right now. Jack was a master at evading any topic he didn't want to talk about, and that seemed to encompass just about every personal question possible. They'd all had rough times in the past. They'd all acted on impulse at some point in a way that threw them into hot water and landed them here, subject to the General's whims.

So what made Jack so damned hard to pin down?

Suddenly Connor reached his limit. Bad enough he wasn't at all sure he could persuade Sadie to marry him. He needed everything else pinned into place—no questions asked.

"You're going to marry Alice," he snapped at Jack. "You're going to get us this ranch—not because we deserve it but because Sadie and Cass and the rest of them—including Alice—do. Got it?"

Jack—mid-sentence—stared at him for a long moment.

And nodded.

JEAN FINNEY. HOW on earth could she have forgotten Jean Finney? Sadie glanced at the greenhouse clock again, and rummaged through the cupboard where she kept her remedies. She wouldn't find what she was looking for, of course—a week ago, when she'd handed Jean a bottle of the elixir in her stores, she'd known it was the last one, and that she'd have to think of something before Jean came back for a refill.

At twelve weeks pregnant, it was crucial she get it. Jean had first come to her last summer to confess that barely two years into her marriage, she'd had three miscarriages. Sadie had seen the desperation in her eyes, heard it in her voice and known she'd do her damnedest to help. She'd made Jean take six months off trying, while she concocted mixtures of herbs to support her body's reproductive health. Jean had quickly fallen pregnant when Sadie had given her the go-ahead to try again, but as she'd said, it had never been getting pregnant that was the problem; it was staying that way.

As Sadie gathered the ingredients for the tonic, she knew it was no good. She could mix them in exactly the same way as she had before, but without that connection she normally felt to the plants, the balance would be wrong. And with Jean, the balance simply couldn't be wrong.

"Mom—what should I do?" she whispered aloud, her hands trembling. Jean always came at eleven o'clock and it was past ten. She had the roots and herbs laid out before her on the table. The sterilized bottle. All her tools to prepare the tonic.

But it was no good.

"Mom?"

Sadie gripped the edge of the table, closed her eyes and tried to calm her mind. What would her mother do in this situation?

"Mom, I need help—"

The greenhouse door whipped opened and Sadie gasped, opened her eyes and saw Connor.

"Sorry; I didn't mean to interrupt... Were you praying?" He slowed to a halt.

Sadie supposed she had been, in a way. She'd asked her mother to send help—but all she'd gotten was—

Sadie stared at Connor. Let go of the table. Took a deep breath. "Come here," she ordered.

His brow furrowed. Was he suspecting a trap? "Okay." He moved through the narrow space between the tables loaded with seedlings, and came to join her.

"I need help," she said.

"Anything."

His quiet assurance took her breath away, and Sadie clutched the edge of the potting bench again, battling vertigo. She'd been rude to him for days but he was ready to do anything she asked. Why was that? Why was he here?

"I need you to stand behind me." Her voice betrayed her nervousness, and Sadie fought to steady it. After a moment, Connor did as she asked, moving behind her.

"Like this?"

He was so close, Sadie shivered with awareness, bit her lip, reached behind her and lifted his hands near her waist. "Hold on to me." She sucked in a breath when he settled his hands lightly but firmly on her hips. Even though she'd been ignoring him since their last fight, her body had taken notice whenever he was near, and Connor had done whatever he could to stick as near to her as possible.

Now every nerve in her body was at attention, and desire tugged deep inside her. She wanted him to kiss her again. She'd missed the taste of his mouth on hers.

Missed this aliveness he passed to her when they touched.

She wanted him, she admitted to herself. No matter that he was a player. That he would break her heart.

"That's it. Stay like that," she managed to say.

Focus, she told herself, but it was difficult. Not only

had his touch turned on the world, as if he'd turned up the volume on a radio, but it set her nerves buzzing with a sweet ache for him to do far more than hold her so innocently. She swallowed, made herself reach out and begin to prepare the herbs and roots she needed to make the tonic for Jean. As soon as she touched them, instinct told her everything she needed to do, and for the first time in weeks her hands moved over the ingredients and implements on the table with the confidence they'd always used to hold. Creating the tonic felt so right, Sadie knew this was the work she was meant to do. Knowing exactly how to measure and add the herbs was like coming home, and tears of gratitude started in Sadie's eyes, but she didn't have time for that. In fact, she barely had time—

Connor lifted her hair away from her neck and kissed her.

Sadie nearly dropped the bottle she'd begun to fill. She couldn't describe the sound she'd just made, half a sob, half a plea for more.

But she couldn't do that right now. "Hold still," she hissed, and kept working. Connor held still, his mouth still pressed to her neck, and they were standing like that when the door opened again a minute later.

"Oh, sorry! I'm early—" This time it was a female voice.

Jean's.

Sadie elbowed Connor away, and immediately the connection went out, making the world feel so gray and mute she wanted to scream. "I was just finishing up your tonic."

"I can see that." The amusement in Jean's voice made Sadie blush.

"Connor was... helping."

"I can see that, too."

Sadie swung around to stopper the bottle and hide her burning face. When she had control of herself, she turned back. "You can't use this until tomorrow," she told Jean. "I just finished it and it needs time to steep."

"I've got enough for today. Thank you, Sadie. And cross your fingers for me—I've never made it this far before."

Sadie knew the next two weeks were the dangerous ones. She gripped Connor's hand suddenly, needing to check one last time. Instantly, she knew the mixture was correct. She knew, too, it was crucial Jean have it. Handing it over to the woman, she let go of Connor and gave her friend a quick hug.

"I know there's no guarantee," Jean said. "I know my body will do what's right. But I'm hopeful this time—"

She didn't finish her sentence. She didn't need to.

"I'm hopeful, too," Sadie said—and meant it with every fiber of her being. She refused payment like she always did in cases like these. You couldn't put a price on a pregnancy.

"I'll see you next week!" Jean waved on her way out.

"Rest a lot," Sadie called after her. "Get that husband of yours to help you out."

"Will do!"

When she was gone, Sadie turned back to Connor. "Thank you."

"You going to tell me what that was all about?"

"I'm not sure I can explain it," she answered truthfully.

He took that in, and Sadie wondered what he was thinking. She wished he would touch her again, but squashed the thought. Not when she knew what type of man he was.

"Tell me this, then," he said finally. "Did I help?"

"Yes." He'd definitely helped. She couldn't have done it without him. "You might have saved a baby."

Just for a second something shifted in his eyes. A softening—before he covered it up by moving closer.

"Thank you for letting me help you. It's what I came here to do." He pulled her into an embrace.

She resisted. "How many other women are you helping right now?" she made herself ask. She wasn't going to be won over with a kiss or two and an assist with an herbal remedy.

"None. Sadie—" Connor sighed. "Lass, I've never done serious. I've never done long term. Lila and Bridget know that. They flirt with me, I flirt with them, we see each other when we see each other, have a little fun—"

Every word he said felt like a knife to her heart. He was just like Mark. It was all a game—a chance to get what you wanted by using the other person.

"It's not like that with you."

"Of course not," she said sarcastically, pulling free

of his arms. "Of course I'm the one woman who's different. The one woman who's changed your mind about everything."

Did he think she was stupid?

"You have every right to doubt me." Connor hooked his thumbs in the belt loops of his jeans. Shrugged. "I'm being honest about who I've been. And I'm being honest about how I feel about you."

"Why should I believe you?"

"Because I'm telling you the truth; just like I've always told the women I date. Hell, Sadie—I'm single. In the Air Force, I put my life on the line every time I went on a mission. If I wanted to flirt—or fuck—" He got a hold of himself. "No one got hurt but me. I made sure of that. Lila and Bridget have their own reasons for not wanting something permanent."

"How can all of you be so… calculating?" She'd never been like that with her affections. She either fell for someone or she didn't. To choose how much to want someone—to simply fuck someone just for the sake of fucking—the idea was completely foreign to her.

Connor chuckled, but it wasn't a happy sound. "That's just it; this isn't me being calculating. This is me—caught—in something I hadn't looked for."

That didn't make her feel better. So he hadn't wanted to fall for her. Hadn't wanted to be a one-woman man. Didn't that mean he'd struggle to break free of the feeling?

"Let me help you. I'll do anything you ask. That's why I'm here." He put his arms around her. As he pressed kisses to her forehead, her cheeks, her chin and finally her mouth, Sadie closed her eyes and tried to sense what was true as her connection to her surroundings turned on again.

Was he here to help?

All this time she'd thought Connor had come to take her place—to step into her shoes so that she could leave the ranch. What if she'd been wrong? What if he was here to do exactly what he'd just said?

Help *her*.

She wanted to believe it.

She clung to him as his kiss deepened, and for once she didn't fight it. Instead she let down her defenses, let herself feel his strength—let herself sag against him. She was rewarded when his arms tightened around her. This was nothing like the offhand way Mark used to kiss her, or the selfish way he used to touch her—as if he could take without giving anything back.

Connor had opened to her as much as she was opening to him. He was fully present, and his attention nurtured her as much as the rain did the plants growing out in the gardens.

When he finally pulled back, his breathing was rough and so was hers. "Will you let me stay, lass?" he asked in a light burr.

"You'll do what I tell you? No questions asked?" She couldn't possibly explain what she needed him to do.

"No questions asked."

"You'll help with the garden?"

"Anything."

Why not take him at his word? Why not take one more chance?

Surely her heart could survive being broken one more time.

"Okay. You can stay. For now."

CONNOR WASN'T SURE what he'd expected when Sadie took his hand in the greenhouse. In a way, he hadn't expected anything. Sadie was so full of contradictions he'd stopped trying to puzzle her out, but part of him had hoped against hope they might make love.

Instead, they spent the remainder of the day working together, first in the greenhouse and then in the garden outside, Connor struggling to keep his libido under check. This close to Sadie, he couldn't help want her all the more. He helped fetch and carry various types of soil amendments and fertilizer and had jiggered the irrigation system to Sadie's requirements, but mostly he watched her as she worked. Once he realized she wanted to keep a connection between them—touching him frequently as she added the amendments to the soil around one plant, sprayed a homemade concoction to rid another of aphids and adjusted the water near a third, he made a point of touching her arm, her shoulder or her back so she didn't have to interrupt her work. He had no idea why they were doing this, but he figured touching each other couldn't be a bad thing. Maybe it was her funny way of building a connection to him. Maybe it was a test.

If it sped them toward his goal of getting to know her—getting to marry her, he didn't care.

By the end of the day he was burning with need for her, but while Sadie allowed him to kiss her good-night, she broke away from him when he tried to angle her into the guest room for a more intimate encounter.

"I'm... not ready for that."

There was something so raw and truthful in her voice Connor didn't feel played. He knew she'd been through a lot. Knew the man who'd dated her before him hadn't treated her well. Knew the texts she'd seen from Lila and Bridget made her doubt him. He couldn't blame her. Connor hated the thought that any man had touched her, but he got that anger under control. Sadie needed his gentleness.

"I can wait," he made himself say. He hoped he was right.

She laid her hands on his chest and he struggled to stay still. He'd never waited before. He'd either been with a woman or hadn't. He realized now how much sweetness he'd missed. Anticipation was a heady sensation.

"I like to touch you," she said simply. "I shouldn't, but I do."

She was killing him. "Know what you mean." His hands ached to cup her breasts and feel their softness, but in this situation he needed to keep a cool head.

"I think..." She met his gaze and searched it. "I think... maybe."

He stilled. Such a simple statement—but he couldn't

think of another that had affected him so much.

She didn't trust him yet, but she'd left a little opening to her heart he might be able to pass through. He'd prove to her he could be the man she wanted. Fast. Because he wasn't sure how much longer he could hold back. Bit by bit his desire for Sadie had crept up on him until it consumed him, making clear thought difficult.

"Any time," he added. "You come looking for me, I'll be here. I'll be here tonight, as a matter of fact."

Sadie grinned. "Really. You'd like me to look for you tonight?"

She really was killing him. "Yeah," he admitted. "I'd like that. But like I said, I'll wait."

Sadie's lips parted. For a moment her own desire was visible on her face. Relief swept through him. He was right; he hadn't lost her irrevocably with those damn texts on his phone.

He forced himself to pull away. "I'll see you tomorrow."

Sadie nodded and slipped down the hall to her own room. She hesitated in the doorway almost long enough to make him think she'd changed her mind, before heading inside and closing the door behind her.

After a night full of dreams so erotic he woke up more frustrated than rested, Connor took an ice-cold shower, and spent several hours working with Lena. He'd just come back to the house mid-morning when a familiar red Ford truck pulled up and parked, and a man climbed out of it just in time to head Jo off as she approached from the carriage house.

"Who's that?" Sadie asked, coming to the door.

"Grant Kimball. He wants one of Jo's puppies," Connor said curtly. He didn't like how often the man was coming around.

"Are you sure? Looks to me like it's Jo he's interested in."

She was right.

Grant didn't seem to be in any hurry. He'd leaned against his truck, cocked his hat back and was chewing the fat with Jo.

"Something about that guy rubs me wrong," Connor told Sadie.

"I've never seen him before. Is he new in town?"

"Near as I can make out. I'm going to make sure he isn't bothering her." As he turned, Sadie held out a hand to stop him.

"Take it easy. I'm all for letting this guy know Jo's got people who care about her; I don't want anyone to hurt her again. But if he's just flirting, don't scare him away. She could use a good relationship right about now."

Connor was sure that was true, but that relationship was supposed to be with Hunter—not Grant. He kept going and arrived at Jo's side in time to hear Grant say, "I'd like to get on your list for next time."

"That list is a mile long," Jo told him. "Could be years before your name comes up."

"Then I guess I'll have to keep stopping by to see where I'm at."

A faint flush on Jo's cheeks told Connor she liked

the attention Grant was paying her.

Connor didn't like it. "There's no need to pester the lady. She'll call you up when it's your turn. Do you have this man's phone number?" he asked her.

"Not yet." She dug out her phone and passed it to Grant to put his information in.

"Your address, too," Connor said. "So she knows where to bring the dog." And he knew where to go to find out more about Grant.

"I'm kind of in between places right now," Grant said evenly. "But here's my number." He handed the phone back to Jo. "Where are they at, anyway? The puppies."

The flicker of Jo's gaze to the carriage house betrayed their whereabouts before she even said a word. Connor stifled a curse. He didn't like the idea of Grant knowing where the dogs were kept.

"Mind if I see one?"

"Yes, she minds," Connor said, stepping between them. "Jo takes her business seriously. She knows every family before she gives them a dog. When she gets to know you, she'll be ready to talk business. Got it?" He'd made all that up, but he had a feeling it was mostly true.

"Sure," Grant said after a long moment. "I can see you all are busy. I'll come back another time. So we can get to know each other," he said to Jo.

Jo nodded.

Grant got back into his truck, started it and peeled out.

"Lunch is ready," Sadie called from the porch.

"What was that all about?" she asked when Connor and Jo reached the back door.

"He wants a dog," Jo said.

"I'm not sure that's all he wants," Connor said darkly. "Jo, don't trust that guy. Something's off about him."

"I think he's kind of nice. And he likes dogs."

"Just be careful," Sadie said.

"I will. I'm not an idiot."

Connor sighed. Jo was no dummy. And maybe his dislike for the man was simply due to the circumstances they were in. Jo was meant for Hunter, not Grant. "Just go count those dogs. Make sure they're all where they're supposed to be." He couldn't overplay this, and he couldn't explain about Hunter, either. He'd do what he could to squash the budding relationship between Jo and Grant, but he'd also tell Hunter what was happening. Maybe the General would send the man early.

"The door's locked." But Jo set off toward the carriage house. Connor took Sadie's hand and guided her along with him as he followed Jo. When Jo opened the door to the room where the puppies were living, she counted quickly. "Five. Everyone's here and accounted for."

Connor dropped to his knees and let the puppies overrun him. Max in particular liked to lick his nose and Connor laughed and shoved him gently aside, only to have the puppy come back for more.

"He knows he's yours," Jo said, softening a little.

"You gave him a puppy?" Sadie sounded surprised.

"Max likes him."

"But—"

"Max likes him," Jo said again obstinately. "Arnold Meyers will have to wait."

Connor looked up to find Sadie watching him speculatively.

"People wait for years to get one of her puppies," she told Connor when they finished up and left the carriage house, Jo hanging back to secure the door. "I've never seen her play favorites like that before."

"Max likes me," Connor said with a grin.

Sadie's answering smile warmed him right to the core.

ALL DAY, SADIE puzzled over Connor in her mind. She didn't know how to reconcile his kindness and consideration with the man who collected women like playing cards and lied to his parents about getting married. He put up with her strange requests all afternoon, working in the garden side by side as if they were tethered together, but not pushing her past her comfort zone as far as their physical relationship was concerned.

Could a player show such restraint?

Would a two-timer be so gentle around her? And around Jo's puppies? Mark certainly wouldn't have been.

After dinner, he helped her with the dishes, and afterward led her out onto the back porch, but when he bent toward her as if he'd snatch a kiss, Sadie pulled back.

"Nope."

"Why not?" His tone was light, but his question was serious.

"You know why not. I'm not some woman you keep around for fun." He was hard to resist, especially after she'd spent the day so close to him, but she needed to resist him.

He didn't pretend not to understand. "Like I said, while I was in the Air Force I didn't want anything serious. I wasn't ready for it. That's changed." He pulled out his phone. "I probably shouldn't show you this. It won't make me look good." He tapped it a few times and showed her the screen. She read texts he'd written to several women making it clear he needed to end their flirtation. "I've met someone," he'd written to each of them. "I have to take this seriously."

She wasn't sure how to react. She was pleased to see the messages but... "You were flirting with all those women at once?"

"I told you it wouldn't make me look good." Connor shrugged. "I told you why I kept things light. My line of work can get... grim."

"You haven't told me much about your line of work."

Sadie sat down on the wicker couch. Connor joined her.

"It's my job to save pilots who go down behind enemy lines—among other things," he said, as if that explained everything.

"Sounds dangerous."

"Know a job in the military that isn't?" he asked her.

"No, but that sounds more dangerous than most."

"It can be."

"Thinking about something specific?" She could tell he was.

"My last mission was... interesting." He shifted closer to her and the rattan couch creaked. "We dropped into Syria, looking for a plane that went down. We found the plane, but the pilot was missing. I have to admit I expected the worst—that he'd been found by enemy forces. Taken hostage."

Sadie suppressed a shiver that traced down her spine. She could only imagine the wreckage of the plane, the sere landscape and their desperate search.

"Then a man came—an old man. A Syrian. Halil." Connor shook his head. "He kept beckoning to us. 'He's over here, over here!' We didn't know if it was a trap. He was ancient. Thin—you wouldn't believe how thin. We followed him."

Sadie bit her lip. Connor must have known he could be killed at any time—

"It wasn't a trap. He led us to a makeshift camp. Just a tarp and a little fire. Hardly anything. But he and his wife, Fatima, had been tending Shaw—the pilot— doing their best to save him. He would have died if they hadn't."

Connor took another sip, but all Sadie could do was watch him. "Why did they do it? Wouldn't they have been in danger?"

"Damn straight." Connor nodded. "They were refugees on their way to the border where they hoped to cross to safety. They knew damn well plenty of people in the area wouldn't be sympathetic to Americans. That's why they carried him to their camp. They were trying to hide him. Fatima was as old as he was—I have no idea how they carried Shaw."

"That's amazing."

"You have no idea." His gaze was distant, and she was sure he was back in Syria again.

Connor chuckled suddenly. "In the middle of all that, he wanted to do things right; to introduce himself. He told me his name, then his wife's. He was so proud of her."

"What was she like?" Sadie didn't want to move. Didn't want to break the spell. She wanted to know exactly what had happened.

"She wore a long dress, a head scarf, but her face wasn't covered. I think she must have been beautiful when she was young. She still was in a way. Frightened, though. Or maybe just shy. But I swear, when Halil looked at her, she smiled and you've never seen anything like it. Those two were in love. In the damn desert, starving probably, trying to walk to safety— eighty if they were a day. Totally in love. Halil told me they'd been married for sixty-two years. You know what he said?"

Sadie shook her head.

"Find a good woman. Make her your everything— your life. Then you will know peace no matter where you go."

"What happened to them?" Sadie knew Connor

probably had no idea.

He hesitated so long she thought he wouldn't answer.

"They had hundreds of miles to go to the border. They'd been walking with their family, but they were too slow. They told the others to go on ahead. They knew their chances of making it were slim."

She thought he was done and her heart ached for Connor. It must have been so hard to leave them there—

"I put them on the helicopter. Took them back with us. They saved Shaw." His gaze pleaded with her to understand.

Sadie sucked in a surprised breath. Of course she understood; how could he do anything else?

But that must be why Connor was here. Why he'd gotten in trouble with the Air Force.

"I couldn't leave them. I don't know where they are now. No one will tell me," he confessed. "All I can hope is I did the right thing and they're safe."

"Of course you did the right thing," Sadie cried. "They saved our pilot."

"That's not what the Air Force thinks. So I ended up at USSOCOM under your dad's command."

She took that in. "And the General sent you here to build a walled garden?" What a finish to the man's career. Connor didn't deserve that.

"Gets me out of his hair, doesn't it?" Connor said lightly, but she could tell the whole series of events had made a lasting impression on him. He'd saved the pilot and two refugees.

And lost everything over it.

"What are you going to do now?" She couldn't imagine how he must feel.

"Build you a walled garden, for starters," he said simply. "Don't feel bad for me, Sadie. I can't think of anywhere I'd rather be right now." He leaned over and kissed her.

And Sadie let him.

Chapter Seven

HOW COULD ONE innocent kiss spark so much want inside him? How could one innocent country girl like Sadie make him want to toss everything else to the wind and follow her everywhere?

Including up off his seat, down the steps and back out into the garden—which was where she was leading him in between kissing him like she could never get enough.

He knew he couldn't.

At first he couldn't figure out her plan. She wandered first in one direction, then in another, with no apparent rhyme or reason until he tore away from a kiss that was driving him half out of his mind, lifted his head and realized she was walking the rows of the garden one after another.

"Lass, what the hell are you doing?" he asked when he finally pulled her to a stop. He wanted more than kisses and she was distracting him from his goal.

"Drawing it out. We'll get to the maze sooner or later." She went up on tiptoe and kissed him again.

"Get to the—?" Hell. Connor gave in. If Sadie

wanted to seduce him in every row of her garden, let her. If she wanted to be with him in the center of the maze, he was down for that. Couldn't think of a better place, in fact. The long summer's day was fading into twilight. No one was around.

Sadie turned a corner and led him down another path. Connor took a chance, put his hand on her waist and skimmed it up her tight-fitting T-shirt to caress her breast through the fabric.

Sadie stumbled, tore herself away from him, but kept a hand on his shoulder, breathing hard while she looked around her. "They can see us from the house—"

But before she finished her sentence, she trailed off and stared at the zucchini plant near her feet. It was by far the healthiest thing he'd seen in the garden since he'd been here, Connor thought. When Sadie grabbed his hand and placed it over her breast, however, all thoughts of zucchini fled his mind. Connor happily obliged her with a firm caress. Sadie's breathing hitched, but she kept her gaze on the ground, then laughed.

"What?"

"They—they like it when we're together. I can feel them… growing. Getting healthier." Connor wondered if she'd lost her mind when she turned in a slow circle, then suddenly shouted, "Is that what you want? A fertility rite?" She paused as if listening.

"Sadie—"

"No, don't even try to defend any of them. You have no idea what this land has been putting me through." She grabbed the hem of her T-shirt and yanked it up over her head, exposing a surprisingly lacy bra underneath.

"Sadie—" Connor glanced around, glad there was no one in sight, glad for the view of Sadie's breasts, if he was honest, but Sadie wasn't making sense. Maybe she was overworked, stressed out by the attack on her house—

"Make love to me," Sadie demanded and flung her arms wide to indicate the whole garden. "It's what they want! What they all want!"

"What who wants?"

"The tomatoes, the carrots, the zucchini—especially the zucchini—"

"Sadie, I... can't." He took a step back to show he meant what he'd said. He'd never thought of Sadie as high-strung, but she'd definitely gone over the edge. "Let's find one of your sisters. Put your shirt on. Maybe a cup of tea—"

Sadie stared at him. Blinked. Looked down at the shirt in her hands.

Blushed a furious shade of scarlet.

"Oh, my God."

"It's okay," he began, but Sadie yanked the shirt back over her head and thrashed around until her arms were through the armholes.

"I'm sorry. I just—I don't—oh, my God." Sadie was shaking and Connor ached to pull her into his arms, but he really needed to know what had happened just now. One minute Sadie had been lucid, the next raving about zucchini. They had to sort this out.

She must have thought so, too, because she made sure to keep a gap between them, narrowing her eyes when he would have stepped closer. She put up a hand to stop him.

"You don't hear it at all, do you? You don't even know—" She backed away from him.

Connor pursued her. "What do you hear? When we touch?" It was a long shot, but with the beautiful woman in front of him all but melting down, he had to take it.

"I hear everything." Sadie hugged her arms over her chest, as if trying to protect herself from his derision. Her eyes filled with tears, and Connor's heart contracted as she fought to express herself. "My whole life when I worked in the garden, it spoke to me. When I touched the dirt I knew if it was too dry or too wet. When I touched a leaf I knew if a plant was diseased or getting too much sun or too much shade. But then… it stopped. Just stopped. Until you came."

Connor didn't know what to make of what she'd said. Didn't all good gardeners read the signs of the dirt and leaves and so on? Did Sadie really feel more than that when she worked with the plants?

"When did it stop?" he asked to buy more time.

"When—" A tear snaked down her cheek. "When Mark—when the shoot-out happened."

Clarity crashed over Connor and despite his intentions, he took a step back. Always Mark. Always this man who'd gotten to Sadie before him.

He wanted to crush the life out of him, whoever he

was. If Brian hadn't already shot the guy, he'd have to go do it himself.

"So when the shoot-out happened, and you learned that Mark wasn't who you thought he was—"

"That's just the thing. I knew exactly who he was. And I didn't walk away. I... helped him. I didn't know what he planned to do, but I knew he was dealing drugs, and I... helped him."

"Helped him?" Brian had told him everything that happened leading up to the shoot-out, and he'd known Sadie was caught in the car with Mark and Howie Warner when they'd been returning home from running a shipment to Bozeman, but he didn't know she took so much responsibility for what happened.

"I should have known what they meant to do," she said as if she'd read his mind. "I should have stopped Mark. I dated the man who tried to kill my sisters— kissed him—let him touch me—that's why the land wants me gone."

"Wait—what?" Connor shook his head. Her admission about being with Mark hit him in a place so primeval his vision had gone red before the rest of her words sunk in. "The land—"

"Wants me gone. At least, I thought it did before you came." Sadie looked at him helplessly. "I know that sounds ridiculous, but Two Willows is different than everywhere else. My mother had this connection to it, and so do I—at least I did. And then I didn't. But now when I'm with you, I do again. I don't hear voices, Connor—it's not like that. It's a knowing. A feeling.

Stronger than anything you usually feel. I get this sense of exactly what the right thing to do is—and what the wrong thing is."

"I don't understand, lass."

She drew in a frustrated breath. "Before you came, the garden was dying. Parts of it still are. The rest is hanging in the balance. I couldn't feel what the plants needed anymore."

He remembered how dusty it had all looked when he'd driven up that first day. He'd chalked it up to too many hot, sunny days, her distraction because of the trouble with Mark and the others, and their race to prepare for Cass and Brian's wedding on such short notice.

But even afterward, when he saw how much care Sadie had lavished on her plants, he'd noticed the blighted leaves, the withered stems and the fruit rotting before it even ripened.

"Some years are better than others, right?" he said, wanting to believe it. What Sadie was hinting at was far too strange.

"No. Not here. Not at Two Willows. Not before I betrayed it."

"You think your garden is... punishing you? Because you fell for Mark even though he planned to use you, take your home and run his operation out of Two Willows?"

She nodded.

Nothing he'd learned in the military prepared him for a situation like this. "So what changed?" Connor managed to ask.

"You came." Her words were a whisper. "The very first time I touched you—"

"What happened?" He was intrigued in spite of himself.

"It was like someone flipped a switch and there it was again. I could hear it—feel it. I could save my plants."

Which was why she kept dragging him around the garden like a wheelbarrow of mulch, he realized.

And he'd thought it had been because she couldn't get enough of him.

The joke was on him, wasn't it? He'd always gotten the women he fancied, even though he was never serious about them. Now he found a woman he thought he could make his wife, and she found him as handy as a pile of manure.

"I think it's because of how I feel about you," Sadie said, knocking him off balance again. "It's not like Mark at all. That was just... boredom. Wanting to be wanted. With you, it's... different."

Connor waited. He didn't think he could stand it if she trotted out some line about true friendship or crap like that.

"It's because... I feel... I feel..."

There was that blush again. But she hadn't finished the sentence, and Connor didn't know how much longer he could wait.

"I feel like you set me on fire when you're close. Like I could go up in flames if you don't touch me. I want you close to me, Connor. I want... I want you inside me."

Connor tossed caution to the wind, closed the distance between them, cupped her chin in his hands and kissed her.

THEY COULDN'T DO this here, Sadie realized when Connor's hands crept up to her breasts again. She wanted exactly what he wanted, but they were in full sight of the house, the carriage house, the driveway...

Besides, there was something she needed to know.

"The maze."

She didn't have to say anything else. Connor seemed to understand without an explanation. He took her hand and tugged her along, his long strides eating up the ground, leaving her scrambling to keep up. When they reached the entrance he plunged right in, but immediately took a wrong turn. Sadie dug in her heels and yanked him in the right direction. He caught her up in a kiss, took the lead and strode down the rest of the green passage before turning the wrong way again. Sadie took hold of his bicep with two hands and bodily turned him around, keeping the kiss going.

"Lass, did your mother not tell not to push your menfolk around?"

The lilt in his accent tugged at something deep within her. She wriggled around behind him, placed her two hands on his back and shoved him in the right direction.

Except he didn't move.

"Ye'll have to try a little harder, you wee little

thing."

Now he was laying his Irish burr on so thick she had to laugh.

"You want to actually make it to the center, don't you?" Frustrated, flushed with desire, panting from keeping up with him, Sadie pushed her hair away from her face and tried again.

Nothing.

"Aye, but under my own power. 'Tis a shameful thing when a man lets himself be pushed around by a lassie—fuck!"

Sadie had elbowed him under his rib cage with a karate-chop-like movement she hadn't known she knew how to perform. Connor spun around, looped an arm around her waist and tossed her over his shoulder.

"If you're in such a damned hurry, you should have said so up front."

There. Now his voice was back to normal. His mock anger made her smile, as did seeing the maze from this angle, jangling on his shoulder as he barged along the paths, taking first one turn, then another, going around in circles until Sadie couldn't stand it anymore.

"Right. No, your other right!" she called when he reached a turn. "My right."

"Which one?" Connor sounded as frustrated as she felt.

"Left!"

Connor went left. Following her directions, they made it to the center in short order and he set her down between the bench and the standing stone. "See? The man takes charge—that's how it's done."

"You're an idiot."

But he wasn't paying attention. Instead he was staring at her like he'd never quite seen her before. "Where were we?" he mused. "Oh, right—" He took hold of the hem of her T-shirt and whipped it up and over her head. "Right here."

"Connor!"

"Want me to put it back on? Oh, wait, lass—I can't seem to hold it in this stiff breeze." He balled it up and tossed it over the nearest green wall.

Sadie bit her lip as the shirt unfolded at the apex of the toss and gently settled on top of the hedge.

"Whoops." Connor eyed the thick evergreen shrubbery that made up the wall. "How high is that? Fifteen feet?"

"Twenty. I always keep it exactly at twenty feet." She'd have to get the damn ladder out later.

"You're a beautiful woman when you're angry, Sadie Reed." He moved in close.

"Lucky for you, because I have a feeling you'll see me angry more often than not."

"Shh." He kissed her, and Sadie forgot the shirt, forgot their earlier scuffle and the way he'd carried her like a sack of potatoes through the maze's passages. Here they were.

Together.

As his fingertips slid over her waist, up her back to the catch of her bra, Sadie held still and savored the sensation.

"I know you're doing this for the garden," he began.

"I'm doing it for me," she said truthfully.

"But you said—"

"That, too." Her voice was husky with need. "I can't lie—" Not when she knew what it felt like to be used. "I wouldn't have let you near me if you didn't turn the connection back on," she admitted. "But I couldn't be with someone just for that. I'm not like that. Not... removed."

He got her bra undone, slid it off and tossed it away, thankfully not onto the hedge this time, although she thought he might have considered it for a moment. "No, you aren't removed, are you? You don't hide."

She wondered what he was thinking about. That sentence seemed to hold a world of pain. She smoothed a hand over his hair and realized the connection arced between them, too. She could hear—or feel—or know—what he needed in the same way she could feel the growing things around them. A touch, just like that.

A kiss.

"I wish I could sometimes," she told him. She had always been too open with her feelings. It was how Mark had controlled her.

"No, don't wish for that." He traced kisses down her neck, behind her ear and over her shoulder. "Be real—like the garden. It doesn't hide either. It wilts when conditions aren't right. It blooms when they are."

She bloomed under his touch. His kisses kept distracting her from the thoughts she needed to work out, and when he cupped her breasts, lifted them and swept his palms over her sensitive nipples, Sadie thought she'd drown in the sensations rushing over her.

"I don't want to hide from you," she said truthfully.

"I don't want to hide from you either," he told her. "I want—I want you to know me."

Somehow she understood those other women—Lila and Bridget—hadn't known him the way he meant. They both had pasts but now they were building a present together. When she tugged at the hem of his shirt, he lifted a hand over his head, grabbed a fistful of the fabric where it stretched across his back and tugged it off.

He tangled his hands in the waistband of her shorts, undid the button, the zipper and shucked them down. She kicked off her shoes and wiggled out of her panties, standing before him in all her naked glory. When she reached for the buckle of his belt, he let her undo it. He was so hard he was straining against his jeans, and he groaned as she undid his belt and fumbled with the button.

Finally, when they were both undressed, he stooped to reach into his pocket and pull out a condom.

"Are you sure about this?" He let her see what was in his hand, giving her one last chance to back away.

He searched her gaze, as if telling her that though it would kill him to stop now, he was man enough to do it. She had to want this as much as he did.

"I'm sure."

Connor tore open the condom wrapper, sheathed himself as quickly as he could, then lifted her up, took two steps and they crashed into the standing stone. Her back pressed against it, held up by her legs wrapped around his waist, Sadie let him take her hands, lift them above her head and press them with his against the stone's broad expanse.

"Are we—?"

SADIE LEANED FORWARD and kissed him before he could finish his question. She knew what she wanted, no matter what Fate had to say. She pressed her thighs against his hips, lifted up and settled back down, taking him in and allowing Connor to push inside her slowly as gravity urged her down. He let go of her wrists to support her, and she twined her arms around his neck. Sadie held on as he pulled out and pushed in again, moaning with the pleasure radiating through her from this sweet friction.

Sadie forgot everything else but him as he began to move in a rhythm she couldn't help but join. A rhythm that coaxed waves of sensation into a vortex in her body. She willed him to speed up and he did, his strong motions teasing her to a fevered pitch.

With the stone at her back and Connor in front of her, thrusting into her, winding her so tight she didn't think she could last another moment, Sadie knew this was her answer.

She was meant to be with Connor.

No matter what the stone said.

No matter if it said anything at all.

This was where she wanted to be. This was her man.

With Connor she'd save her garden, save her home. Save herself.

CONNOR HAD BEEN aching with need for Sadie for days, so when he thrust into her again, and she arched her back and cried out, her abandon pulled him over the edge into the throes of an orgasm so powerful his vision went black.

When it cleared again, he was struck by Sadie's beauty all over again. Always before when he'd been close to her, she'd shied away from him, or been bent over her vegetables working, or distracted with worry.

For once she was fully present, and she met his gaze with her own.

"That was—incredible," she said, and then, to Connor's horror, she teared up.

"Whoa, whoa—what's wrong?"

He moved to pull out of her, but Sadie linked her ankles behind his back. "Nothing's wrong. Nothing at all; it's…. right. I didn't expect that."

She was a pleasant weight in his arms. Every move he made pressed part of him against part of her. He could stay like this forever.

"What do you mean?" Relaxing a little, he smoothed a knuckle over one bare breast and Sadie moaned, a smile on her face.

"I mean, I thought I was supposed to leave."

"Go to India."

"Right. I thought the garden—the maze—was telling me I wasn't fit to live here anymore."

Connor glanced over his shoulder and frowned. Was the hedge—greener? "Everything looks healthy to me."

She leaned forward until her breasts brushed his chest. "It does, doesn't it? I think that's because of you. Connor... you have to stay."

"Because your garden will die if I leave?"

He was fishing, but she didn't care. She felt silly for trying to hide her feelings from him. "Because I want you to stay."

Chapter Eight

A FTER HE'D MADE love to Sadie slowly and thoroughly a second time, they dressed and returned to the house. Connor gave Sadie his shirt, since hers was out of reach, and when they met up with Lena on the back porch, Lena took one look at his bare chest and rolled her eyes.

"Ready for your close-up?" she asked sarcastically.

Connor simply shrugged and struck a pose. He wasn't ashamed of the muscles he'd gained during his years in the Air Force.

"Not *your man*, huh?" Lena said to Sadie as Connor brushed past her and reached for the screen door.

"Not until today," Sadie said pertly. "Don't you have some cattle to chase around?"

"Just got a phone call from Autumn Cruz. She wanted to know if we'd host the quilting bee here tonight. She's got unexpected guests. I told her that was fine."

"Quilting bee?" Connor repeated, his hand on the doorknob. "They still have those?"

"I forgot all about it! Wait—you said we'd have it

here?" Sadie's eyes widened.

"Why not? We've got plenty of room."

"The place is a mess. Cass would kill me if I let people see it like this!" Sadie ducked around Connor and pushed into the house. "I'll need everyone's help. Lena, get Alice and Jo. Right now!"

"Hell, she sounds just like Cass," Lena said to Connor.

"Lena, I said NOW!"

Lena chuckled. "Now she's channeling Mom."

"Is that Grant Kimball again?" Connor watched as a familiar truck pulled in near the carriage house.

"Yep. And that's Jo—shit."

Connor wanted to echo Lena's sentiment as they both watched Jo practically skip up to the truck, climb in to the passenger's side and drive away with Grant.

"Should we stop her?" he asked.

Lena shook her head. "We can't. She's an adult." But she sounded worried. "She's been talking about him down in the barn. It's Grant this and Grant that. We don't know anything about that man." She glanced at Connor. "Normally I wouldn't be like this. We Reeds are independent. But lately…"

She didn't need to finish her thought. "You're right; we don't know anything about Grant. And that's going to change. Right now." Connor made up his mind. "Text her. Tell her about the quilting bee. Tell her Sadie needs her help—lay it on thick. Does Jo usually take part in things like that?"

"Yes."

"Good. Get her home again. Meanwhile, I'll slip out when you ladies get busy and head to town. See what I can find out." Cab might not have information on Grant, but someone would.

Lena already had her phone out. "I like the way you think."

Sadie stuck her head out the door. "Have you gotten a hold of Alice and Jo yet? Someone needs to deal with the farm stand."

"Doing it right now."

"I need your help, too," Sadie told Connor with a significant look.

Connor joined her inside, and to his surprise Sadie led him upstairs. "We both need to clean up; figured we might as well do that together. No funny stuff, though."

"No funny stuff," he agreed.

There was plenty of funny stuff, but twenty minutes later they were both clean and Sadie was all business as they dressed in the bathroom. "I was lying about needing your help. What I really need is for you to make yourself scarce. Would you mind having dinner in town? I'm going to fix my sisters a snack and then we've got to clear the kitchen so we have room to sew."

"I don't mind at all. I'll get a couple of errands done and eat while I'm at it. When I come home, I'll handle the evening chores. I had no idea people still quilted." He didn't bring up Grant—or the way Jo had left with him. No need to get Sadie worried since Lena was already calling Jo home. He didn't want to spoil her night, either. He'd fill her in on what he found out when he got home and her guests were gone. After all, he didn't have any specific reason to distrust Grant.

"They do here. We're all getting together to make a quilt for Jill Winsor's bridal shower. She asked for one and let us know what colors she likes, so tonight we'll each sew up a square or two. We'll put the quilt together soon and get together for another bee to finish it off."

"I'll get out of your hair then. Have fun tonight."

"You, too. See you... later?"

"I'll be waiting for you."

WHEN SADIE SLIPPED away from the quilting bee late that evening, she headed upstairs, ostensibly to freshen up, but in reality to snatch another moment with Connor. She hadn't seen him return home yet, but it was nearly ten and he'd left over four hours ago. He should have been home ages ago to do the evening chores. With the area near the carriage house full of their friends' vehicles, he'd probably parked out front and slipped in the front door.

All night she had thought about their encounter in the maze, and wondered when they might be together again. Just thinking about it made her tingle all over, and made it hard to focus on the chatter of the women around the table. They talked about the usual things: Jill's upcoming wedding, and the chances the young couple had for happiness—which everyone reckoned were strong. The harvest festival and whether or not the old Revolutionary War re-enactments should continue or be abolished—some women begrudged the time it took their boyfriends or husbands away from them and the emphasis on fighting, others enjoyed the re-enactments themselves, and looked forward to them. The settling of the extensive Cooper family on a ranch that had been left alone for years. Overall, the women at the table agreed it might mean trouble.

Sadie knocked lightly on Connor's closed door, but there was no answer. She knocked again, but again he didn't respond. She knew he could be anywhere on the ranch, perhaps still out with the animals. Lena had slipped away some time ago and hadn't returned, but then she'd never been one for quilting. Probably hiding down in the barn with Connor. Sadie pulled out her phone and called him, turning toward her own room. But when she heard a sharp buzzing sound from behind her, she turned back, and pressed her ear against the guest room door.

Connor had left his phone in his bedroom again. Maybe he was here after all. Sadie hesitated, then curiosity won over common sense, and she turned the handle and opened the door a crack. Connor wasn't in his bed, and when she opened the door farther she could see he wasn't at his desk, either. In fact, the room was empty. But his phone lay on the dresser where he'd left it. So she couldn't call him. She wouldn't sneak a peek at his messages, either, she decided. She was done with that.

Although she had to admit she was curious… and a little worried. She couldn't help but think about all of Mark's lies. At first he'd hidden his exploits with Tracy.

Only later did he flirt with her openly... and take Tracy home instead of her.

Sadie's cheeks burned at the memory and she was glad no one could see her here in the guest bedroom. Maybe she wasn't as over her past as she thought she was. For the first time she admitted to herself how badly it had hurt when Mark had treated her that way. She'd put up a front for him, pretending she didn't care, but she had. Every look he'd exchanged with Tracy had felt like a knife in her heart.

Of course, it had been worse after the attack. Bad enough he'd thought so little of her he'd treated her that way, but for him to try to kill her sisters—

She could barely breathe when she thought about what had happened. She loved her sisters more than she loved herself. What if he'd succeeded? What if they'd died and she'd had to go on—

Alone?

Sadie reached for the door frame and steadied herself.

If she chose to be with Connor, she'd leave herself vulnerable to that kind of pain again.

Sadie went down the hall and checked in the bathroom. It was empty, too. On a whim, she called Lena next. "Where are you?"

"I just got back from the barn. Where are you?"

"Upstairs."

"Get your ass back down here and start sewing. If I have to do it, you do, too."

"Was Connor still down there when you went to

check on the animals?" Sadie held her breath.

"As far as I know, he hasn't made it back. I went down for some fresh air, but none of the chores had been done, so I did them."

"That's weird—he said he'd be back to do them. I wonder where he is?"

"You've got it baaaad," Lena sang.

Sadie cut the call and pocketed her phone. Lena was right; she did have it bad, and that made her anxious. Why hadn't he called her if he knew he was going to be late? He could have borrowed a phone.

He's a grown man, she told herself. *You don't own him. He doesn't have to report his whereabouts to you at every minute.* She would hate a relationship like that.

But as she headed back downstairs, she admitted to herself she wasn't just disappointed. She was worried. Not about his safety, but about what a man like Connor might choose to do when left on his own. She couldn't help remembering the women he'd been texting before. Couldn't help remembering the way Mark had played her.

And she didn't like that feeling one bit.

IT WAS AFTER ten when Connor entered the Dancing Boot, pushed his way through the crowd and angled up to the bar. He'd done his errands, had dinner at Del-Monaco's, waiting a long time for his meal since the restaurant was so crowded, and realized afterward he couldn't call the ranch to let Sadie know he'd be late because he'd left his phone in his room. He knew Lena would check the animals and do the chores since he wasn't there, but he'd have liked to call and tell her all the same.

Instead, he persisted in his attempt to learn about Grant, figuring Sadie was too busy with her guests to miss him. He spent a fruitless couple of hours monopolizing a pool table at a dive bar called Rafters before someone told him the real action was going on here.

He ordered a shot of Jack Daniel's, frustrated by his lack of progress learning more about Grant Kimball.

"It's on the house," the pretty bartender said when she placed it in front of Connor.

"Really?" He grinned at the brunette behind the bar. Things were finally looking up if the booze was free; he'd already spent plenty on dinner and alcohol tonight. The bartender was dressed for work in a skintight T-shirt that left little to the imagination and a pair of poured-on dark jeans.

"Really," she purred.

Too late Connor realized she meant it as an opening salvo in a flirtation. Her smoky eyeshadow and painted lips were a far cry from Sadie's fresh-faced good looks, and he remembered Cab's admonition—this was a small town. Just talking to the woman was bound to be trouble.

On the other hand, he'd scored a big goose egg as far as gathering any intel on Grant so far tonight. A bartender could be a gold mine of information. He couldn't pass up this opportunity.

Or a free drink at the tail end of a frustrating evening. He'd had more than a few at Rafters, and had left his truck there and walked the few blocks to the Boot. He'd have to take a cab home at the end of this night. If he arrived there empty-handed, he'd really feel like a fool.

"You look like you've had a hard day." The bartender rested her elbows on the bar, her chin in her hands. "Want to tell me about it?"

"Thanks, lass." He thought he did. Laying on his accent, he continued. "Been a bit of a rough one."

She nodded. "Tell me about it."

"Rough one for you, too?"

"You could say that." For a moment her smile faded, and Connor realized she was older than he'd first thought. She looked like a woman who'd seen too many opportunities pass her by.

"Man trouble?" He asked half because it made a good lead-in to asking about Grant, but also because he felt for her. The world wasn't kind to everyone. You made a few mistakes and suddenly you couldn't come back from them.

"What else?" She shrugged. "I seem to have a knack for picking the wrong ones."

"A common ailment." He leaned closer. "A friend of mine's done something like that—picked a man I don't think is good for her. That's why I'm here. Need to have a word with him, but he's nowhere to be found."

He downed the shot.

The woman poured him another, ignoring the

shouts of a bunch of young cowboys at the far end of the bar who wanted another round. She put it in front of him. "This one's free, too."

"You're generous tonight, lass."

"You're pretty fucking cute. And you look single. What do you say—will you take me away from all this?"

Connor choked on the shot he'd just lifted to his mouth. Shit. He'd almost dumped the alcohol down his front. Just what he needed; to come home to Sadie smelling like he'd bathed in it. He'd have to walk a fine line with this woman. She was reading far too much into their banter.

The cowboys were beginning to kick up a fuss. "Hold that thought," the bartender told Connor. "I'll be back. I'm Tracy, by the way. Don't run off, now." She touched his arm and sashayed down the length of the bar to serve the young men. He watched her go, the alcohol giving his tawdry surroundings a pleasant glow.

A hand clamped down on Connor's shoulder, and he turned to find a cowboy he didn't recognize behind him. The man was tall, rugged, dressed in jeans and a black shirt, a black hat in his hand.

"Let's go take a walk," the man said. He strode off and the patrons in the bar rushed to part around him as he passed.

Connor, taken aback, hesitated and glanced at Tracy's receding figure again before he pushed off his stool to follow the man. He'd be back for another try before she even noticed he was gone, he told himself.

Outside, the man was waiting for him, his hat on his

head, but he set off again when Connor reached him and turned the corner. Only when they were out of sight of the entrance did the stranger thrust out his hand.

"Name's Steel Cooper."

"Connor O'Riley." Connor shook with him, wondering what this was all about, trying to sober up a little.

"You're staying at Two Willows?"

"That's right."

Steel kept his gaze over Connor's shoulder, scanning the street while they talked. "Tracy Jones is no friend to the women there. If you are, I'd give her a wide berth."

"I was just having a drink, mister."

"You were trying to get in her pants."

Ouch. Was that what it had looked like? And if Steel had noticed, had anyone else? "What's it to you?"

"Nothing." The other man surveyed him with a mixture of exasperation and contempt. "Thought you were at Two Willows to help the Reeds."

"What do you even know about it?" Connor didn't like the turn this conversation had taken. He knew Brian had opened up to some of the other ex-military men in town when things heated up a few weeks ago. A few of them had helped out the night of the shoot-out. Had they spread their business far and wide? He'd have to have a word with Brian when the SEAL returned.

"More than I want to. Look, the Reed girls practically shut down the supply of drugs in this town. People are pissed. They're talking. And Tracy isn't their friend. Do I need to draw you a picture?"

"I think you do. Cut to brass tacks. What the hell

are you trying to say?" He felt far more sober than he had just a minute ago. The comment about trying to get into Tracy's pants still chafed. Couldn't a man have a minute alone around here? Was everyone going to have an opinion on the way he conducted his business?

He supposed so. Small town and all that.

Steel stepped in closer. "Let me put it this way. That woman you're chatting up in there? She was Mark Pendergrass's girl, too. Didn't like Sadie horning in her action. Doesn't like the idea of Mark serving time—or being shot."

Connor's gut tightened. "Mark Pendergrass? The one who—"

"The very one." Steel backed off. "That's all I got to say to you." He touched his fingers to the brim of his hat.

"Wait." Connor's mind was racing. "What's all this to you?"

The cowboy shook his head, turned on his heel and walked away, melting into the shadows of the narrow street until Connor couldn't see him.

He looked back toward the Dancing Boot.

Decided it was time to go home.

IT WAS LATE by the time the women all trooped out onto the back porch to head home. Stars twinkled overhead and it was the kind of soft summer evening that called for a glass of lemonade and an hour or two on the back porch before bed.

Sadie was too busy worrying about Connor to enjoy

the stars, however. With each passing minute, her imagination went a little further afield. Had he found someone he liked better than her?

"We should do this more often," Autumn Cruz said. "We can meet at my place next—"

"Hey! Get away from there!" Jo broke from the crowd, clattered down the steps and took off running toward the carriage house, which stood far enough from the house to be shrouded in shadow.

As the other women murmured with shock, Sadie pushed through them to try to see what had riled Jo. Sometimes foxes came to try for the chickens in the coops out behind the carriage house. Even coyotes sometimes made their way onto the ranch, but not very often.

When she heard a man's angry shout, she took off after her sister. The thought of Jo facing a stranger, alone, after what had happened just weeks ago—

Footsteps pounded behind her and she realized several of the other women had followed her. As she rounded the side of the carriage house she caught sight of a man scuffling with Jo. She couldn't make out more than his silhouette in the dim light, but before she could reach them, a gun went off, several of the women screamed and Sadie ducked. Inside the carriage house, all the dogs began to bark.

The man swore and took off running.

Sadie couldn't breathe. Who had fired…?

Lena ran past, her pistol still in her hand. Several other women rushed by in pursuit of the man. By the time Sadie got to Jo, Lena had shoved the pistol into her shoulder holster and helped her up. Spending so much time on the range by herself, Lena tended to be armed.

"What were you thinking?" Sadie screeched at Lena. "You could have killed her!"

"I didn't aim at them; I pointed into the air. Jo—are you okay?"

"That's right, run, coward!" Claire Lassiter shouted in the direction the man had disappeared. She and the other women trailed back, obviously discouraged. "He got away, whoever that was."

"Are you hurt?" Sadie asked Jo again, her heart still beating much too fast.

"No. Just…pissed!" Jo straightened and scrubbed her wrist over her cheeks where Sadie spotted the glint of tears. "I thought I saw something near the carriage house. I thought it would be an animal, and it would run off when it saw me. But it was a man—and he grabbed me!"

"Let's get back to the house."

"I need to check on the dogs."

"Did you get a good look at him?" Lena demanded as Jo fumbled in her pocket for her keys.

"No." Jo shook her head, taking two tries to unlock the door. "He had a ski mask on. I think he was on something—drugs. He was wired."

"We should call Cab," Autumn said.

Sadie nodded. She pulled out her phone and placed the call, but while she waited for someone to answer, she said, "We should really get inside."

"Not until I check on the dogs."

Sadie was thankful for the presence of all the other women as she waited for Jo to check on the animals. Only when she had determined they were all safe, and had locked them back in again, did Jo consent to return to the house.

Everyone stayed to give their statements when Cab arrived, and he spent some time checking out the carriage house and its surroundings.

"Can you bring the dogs inside for the night?" Cab asked Sadie. "I'd like to keep this area as intact as possible and come back in the morning to check it again."

"I can do that." Her sisters helped move the animals inside and down into the basement, where it was easiest to set up an area the puppies couldn't destroy overnight. The other women headed home, promising Cab to contact him if they remembered any details they hadn't already mentioned. When they were gone, and Lena was inside brewing a strong pot of coffee for the all-night vigil she insisted on mounting, Cab asked Sadie to walk him to his cruiser.

"Where's Connor tonight? I'd have thought he'd be here guarding the place."

"I'd have thought that, too." Sadie tried not to betray the worry and bitterness warring within her. Where was Connor? It was late—he'd been in town for hours.

"You two have a fight?" When she shot him a sharp look, Cab held up his hands in a placating manner. "People talk. He talked," he admitted when she didn't back down. "It's pretty obvious he's carrying a torch for you. He came to see me a while back. He didn't say anything outright, but it didn't take much to see where his attention had wandered."

"I don't know about that." A few hours ago she'd been sure she and Connor were made for each other, and she still wanted to believe that he'd stayed in town this long to keep out of their way while they entertained their friends, but was she fooling herself? Sadie wasn't sure how to tell. After all, she'd proved she wasn't too smart where men were concerned.

"You could do a lot worse."

Sadie turned on him. "You mean I've done a lot worse in the past. I know that, Sheriff. I don't need you to rub my nose in it."

"That's not what I meant at all. I'm just saying he's worth fighting for if you've had a little tiff."

"That's just the thing." Her aggravation mounted. "We didn't have a little tiff. But he's not here. Where the hell is he?"

"You expected him home before now?"

"Yes! No—I don't know." She couldn't hide her frustration.

The sheriff studied her. "I'll keep an eye out for him. I'll be back first thing in the morning, too. Now you get inside, lock those doors tight and keep inside until morning. I'll keep some men here overnight."

"Thank you."

Inside she found Lena cleaning her shotgun. "I'm calling it a night," Sadie told her. "Cab's got some men outside. Try not to shoot them."

Lena didn't rise to the bait. "Get some rest."

But when Sadie headed upstairs to her room, she knew she wouldn't sleep a wink.

Chapter Nine

K NOWING HE'D DRUNK too much to drive home, but not feeling like calling a taxi, either, Connor had decided a good long walk would help clear his head and help him make sense of what Steel Cooper had told him. Besides, he needed time to sort out what to tell Sadie about Tracy—and what not to mention.

If Steel hadn't accused him of trying to sleep with Tracy, he wouldn't have thought twice about his encounter with the bartender, but now he was worried that word would get back to Sadie about him... flirting.

Which he hadn't been.

Except he had, in order to get information out of the woman.

He never really thought about the tricks he'd used to gain intelligence in the past. Or the way he flirted with women constantly, if he was truthful. It came easily, and he liked the extra perks he got when women were attracted to him. A free drink at a bar, an upgrade to first class on a plane...

A fun weekend when he was on leave somewhere halfway around the world from his home.

Now his life had changed. He didn't want fun week-ends; he wanted the whole deal. He hadn't gone to the Dancing Boot looking for anything more than infor-mation. Still, when Tracy started flirting it had felt...

Comfortable.

And he wasn't sure what to make of that. Nor could he stop trying to puzzle it out. He didn't like the answers he came up with. Tracy couldn't hold a candle to Sadie—not just in looks, but in personality, intelli-gence—the whole package. Neither did Lila, or Bridget—or any of the other women he'd dated. So why had he been with them?

Because he didn't think he deserved the real deal?

After all, his mother had sent him packing at ten—

Connor stopped in his tracks, an ancient sorrow pressing hard on his chest. His hands clenched and flexed. His breath came fast.

She'd let him go.

Kept Dalton, but let him go.

Why?

Alone, on the side of an empty road, the darkness pierced only by the glint of starts, Connor asked the question.

But received no answer.

When he patted his pocket, he realized he didn't even have his phone. If he did, would he call and ask her outright?

He didn't know.

But for the first time, he didn't push the painful question away. He let it expand until it filled him—

swallowed him whole. Still, under the vast canopy of the star-studded sky, his pain was just a tiny spark. There was room for him to feel it—and let it go.

He could feel compassion for the child he'd been when he'd left Ireland, feel compassion for the father who'd wanted to go home, and the mother who'd done her best to be fair.

None of them had meant to hurt each other, but they'd all done so anyway.

The same crystal clarity made him realize he'd prolonged his suffering—surrounding himself with women, but allowing none of them near him. Not really.

That had to stop. If he wanted to move forward— to marry Sadie—

He had to open his heart.

Nodding in the dark, Connor started walking again, picking up his pace.

He wanted to get home to Two Willows. To see Sadie. To tell her—

A sheriff's cruiser came around a bend toward him. Its blue and red lights swirled, and a siren tapped on and off. Connor stopped and waited for Cab to pull over, get out, cross the road and confront him.

"I should give you a ticket for asshole-ism," Cab said, giving him a baleful look. "I could do it, too. No one would deny you deserve it."

"What's got your knickers in a twist, Sheriff?" His expansive mood faded fast.

"You think to check in back at the ranch after you decided to go have yourself a good time? Or do you get off acting as self-absorbed as a seventeen-year-old?"

Connor bristled. Here he'd been fielding epiphanies. He didn't need this kind of abuse. "Just needed to clear my head, Sheriff." If Cab had an accusation to make, he could make it. He hadn't done anything wrong.

"Well, while you were clearing your head, someone snuck onto Two Willows property. And those women you left behind took it on themselves to chase him off. He got Jo pretty good."

Connor sobered in an instant. "Someone hurt Jo?"

"Slammed her up against the carriage house. She's a little bruised. A little freaked out, too. Watch yourself going home; Lena's armed and waiting to shoot someone. I've got a unit out there, too."

"What did he want?" He didn't like the sound of this at all. If those drug dealers were back—

"Looked like he was going for Jo's dogs."

Dogs? "Grant Kimball?"

"Nope. Some other guy. No one got a good look at him, but Jo was pretty sure it wasn't Grant." Cab looked him over. "What the fuck were you thinking? The General gave you a mission. A pretty damn simple one. Did you think you deserved a night off?"

"Fuck." He'd really screwed up. Left his post. Left the women vulnerable. What if the man had come in, guns blazing—?

What if he'd hurt Sadie?

Killed her?

Connor swallowed hard. He couldn't lose her—not when he'd just found her—not when he'd just figured out—

"Yeah, now you get it." Cab shook his head. "You're supposed to be with Sadie. So why aren't you? She said you didn't have a fight—she couldn't figure out why you hadn't come home."

Fuck. Fuck. Fuck. "She was worried?" Why had he left at all? He could have hung out in the barn and gotten some work done. Gone to town another time—

"Of course she was worried. She cares about you. God knows why."

Connor braced himself. He knew what the sheriff would ask next.

"Where were you?"

"At the Boot."

"With another woman?"

"No." He'd answered too quickly, and felt even worse. "Yes. Kind of. Look, the bartender is a flirt. She gave me a couple of free drinks, that's all—I was trying—"

"That's all—?"

The sheriff looked ready to haul off and knock him into next week. Worst thing was, Connor was beginning to think he deserved it. His intentions had been good, but he'd gotten too caught up in the game. A misunderstanding between him and Sadie could undo everything.

Cab got his temper under control with a visible effort. "You make up your mind. You're either with Sadie, or you call the General and tell him you're not the man for the job. Let him find someone else. Shit or get off the pot. Got it?"

"Got it." He did. Cab was right; he had to get his head together. He couldn't flirt with anyone anymore. No matter what the cause—for information, or for perks. Not because he'd gotten caught, or because Cab had told him so.

Because that wasn't the kind of man he wanted to be.

He wasn't his father. He didn't want to turn tail and run when things got hard. He didn't want to settle for halfway good enough when everything he wanted was possible. Even if he'd been hurt in the past, even if his own mother had let him go too soon, he was making his own choices now and he was choosing to be with Sadie.

"I've got it," he said again.

Cab backed down. "Good."

"Give me a ride?" Connor asked, suddenly eager to see Sadie—to tell her how he felt. To make sure she understood he wanted a lifetime with her.

"Fuck no." Cab strode off, climbed in his cruiser and took off without a second look.

IT TOOK CONNOR another hour to make it home, nod to the sheriff's deputies as he passed them on his way up the driveway to the house, and announce his presence to Lena before she shot him. Inside, he found the house quiet and he snuck up to bed, hesitating at Sadie's door a moment before he acknowledged to himself it was too late for heart to heart conversations now, and entered his own room. He only slept a few hours before he woke with the certain knowledge he needed to head back to town, get his truck—

And buy Sadie a ring.

He needed to propose today. He needed to settle this now.

And he was going to do this right.

He slipped out past a snoozing Lena, made sure the duo in the sheriff's department cruiser near the end of the lane spotted him and waved hello as he approached and passed them.

The long walk back into town cleared the cobwebs from his brain, and he was gratified to find his resolve remained perfectly firm. He wanted to marry Sadie. Wanted to be her husband. Wanted to make Two Willows his home.

He would break the pattern of unhappiness that his parents had begun. He'd use his wedding to bring them together again, too. He'd do everything he could to throw them together as much as possible while they were here.

He couldn't ask for a better future. He and Sadie would help run Two Willows. He'd have Brian for a brother-in-law. Together with Lena they'd get the cattle operation tip top and he'd do whatever it took to help Sadie tend her gardens and run her farm stand. During the weeks after the disaster in Syria, Connor had thought his life was over. He'd known getting kicked out of the Air Force would put a blot on his future it would be hard to remove.

Now he saw it as a gift. He hadn't known what he wanted until it was handed to him on a silver platter.

He'd make sure to treat Sadie as she deserved and ignore every other woman in the world. No more flirting. No more charming the ladies to get what he wanted. Straight dealing from now on.

When he finally stood in front of Thayer's Jewelers, however, a twinge of doubt insinuated itself into his mind.

If and when Sadie heard the rumors about him and Tracy, would she be angry with him? Would she believe him when he told his side?

If not, he'd do what it took to make her love him again, he promised himself, but he felt another twinge at the word *love*. He'd never told Sadie how he felt about her.

And she'd never said the word to him, either.

They barely knew each other. He hadn't even been here for two weeks.

Connor's heart sank. Was he jumping the gun?

He thought about all the time he'd spent with Sadie. The way he couldn't take his eyes off her when she was near. The way he thought of her all the time when she wasn't.

The way it felt to make love to her.

Sometimes you just knew. That's what his father had said about meeting his mother, right? That he knew she was the one the moment he laid eyes on her.

But his parents' love hadn't been enough to hold them together.

Was he fooling himself if he thought the connection that he had with Sadie could go the distance?

A few days spent in the garden, a few kisses.

An encounter or two—or three. He smiled, thinking of their shared shower yesterday.

A pretty, petite woman with dark hair greeted him. "Feel free to look around. I'm just setting up for the day. We only opened a few minutes ago."

"No hurry." Connor wandered among the glass cases, his worry growing again. How was he supposed to choose a ring for a woman he'd known for less than two weeks?

What if he was just like his father—unable to commit to a lifetime with a woman? What if he had inherited some defect that made commitment impossible? It was strange Sean hadn't married again. In fact, he'd barely dated as far as Connor knew. It was like he'd tried love once, found it too difficult and never tried it again. Like he'd chosen loneliness as the easier alternative.

Connor didn't want to make that choice, but choosing love—choosing forever—

Laid all his worried bare.

He looked at the glass cases around him. Even this first step seemed almost impossible. What if Sadie hated the ring he chose? Would she turn him down? Maybe—

"Looking for something special?"

"An engagement ring," Connor said slowly.

"Right over here. Take your time. I'll pull out anything that catches your eye."

Stunned by the array of choices, Connor tried to focus on one that Sadie might like.

"Who's the lucky lady?" the woman asked.

"Sadie Reed," he said reluctantly. Now it was out there. This woman knew. Which meant he had to go through with it—

Which he wanted to, of course. But—

"Oh, congratulations! What about this one?" She pointed toward a ring Connor hadn't noticed yet. It wasn't nearly as flashy as some of them, but he knew instantly why the woman had chosen it.

"You know Sadie?" he asked as she brought it out and showed it to him. Some of his anxiety drained away as he took it in his hand. Several thin bands wove together around a large diamond. It reminded him of a vine winding around a flower. The woman was right; it seemed made for Sadie.

"Of course. I'm Rose Johnson—Cab Johnson's wife. He's the local sheriff."

Connor choked on the words he'd been about to say, coughed to cover his surprise and got control of his tongue. "I've met him."

Rose smiled. "Sadie loves her garden."

"That she does." He lifted the ring and examined it up close. It would suit her perfectly. "Okay—I'll take it."

"Great." She held out her hand and Connor placed the ring in it. As she folded her fingers over it, her eyes took on a distant look and she hesitated. Then frowned.

"Something wrong?" Connor asked. He looked over his shoulder to see if someone had come in behind him. When he looked back, Rose was staring at him, her brows furrowed.

"Um... I... Do you want me to tell you—you know?" She stumbled over her words and Connor's confusion grew.

"Want you to tell me what?"

Rose bit her lip. "Right, you're new here. You don't know that I... I mean—nothing," she said quickly. "I mean—do you want a case for the ring? Most men do."

"Sure." But Connor was sure that wasn't what Rose meant to say at all. Trouble was, he couldn't guess what she had been getting at. "Is there something I'm forgetting?"

"Do you plan to propose soon?" Rose busied herself pulling out a black velvet box and nestled the ring inside.

"Yes. Today."

Rose kept fussing with the ring, not meeting his eye. "Well... that's wonderful. It's just... I always suggest... that people make sure they've cleared the air first. If they've had any issues in the past. You don't want to carry trouble into an engagement. That's the advice I always give." She spoke quickly—obviously flustered, her words tripping over each other. Something was going on here Connor didn't understand. Rose put the rest of the rings away and motioned him over to the cash register.

Connor followed more slowly. "Did you talk to Cab about me?"

She stopped ringing him up. "No. Why would I do that? I've never met you before."

Connor felt silly. "No reason. How much?"

He finished the transaction as quickly as possible, thoroughly unsettled by the whole situation. Cab must have told Rose all about what had happened last night, even if she wasn't going to admit it. How else to explain the way she was acting?

Which sucked.

Really sucked.

Instead of climbing into his truck and going home when he'd left the jewelry store, he walked three blocks down Main Street to the Sheriff's Department. Inside, he opened the door to the man's office without knocking, "Hey—I need to talk to you!"

Cab looked up with a long-suffering expression. "Get in here and pipe down. People are working." The two men faced off in the small room after Connor shut the door behind him. "What's this about?" the sheriff asked.

"You told your wife what I did last night?"

For the first time since he'd met the man, Cab looked confused. "Come again?"

"Your wife. Rose. Sells rings?" He held up the small black box. "Knows all about my personal life?"

When a shit-eating grin spread across the sheriff's face, Connor wanted to deck him.

"Naw, you got it wrong," Cab said. "I didn't tell her anything. I don't make it a habit to spread around the exploits of Chance Creek's riffraff."

"Then how did she know Sadie and I have had problems?"

To Connor's surprise, the sheriff chuckled. "Let me guess. You bought a ring and she held it for a second? Gave you a set of orders for what to do next?"

"That's right."

"Just a parlor trick," Cab said lightly. "She gets... hunches. When she touches an engagement ring. Whether or not the couple will make it for the long haul."

Connor remembered her frown. Her furrowed brow. He shook his head. "She doesn't know anything about me and Sadie—"

"Like I said, she gets hunches. Whether or not you pay attention to them is your business."

Connor sagged. He jammed his hands in his pockets. "She said to clear up any misunderstandings before I propose."

"Sounds smart to me." Cab took a seat behind his desk and waved Connor to one of the chairs.

Connor shook his head. "I've got to go."

"Hey," Cab called after him as he headed for the door. "Good luck. With your proposal."

"Thanks."

IT WAS NEARLY noon by the time Connor returned to the ranch, and Sadie was so furious she thought her blood was boiling in her veins. By the time Connor had come home last night it was long past midnight. She'd heard his heavy steps in the hall, heard him pause in front of her door. He hadn't bothered to knock or come inside. Hadn't bothered to excuse his absence, and this morning he was gone before she even woke up. Avoiding her, obviously.

What had he done to make him feel so guilty he had to leave the house so early? And who had he done it with? That's what she wanted to know.

She made herself stay in the kitchen even as his truck pulled in and parked. She was in the middle of setting the table for lunch, putting out the fixings for sandwiches and a large bowl of salad. Despite her fury at the way Connor had treated her in the last twenty-four hours, it was still her job to run the house, stock the farm stand, make herbal remedies and make sure her sisters were fed. Everyone was busy, and she was determined to do her part.

Even if she was being cheated on.

Again.

Connor entered the back door and let it shut behind him. "Sadie, got a minute?"

"No. I don't."

She bustled to the refrigerator, opened it, but wasn't sure what to take out. She was shaking so hard that when she finally spotted a jar of mayonnaise, she had a hard time grabbing it. She turned to place it on the table, and found Connor directly behind her.

"Listen, I know I fucked up—"

"That's right. You fucked up. It's common courtesy to let someone know when you plan to stay out all hours."

"I didn't mean to stay out so late—"

"I was up until nearly one-thirty in the morning."

Connor looked sheepish. "It was closer to three by the time I got home," he admitted. "I got delayed a couple of times, and—"

"I can only imagine."

"That's just it," he said. "I don't want you imagining, because it was nothing like that. Not really."

"*Not really?* That makes me feel a whole hell of a lot better," she snapped. Ducking around him, she placed the mayonnaise on the table, and realized she didn't have an appetite anymore.

Jo came into the room. "Is it almost lunch? I'm hungry." She stopped when she caught sight of Connor. "Am I interrupting something?"

"No—"

"Yes—"

"Sadie, step outside," Connor said. "I've got something I need to say to you."

Sadie's heart plunged into her stomach. Something he had to say to her? There was only one thing it could be. He'd thought about it, and realized they had nothing in common. Realized he didn't want to stay here on this ranch in the middle of nowhere. Realized she wasn't all that interesting, after all.

He'd probably realized that last bit in between the legs of another woman.

"This'll just take a few minutes." He held out his hand, but she didn't take it. Instead, she skirted around him, stalked to the back door and headed outside. Best to get this whole thing over with and out of the way. Then she could get back to being single—the way she planned to spend the rest of her life.

When would she learn that if you cared for someone they could crush you? The minute you trusted them, they'd walk out of your life and wouldn't come back—

Or stay in your life and flaunt their other conquests—

Connor followed her, but he didn't stop on the porch. He led the way down the steps, across her gardens, around the greenhouse into the staked-out perimeter and partially built walls of the enclosed garden out behind it. It was far from finished, but it did provide a bit of privacy. Sadie gritted her teeth and followed along.

"Say what you need to say," she told him. She didn't want to spend a minute more with him than was necessary. He'd already showed he couldn't be trusted. And she had a feeling she'd hear a lot worse in the next few minutes.

"I went out last night to find information about Grant. I tried a couple of places but it wasn't until I got to the Dancing Boot that it seemed like I could get someone to really talk to me. The bartender—well, she began flirting with me. Giving me drinks—that kind of thing."

Sadie felt her cheeks burn. Bartender? "You mean Tracy?" Her voice didn't sound like her own. It was flat and hard—betraying the feelings she wanted to hide.

"That's right. I guess you know her?"

"Of course I know her." Tracy had flaunted her relationship with Mark at every opportunity, rubbing

Sadie's nose in it.

"I didn't mean anything by talking to her. Like I said, I wanted to see what she knew about Grant."

"If it didn't mean anything, why do you look so guilty?" She couldn't keep her anger out of her voice. He did look guilty, and that sent her fears into over-drive. If he'd cheated on her, she didn't know what she'd do.

"Because—" He shrugged helplessly. "I let her think I was flirting back to her. I wanted information and I thought I could get it that way. But then I realized how that might affect you. I don't want to do anything that hurts you, Sadie. I want to be the kind of man you trust."

"Are you? Trustworthy?" She could hardly force the words out. What exactly had he done with Tracy? And had Tracy known what he meant to her? Sadie still couldn't forgive her for sleeping with Mark when she'd known Sadie was dating him—even if he'd turned out to be a killer. It meant she wasn't enough to keep a man's attention. If Mark could stray, then Connor could stray.

"Yes. I swear, Sadie."

How could she believe him? "You were out nearly all night—"

"Not with her. I walked home. It took a while."

"Yeah, that would." But she wasn't convinced.

"Look. Nothing happened. I didn't want anything to happen. I just… got…"

She waited for him to finish his sentence. "You got

what? Horny? Lazy? Selfish?" If he was going to break her heart, she wanted him to get it over and done with.

"Not any of that." He took a deep breath. "Thoughtless, I guess the word is. I haven't spent a lot of time thinking about long-term commitments. You have to understand, I've seen what a failed marriage can do. I've seen the worst of it. When my parents split up, they didn't just move across town from each other. My dad took me to Texas, and my mother and brother stayed in Ireland. They told us it wouldn't be so bad; that we'd talk all the time. That nobody was really losing anybody else. They lied." He lifted up his hands. Dropped them again. "I can't tell you how that felt; losing my country, my home, my family—my brother— all at once."

Sadie softened, understanding that pain all too well. Hadn't she lived through something similar? Hadn't her father disappeared into the Army? Hadn't her mother died when Sadie was eleven? Hadn't she spent the last few weeks imagining every hour of every day what it would feel like to leave Two Willows—and her sisters? She knew exactly how heartbreaking those kinds of separations could be.

"I don't let women get close. Ever. But I want to be close to you." He shrugged. "I walked home because I needed to get my head on straight. To understand myself—damn it." He jammed his hand in his pocket and pulled out his phone. Glanced at the screen. "I've got to take this. It's from USSOCOM. It could be your dad."

ISSUED TO THE BRIDE ONE AIRMAN | 183

Sadie wanted to grab the phone away. She wanted him to keep going, because she was beginning to understand he was struggling with commitment as much as she was. They'd both been burned and they were both trying to heal. Trying to move forward with hearts that had seen too much damage. They needed to talk about this.

But she knew Connor hadn't separated from the Air Force yet. If USSOCOM was calling, he had to answer.

"O'Riley here," Connor said into the phone. "Yeah." There was a long pause. "No shit." He raked a hand through his short hair. "Really?" His voice rose with excitement. "Yeah, patch him through." He turned to her. "You won't believe this—" He turned his attention back to the phone. "Halil? Is that you? Where are you?"

Halil? Wasn't that the name of the man Connor had met on his rescue mission? The one who'd sheltered the pilot? The reason Connor been reassigned to USSO-COM?

"Canada? No kidding! That's terrific!" Connor listened intently, and as he did so a wide grin spread across his face. All traces of his frustration dropped away, reminding Sadie what a handsome man he was. "Your family is there, too? That's amazing. No, don't thank me. I didn't do anything. You're the ones who saved Wesley's life. I'm in your debt." He listened again, and Sadie couldn't help soften a little more. Connor was smiling like a madman. His happiness tugged at her heart. He looked younger when he smiled. Hopeful. She wanted to feel hopeful, too.

Maybe she should let herself feel that way. After all, Connor had freely admitted he'd flirted with Tracy without meaning to. He could have simply covered it up with a lie. He had come home last night; she'd heard him in the hall. He'd said he wanted to commit to her.

Was she creating a situation out of nothing but her own fears?

When he finally hung up, Connor turned to her, grinning. "You won't believe this! That was Halil—the man I told you about. The man who saved Wesley Shaw's life. The one I took to Iraq in the helicopter."

"He's all right?"

"More than all right. Somehow he tracked me down, which is a miracle; no one's supposed to tell anyone where I am. One of the guys back at USSOCOM patched him through. He wanted to tell me they made it to Canada. His whole family, grandkids and all." Connor's voice cracked, and he cleared his throat.

She'd never seen him so close to losing control of his emotions, and she had a feeling Connor didn't often let them get the better of him. "Connor—"

"That phone call just made everything worth it," he went on when he could speak again. "Getting kicked off my team, getting sent to USSOCOM. Getting booted from the Air Force, whether my record gets cleared or not. I want to stay here—with you. But even if you decide you're done with me, it will have all been worth it. Halil is safe. So is his wife—his children. Grandchildren."

This was the man she'd fallen in love with. The man who valued other people more than himself. He'd taken such a risk to save Halil and his wife. He could have simply left them, but he'd done what he thought was right.

Sadie ran over his words in her mind. Last night he'd gone out looking for information about Grant—to protect Jo, a woman he'd only known for a short time. That's the kind of man he was. He took responsibility for the well-being of the people around him, even if he didn't have to. Maybe he'd flirted with Tracy along the way.

But he'd come home to her, confessed his transgression and was looking for her forgiveness.

What kind of woman would she be if she didn't give him another chance?

"I'm not—I'm not done with you," Sadie heard herself saying. "Not if you can look me in the eye and tell me nothing happened with Tracy."

Connor took her hands, looked her straight in the eye and said, "Nothing happened, lass. Nothing ever will. I'm yours."

Sadie shivered, and not just because that shimmer of awareness rushed through her as it always did when they touched. She felt as if the ranch itself was telling her to believe Connor. That he belonged here as much as she did.

She wanted to lean closer to him. To kiss him.

She wanted to believe him.

But she was afraid.

Connor must have read her fears in her eyes. His jaw tightened. "Lass, I promise. I'm your man. Yours; not anyone else's."

Sadie swallowed. Gave in. As much as she'd been hurt before, she had to try again or risk losing the one man she'd ever met who stirred so much want inside her. If she didn't, she might be safe, but she wouldn't be whole. Not if she turned her back on love.

She went up on tiptoe and kissed him. "I'm glad Halil is safe."

"Me, too." His voice was rough. "But even gladder to be with you."

CONNOR'S HANDS SHOOK as he pulled the small, black velvet box from his pocket. It was time. He couldn't wait any more to find out Sadie's answer, and with the news of Halil and Fatima's safety, he felt there would never be a more auspicious occasion.

He took Sadie's hand. "When I came here, I didn't know I'd find the woman I'd always been looking for. In fact, I didn't know I was looking for one. My past didn't set me up to believe in marriage, but all that's changed now. I want to share my life with you.

Sadie shifted, as if she would say something, but Connor didn't wait for her to speak. He felt that he needed to get all of it out, before he lost his nerve. Or before he lost the words to best explain how he felt.

"I think some men underestimate what it will take to make a good husband. But I'm on the other side; I've always overestimated it. I've made it into something so big and so difficult I never felt myself worthy. What Halil and Fatima taught me was that the only thing you need to make love work is the willingness to keep trying. The willingness to keep loving—despite the difficulties that life throws at you, even if those difficulties seem insurmountable. I asked Halil how his marriage had lasted for sixty-two years—just making small talk, you know? Trying to keep everyone calm on the chopper ride. He laughed at me. He said, 'Every morning I wake up and look at my beautiful wife, and I thank God that she's there beside me. If it wasn't for her, I would be alone. I don't want to be alone.'"

Connor squeezed Sadie's hand. "What if it's really that simple? I look at you now, and I thank God that you're here. If you weren't, I would be lonely. And I don't want to be alone, either." He lifted her hand, and showed her the velvet box. As he sank down to one knee, her eyes grew large. She opened her mouth to speak, but again he interrupted. "So, Sadie Reed, would you do me the great honor of becoming my wife? Would you go through life by my side? Would you allow me to be your best friend, your protector, your partner and the man who wants to dedicate his life to making you happy? Because that's what I'm going to do. Because I want you to wake up every morning, and look at me, and be grateful that I'm there with you. I want you to feel that with me you're not alone. Sadie, will you be my wife?"

The seconds that followed his proposal were some of the longest of his life. Sadie kept searching his gaze.

She hesitated for a long moment, and Connor's heart began to sink. Had he jumped the gun? Should he have taken more time to clear things up before he proposed? Rose's words kept ringing in his mind.

But just when he began to lose all hope, Sadie squeezed his hand back. "Yes," she said. "Yes, I will."

IT FELT SO natural to let Connor slide the beautiful ring he'd chosen onto her finger and to melt into his arms as he stood up and embraced her. As their mouths met, Sadie felt as if the world was singing a Hallelujah chorus. Joy ran through her veins as their kiss deepened, and when Connor pulled her down to lie beside him on the grass, she was all too happy to let him.

A bright blue sky above them was studded with puffy clouds like sailing ships, and for a brief moment, Sadie thought about what she would be giving up—the chance to travel the world, to be fancy free—

But really she wasn't giving up anything she wanted. She and Connor could travel together someday—and the best part was Two Willows would always be waiting for them when they were ready to come home.

Meanwhile they'd finish this walled garden, and for the first time Sadie pictured it in all its glory as it would be one day. Graceful trees, masses of flowers, stone walkways—maybe a fountain.

But always, always this patch of grass where they lay right now. Because this is where they'd seal their promise to each other to spend their lives together.

Sadie tugged Connor on top of her, enjoying the

press of his body on hers, as if he was tethering her to the land she loved so much. The metaphor pleased her, and she was glad Connor was a man who wanted to keep her at Two Willows rather than take her away from her home.

When she felt his hand tug at the hem of her shirt, she helped him pull it up and over her head. Connor glanced toward the house, but she told him, "I don't think anyone can see us behind the wall." She arched her back and he slid his hands underneath to undo the clasp of her bra. When he tugged it off her, set it aside and palmed one of her breasts, Sadie closed her eyes and gave herself up to the sensation. She sighed blissfully when he replaced his hand with his mouth, teasing her, circling her breast with kisses, nipping tenderly at her sensitive skin.

When he eased lower, trailing kisses down her belly, Sadie wrapped her fingers into his hair, remembering what he'd said. He wanted to wake up grateful for her. Wanted her to wake up grateful for him.

If he planned to treat her like this she'd be grateful all her life.

He undid the button of her jeans, and she lifted her hips so he could shimmy them down, kicking off her shoes and helping him untangle her legs from the thick fabric.

"You're wearing too many clothes," she told him.

"We'll get to that. In time." He tugged down her lacy panties, tossed them aside with the rest of her clothes, parted her thighs and bent to taste her.

The sound that traveled from her lips was part hunger, part joy. Sadie was hungry for him—wanted him inside her right now. But Connor seemed to think he should take his time.

And maybe waiting wasn't so bad.

As his mouth brushed over her, his breath warming her, Sadie moaned again. He began a teasing kind of sensual torment that made Sadie twist the fabric of his shirt in her fingers. With every touch he heightened her desire, until she couldn't take it anymore.

"I want you inside me," she insisted. "Now."

"Plenty of time for—"

"Now!"

Connor chuckled. "All right." In a flash he'd shucked off boots, jeans, boxer briefs and even tugged his shirt up over his head in a one-handed maneuver that Sadie barely had time to marvel over before he'd kneed her legs apart and set himself in just the right place to cause her to sigh all over again.

He pulled a condom out of a pocket in his jeans, got it on before Sadie could even offer to help.

"I'm glad you're always prepared," she said with a wry grin. "Do you restock every morning?"

"I'm an optimistic man."

The laugh that bubbled from her throat dissipated all her remaining tension. She relaxed, fully accepting Connor's love—and enthusiasm. Maybe she'd been making this more difficult than necessary all along. Maybe love was easy if you let it be.

"This more like it?" he asked as he settled between

her legs.

"Hell, yeah." Maybe she was taking a chance. A chance she hadn't anticipated she'd take with her heart ever again. It was terrifying—

When Connor pushed inside her, Sadie gasped.

It was heavenly—

She surrendered to him fully, loving the feeling of him between her legs—the way his arms boxed her in. The way he took control and the whole world came alive as they touched. She knew Connor could coax pleasure from her body like a virtuoso playing a fine violin. As he began to move inside her, she relaxed and let him press in deep, loving the connection between them and wanting to give him as much pleasure as he was giving her.

She caressed her hands over his hips, glorying in the muscles that bunched and released as he moved. Connor was a thing of beauty—with a body hardened by war and experience. She believed him when he said Halil and Fatima's safety made it all worth it. She was beginning to see that Connor was a man who'd closed his heart for many years—but was ready to open it again—to her.

This was a man she could spend a life with. A man whose very touch put her in harmony with all creation. They created magic together.

The way he moved inside her felt like magic.

Connor sped up and Sadie pressed her fingers into his skin, urging him deeper—harder. As Connor pumped into her, she opened to him, lifting her hips to meet him halfway with each stroke.

He slid a hand underneath her bottom and lifted it higher. Sadie sighed as he pressed in, pulled out and pressed in again.

He felt so good. Felt so right. She arched her back and he bent to take one of her nipples in his mouth. Sadie had no idea how anything could feel this good. As she crashed over the top into a series of shuddering waves of ecstasy, she clung to Connor, needing to feel him, needing to know he was here with her, in this most intimate of moments, when she was truly open.

"I'm here," he whispered, kissing her neck. "Right here. Right—" Connor came, grunting with his release, working himself in and out of her with a slow, deep rhythm that took her right over the edge a second time.

"Connor—" She clung to him more tightly, her mouth pressed against his shoulder, thinking the waves of her orgasm would never stop.

When they did, she collapsed back, Connor following her—allowing his weight to rest fully on top of her until she wriggled beneath him and he disengaged, then slid to the side. Both of them were breathing deeply. "How was that?" Connor asked her.

"Fabulous. Can we do it again?"

"Give me a minute to rest up. You'll be the death of me, lass."

Sadie smiled. "Will you take me to Ireland someday to meet your mother?"

"You'll be seeing her soon enough," he reminded her. "In about a week. My dad, too. Don't forget they're expecting a wedding." He smiled roguishly. "In about... four weeks. Think we can make that work?"

She held up her hand and touched the ring that graced her finger. "I think so."

Chapter Ten

"**H**ELL, YOU REALLY did it?" Logan asked, peering into his laptop camera until his face filled Connor's screen. Connor was seated at the desk in his room, trying to keep his voice down so none of the Reed women would overhear him. Sadie had spent the night with him, but she'd gotten up early to get a real breakfast going. He should be working on the wall, or down in the barns helping Lena, but he'd told her he had something to take care of first. After a quick visit with Jo to see the puppies, he'd come back to his room and shut the door.

"I did. The wedding is in about four weeks." He couldn't express how much satisfaction that gave him. Never in a million years had he expected to move to Montana, become engaged—and be happy. His role helping with the cattle would expand, of course, but he hoped there were more things to build at Two Willows. He found working with the granite, building the walled garden, oddly satisfying.

"Congratulations," Hunter said.

"I bet it's my turn next. Watch out, baby girl. You

don't know what's about to hit you! A big ol' dose of Logan love." Logan turned to one side and Connor could only guess he was looking at Lena's photograph.

Jack grabbed something and chucked it at Logan, the first time Connor had ever seen him completely lose his temper. With each of them occupying a different box on his screen, the effect was comical; the bottle of water left Jack's hand in one box and hit Logan in another one. Connor couldn't help but remember when he'd been back in that rectangular office with them, wondering what was to come next.

Now he had a home—and would have a wife in four weeks. It was nothing short of a miracle.

"Have you told the General yet?" Hunter asked.

"He's my next call."

"We'd better let you get to it. Don't drop the ball now, O'Riley. You're nearly to the goal line."

"I won't drop the ball." Connor signed off and made a new call. When the General's face appeared on his screen, the man was frowning.

"What's wrong?"

"Nothing, sir. I've got good news, actually. Sadie agreed to marry me. The wedding is four weeks from Saturday."

For a long moment the General had nothing to say. Then the strangest thing happened. Half a grin tugged up one corner of his mouth. The half smile disappeared almost before it started, but Connor's fingers tightened on the arms of his chair. He'd never, ever seen the General smile.

Had anyone else ever seen it?

The other guys would never believe this. And Sadie—was the General different with his girls? From everything he'd seen, the answer was no. Sadie and her sisters avoided talking about their father, and when they did their attitudes weren't friendly. How would Sadie feel if she knew the General had ordered him to come here and marry her?

"Will you be able to make it?" He wasn't sure what answer he wanted, but when the General quickly shook his head, Connor was relieved—then disappointed on Sadie's behalf.

"Why not?" he asked.

"We've got teams working all over the world. Trouble's heating up around the globe. I can't leave USSOCOM now."

"With all due respect, General, there are other men who can do your job for a couple of days—"

The General cut the call.

Connor stared at the blank screen. He thought about that smile. Then the General's palpable anger as he'd reached out to put an end to their conversation.

The General had missed Cass's wedding, and he wasn't coming for Sadie's either. Was he worried the women would figure out his ruse if he did?

When his phone buzzed, he picked it up thinking maybe it was the General again, but it was a text from Lila.

Hey baby. Busy?

Connor nearly tossed the phone away. Instead, he answered her.

Stop texting me. I'm getting married. It's over, got it?

A knock sounded at his door. "Connor?"

Hell. Connor turned off his phone, jammed it in his pocket, and went to open the door. Sadie stood in the hall.

"Breakfast is ready."

He waved her in, shut the door behind her, led her to the bed and sat down, patting the comforter beside him. Sadie sat down, too.

"What's wrong?"

"I just talked to your father," Connor said.

She straightened. Her eyebrows rose and he could read the question in her face.

Connor shook his head. "I'm sorry. He—"

"He won't leave USSOCOM. He doesn't want to set foot on Two Willows—even for my wedding." She wilted again.

"I can't believe—"

"I can. The General is the one who taught me to be disappointed by men," she said sharply.

Connor pulled back and Sadie's expression softened.

"I'm sorry. That wasn't fair." She reached for his hand. "He's never been here for me—for any of us. I don't expect any different. That's probably why I didn't expect much from Mark—or you, at first."

"I'm not going to disappoint you," Connor told her. "I'm going to change the way you think about men."

"You already have."

Connor kissed her. "You've got a ring. My folks have booked their flights. What else do we need to do to get this shindig off the ground?"

"Lots." Sadie made a face. "Tons, in fact. You know, Mia Matheson does wedding planning. Should we ask her for help?"

"Hell, yeah. Let a planner do the work. We can have the fun." He flopped back on the bed and pulled her down on top of him. "I suppose there are a few things we should talk about, too."

"Like what?"

He tucked her hair behind her ear. "You've never said if you want kids."

She propped her chin in her hands, elbows planted on his chest, and thought about it. "Yes. I do. Two girls and one boy."

"How about two boys and a girl?" Connor countered. "Don't want to be outnumbered."

"You're going to be outnumbered," Sadie told him as she began to get undressed. "Get used to doing what you're told. Now make love to me."

"Yes, ma'am."

WHEN SADIE SET out toward the walled garden later that morning to help Connor, she couldn't help the spring in her step. Their bout of lovemaking had left her glowing, and after Connor had taken a quick rinse and headed downstairs for breakfast, she'd luxuriated in the tub for a time before showering off the bubble bath and washing her hair. Freshly dressed, her still-wet hair pulled up in a ponytail on top of her head, she made short work of feeding herself and cleaning up after the meal, all the while looking forward to a morning spent working with Connor.

Outside, the day was lovely, and Sadie increased her pace, eager to reach Connor. But halfway across the garden, a sage plant whispered it was thirsty, and she stopped automatically to shut her eyes and listen to what else the garden had to tell her.

And that's when it hit her. She could hear the garden—hear the growing things.

And Connor wasn't anywhere close to her.

Sadie wobbled and sat down hard in the dirt. Messages came from all around her: aphids in the peonies. Mold on the zucchini. The tomatoes were almost past-ripe and needed harvesting.

Sadie laughed as tears started to her eyes. It was back. Her gift was back—which meant—

She lurched to her feet and raced to the greenhouse. Inside, she gathered what she needed, the roots and herbs speaking to her as well. It was back—her knowledge was back. Her intuition.

Her ability to heal.

She was still hard at work a half hour later when Connor let himself into the greenhouse. "Sadie? Everything all right?"

She turned to him and smiled, hardly able to contain her joy. "I can do it. I can make my remedies. Jean is due any minute and I've made her tonic." She held it up, knowing he couldn't possibly understand.

"You need me to hang close?"

"No!" Connor's frown had her backtracking. "I mean, I love it when you're close. Be as close as you want to be. But—I can do it again. Myself!"

He moved toward her. Linked his fingers through her belt loops and tugged her to him. "So you don't need me anymore? Is that what you're trying to say?" he growled, then kissed her nose so she knew he was kidding.

"No." She needed him now more than ever. She kissed him back, buzzing with as much anticipation as she had the first time they'd gotten close. "This means I'm happy."

"That kind of turns me on."

"Then you'd better lock that door." Sadie checked the time. They had a half hour. Enough time if they were quick. Before Connor was gone and back again, she'd shucked off her clothes, and when he turned around and stopped, a smile spreading across his face at her nakedness, she pushed up to sit on the edge of the table. "Time's wasting," she told him.

"Then I'd better hurry up."

When Connor was naked, too, and positioned himself between her legs, Sadie didn't need any foreplay. She was ready for him. Aching for his touch. Like she always seemed to be when he was near. So when he lifted her up to press against him, she wasted no time in wrapping her legs around his waist and pulling him inside.

"Wait—condom."

"I'm on the pill," she told him. "I've been checked out. We are getting married, after all."

"I've been checked out, too. And you're right; pretty soon you'll be my wife."

He slid inside her and Sadie relished the idea there was nothing between them this time. As the two of them joined, she felt she was pledging her life to him already. He was so strong he could hold her up and ease in and out of her with such slow precision, Sadie was close to losing control almost from the start.

When he tilted her head back and kissed her neck, still sliding in and out of her with long, strong strokes, the pressure built inside her until she couldn't hold back anymore. Her orgasm rolled through her in waves as strong, steady and persistent as the ocean, and Sadie was shaking by the time Connor grunted and came inside her, crushing her to him as he gave in to his release.

Afterward, Sadie didn't want to let him go. But soon they'd have company. "Come on—I need to go clean up quick. Jean will be here in a minute."

"All right." They dressed as fast as they could and raced back to the house, laughing like teenagers as they barged through the back door, into the kitchen, down the hall and up the stairs.

"Come find me when your friend is gone," Connor told her when they'd climbed into the shower for a quick rinse. "I don't think I'm done with you yet."

She didn't think she was done with him, either.

"YOU'RE NOT COMING back to Ireland, are you?" Connor's brother's disappointment was palpable even over the phone. Connor was a little surprised. As far as he knew, Dalton had always seemed to enjoy having their mother to himself. He'd certainly enjoyed becoming lord and master of *Ard na Greine*, their mother's property, and the small herd of cattle the family owned.

"No. Two Willows is going to be my home."

"Always thought you'd return in the end. Mom gave up years ago, but I never did."

His brother's words twisted a knife in Connor's gut, as did the pain in his voice. "You never said anything." Connor couldn't figure out what Dalton was up to. Surely he'd know it if his brother had missed him. All these years it had been like Dalton hardly cared.

"She said I wasn't to go driving a wedge between you and our dad. I always said Dad was the one who did that."

Hell. Connor clutched his phone more tightly, wanting to crush it if he was honest. "I never wanted a wedge between any of us," he said forcefully. He paced the back porch, not believing what he was hearing. "Why would Mom try to keep us apart?"

Dalton sighed. "I don't think that was her intention. I think she was trying to be fair to everyone."

"Well, it didn't feel fair from where I was standing in Texas."

"Didn't feel fair here in Ireland, either, brother."

Brother. Connor didn't think he'd ever heard Dalton say the word. God, he'd missed his older brother when his dad had taken him to Texas. He couldn't understand why Dalton hadn't followed them somehow, even though he'd known his brother was as helpless as he was in the situation. By the time either one of them was old enough to change anything, it was already too late—their relationship had been strained.

He let his gaze run over the walled garden taking shape out past the greenhouse. He wished Dalton could see it. "You're coming for the wedding, aren't you?"

"I don't know. Someone should stay here and keep watch on the place."

Connor didn't think his hesitation was worry about the ranch. Dalton wasn't sure he'd be welcome after all this time. Connor understood. "You have to come. Get old Seamus to watch the place. He can handle it for a few days." Seamus had practically grown up on *Ard na Greine*. He knew all its ins and outs.

"I don't know."

"Dalton, as your only brother, I'm asking you to come to my wedding. I want you to stand up with me." Connor hoped Dalton understood what he was really trying to say. He needed Dalton here. Needed to fix the past and reconnect with his family.

He heard a bird chirping in the hedge maze as the silence on the other end of the phone stretched out.

"There's not much else you could have said to get me on that plane, you know."

"I know." He did know now. He'd never considered that it was Dalton's pride that kept him so distant over the years. That Dalton had been hurt as much as he had by their parents' choice. "I've missed you, you know. Never forgot what it used to be like."

"Didn't think you had time to miss me, so busy on that ranch. Big enough to be its own state, isn't that what you told me once? Or maybe ten times?"

Connor winced. "I didn't mean to brag," he said truthfully. "Just couldn't believe the size of it myself. I grew up the same way you did, remember."

"But you're the one Dad thought could handle the change."

Connor closed his eyes. He'd never guessed how much pain that had caused his brother. "You're the one who got to stay with Mom. With Gran and Grandad."

"Yeah, I guess." They were both quiet for a long time. "Do you ever want to ask them what the hell they were thinking?" Dalton added.

"Yeah, I used to," Connor said. "I changed my mind."

"Why?"

"Because you know what? They've already suffered enough. We all have."

"You got that right," Dalton said.

"Could we start again, do you think?" Connor asked him. "Go back to what we were? I could use a brother right now."

"We could try. Lot of water under the bridge, though," Dalton added.

"Sure and can't we catch each other up over a pint of Guinness?" Connor laughed, letting a little of his brogue shine through to remind his brother they weren't so different after all. "Come on, Dalton—we'll have a grand time."

"Okay, okay—I'll come to your wedding. And I'll be proud to stand up with you."

"Good." Connor grew serious. "I do miss you."

"Yeah, me, too."

LATE THAT AFTERNOON, when Sadie was frying chicken and topping and tailing green beans for a side dish, Jo padded into the kitchen on bare feet. She opened the refrigerator, pulled out a pitcher of lemonade and poured herself a glass. "I didn't think I'd ever say this, but I've kind of gotten used to Cass being gone."

"She'll be home soon."

"You've done a good job stepping into her shoes."

"You think?" Sadie looked around the kitchen, sure the first thing Cass would do when she got home was scrub the place from top to bottom.

"I've been thinking it over," Jo said casually. Too casually, Sadie thought. She watched her sister out of the corner of her eye as Jo went on. "I want to give Grant one of the puppies."

Sadie stilled. "Aren't they all spoken for?"

"Yes." Jo moved the glass around on the table. "But one of the families is out of town. They don't even know they're due to get one."

"You've already given one to Connor."

"I know."

"What is this really about? I know you don't want to damage your reputation as a breeder and a fair dealer."

Was Jo sweet on Grant? After the disaster with Sean, she felt protective of her sister, and they knew so little about Grant. Connor had told her he hadn't managed to learn much that night he'd gone to the Dancing Boot.

"He's had it hard. He doesn't have family—not like us. That's why he left Tennessee—he wanted to find somewhere he could make a home for himself. I feel like he could use a friend."

"Where is he staying?" Sadie stalled for time. She needed to get a better feeling for the circumstances. Something about the man bothered her, and she liked most people.

"He's renting a cabin the Coopers own in Silver Falls."

"Silver Falls? The Coopers' ranch is right here in Chance Creek."

"It's some other property they own, I guess. I'm not sure exactly where it is."

Sadie wasn't sorry Jo hadn't been there yet. The Coopers had a reputation for lawlessness.

"If he's mixed up with the Coopers, I wouldn't give him a dog. First of all, those dogs are worth money; you spend a lot on their food and vet bills and care. You need to earn that back. Second of all, you have customers who've waited their turn. Third—" She hesitated. She needed to word this next bit carefully. Jo waited for her to continue, still playing with the glass of lemonade. "Third—the Coopers have a reputation for neglecting their animals—and people, for that matter. Maybe you need to take a step back from Grant."

"What if he's not like the Coopers?" Jo asked.

It was progress, Sadie thought. A month ago, Jo would have run from the room in a snit if someone had questioned her choice of boyfriend. She'd grown more cautious.

"Then give him time to prove it. But don't give him a puppy."

Jo nodded. "Okay," she agreed. "I won't. I'll tell him again they've all been promised."

"Which they have." Sadie thought a moment. "Do you want me there when you tell him?"

Jo looked surprised. "No. I'll be fine. He knows it was a long shot."

"When will you let them go to their new owners?"

"The day before your wedding."

Chapter Eleven

"I'M LOOKING FORWARD to seeing your spread, son," Sean O'Riley said when Connor picked him up at the airport just over a week later. He was a bear of a man, tanned so deeply by the Texas sun his skin was tough as leather. His blue eyes were deep-set, but piercing, and there was little they missed. Connor always wondered what they saw when they took him in. He knew his father loved him, but wasn't sure how he stacked up to his dad's expectations. Sean had been disappointed deeply during his life and it was hard for Connor to remain confident he hadn't added to those disappointments.

He was glad his dad seemed positive about him settling down in Montana, however. He'd figured his father would make a fuss about him not choosing Texas, but he had begun to get the sense that Sean's days overseeing the ranch there might be numbered. His dad was getting older. Slowing down. And Connor had a feeling he might be thinking about his future in broader terms than before.

It gave him satisfaction to know he'd get to show

his father something permanent he was building on the ranch. He felt sure Sean would appreciate the workmanship he'd put into the walled garden so far. He still had a long way to go before it was done, but with Sean and Dalton, and soon Brian, around, he still hoped to finish it before the wedding.

He thought Sean would like Max, too. His father had always had a soft spot for dogs. They'd never owned one when Connor lived at Valhalla, but there were plenty of them on the ranch, and all of them made a favorite of his father. Sometimes Connor had envied those dogs, and the comfortable way Sean had interacted with them. He seemed far more at ease with the four-legged critters than with his own son.

"That's my bag." Sean pointed to a black suitcase that had seen better days. Connor grabbed it off the belt.

"Just the one?"

"That's it. Let's find your truck and get out of here. I could use a drink."

"We can't leave yet. We're picking up someone else."

Connor's words stopped Sean, who'd already begun to head for the doors.

"Who?"

Connor sighed at his dad's suspicious tone. "Your wife."

"I don't have a wife."

"Ex-wife, then. Mom. Remember her?"

His father folded his arms over his chest. "You

didn't tell me Keira was coming."

"Of course she's coming. It's my wedding."

"She's never come for anything in the past. Missed your graduation, all your military revues—"

"In every case I had visits scheduled with her right afterward. Plane tickets to and from Ireland are expensive. You know that. You never made her feel welcome, either."

"Don't you start—" Sean broke off. "Hell, I'll take a taxi. You wait for your mom."

"What about Dalton? Don't you want to see him?"

That brought Sean up short. "Dalton's coming, too?"

Connor nodded, taking in the emotions crossing his father's face. Interest. Hope. Regret. Worry.

"I thought you two didn't talk."

"It's you and Dalton who don't talk, Pops."

"Don't call me that." But Sean's words were automatic. Connor could tell he was mulling over the news. "You'll need room in the truck. I'll grab that taxi."

"You'll stay here and get the awkward part over with—away from Two Willows. Just because you and Mom—or you and Dalton, for that matter—can't have a civil conversation doesn't mean the Reeds should have to suffer."

Sean stepped nearer. "It's a wonder you've invited me here at all, the way I act so badly."

"I hoped you'd surprise me." Connor glanced over Sean's shoulder. "Their plane is due in ten minutes. Sit down, take a load off and do this for me."

Sean's shoulders were bunched with anger, but he took a seat, his arms still crossed, and studiously watched the muted television screen hanging nearby. Connor supposed it was too much to ask for his father to change his attitude all at once, but he'd hoped for better.

The ten-minute wait seemed more like a couple of hours, and by the time he'd dragged his father back to where passengers entered the hall, his stomach was knotted with concern. They'd get through this wedding. His family wasn't a bunch of reprobates who couldn't keep it together for a few weeks. But his dreams of a reconciliation slipped further away with every moment.

"There you are," his mother cried several minutes later when she entered the arrivals hall. She embraced Connor hard, pulled back, looked him up and down and embraced him again. Keira was a tall woman with dark hair that framed her face in thick curls. To Connor she'd always looked more like an artist than a rancher, but he knew his mother was strong and capable. A woman who knew how to get things done.

Dalton shook his hand and Connor clapped him on the back. His brother matched him in height, if not brawn. He'd inherited their parents' dark hair and blue eyes.

"Glad you could make it," Connor said. "Can't wait for both of you to meet Sadie. She's—"

But his mother had spotted Sean. "Connor—you didn't say—"

Dalton went straight to the point. "Have you lost

your ever-lovin' mind, Connor?"

"That's what I said." Sean joined them. "Keira. Dalton." He made no move to hug his ex-wife or shake hands with his son, and Connor's heart sank another inch. He could handle the family's rancor, but Sadie would hate it. She was already hurt that her father wouldn't attend her wedding. If his family was going to be there, they had to behave.

He lost his patience. "Look, all I'm asking you to do is take a single car ride together. Mom and Dalton, you two are staying at the Cruz ranch. Autumn and Ethan Cruz run a guest house that's second to none, according to Sadie. They'll spoil you rotten, Mom. Dad, we've put you at the Evergreen Motel in town, just like you asked. It's less than three weeks until the wedding. Three weeks until you all fly home again. You can stand that. I'll pick you up first thing each morning and you'll spend the days at Two Willows. Behaving yourselves. Remember you're here for my wedding, and remember my bride deserves your respect. If you can't be on your best behavior, then go home. That means all of you."

A long silence greeted this pronouncement, but when he led them back to the lone carousel to wait for his mother's and brother's luggage, all three of them followed.

A half-hour later, when he pulled into the driveway of Two Willows, the truck was as silent as it had been since they'd left the airport. Connor parked the truck and killed the engine.

"Best behavior," he threatened them again.

"I thought you were taking me to my motel," Sean said.

It would have been the smarter move, Connor knew. But he needed to get his family invested in the idea of his wedding, which meant introducing them to Sadie—right away.

Sadie expected them, and when he led the way inside, he found she and her sisters had laid out a spread fit for a king on the long, scarred kitchen table.

"Come in," Sadie said, meeting them at the door. "I'm sure you're all hungry after your trip."

Connor made the introductions and his mother, father and Dalton all behaved themselves well enough as they said their hellos, washed up and sat down to the meal. He saw them take in the homey kitchen, their gazes stopping in surprise at the bullet grooves on the table, but none of them mentioned the damage.

Once they sat down, however, things deteriorated.

Sadie had made the mistake of setting his mother and brother directly across from Sean. After she had inquired about their flights and their health, everyone subsided into silence until the scrape of knives and forks was the only sound in the kitchen.

"Have any of you been to Montana before?" Sadie asked brightly, shooting Connor an imploring look.

All three of his family members shook their heads.

"It seems nice so far," his mother said.

"Can't hold a candle to Ireland, though," Dalton said.

His father harrumphed. "Anywhere in the good ol'

USA outshines that little backwater—"

"Dad!"

Sean subsided and Connor tried to eat his meal, but the food tasted like dust in his mouth. Why had he thought bringing his folks here was a good idea?

Jo snorted.

"Shh," Sadie said.

But Jo couldn't seem to get herself under control. A funny little sound escaped her, and a smile twisted her lips.

"What?" Connor regretted his tone immediately, but instead of taking offense, Jo laughed.

"All we need is the General here to cap off this love-fest."

Sadie clapped a hand over her mouth to hide her smile. Lena guffawed.

Connor's lips twitched despite his irritation. Jo was right. With his prickly attitude, the General would fit right in.

"I apologize for my family's lack of manners," he said to Jo. "Seems they were all raised in a barn."

"Connor's right; we're not showing off our best manners today." Keira gave her husband and son a reproving look. "Family differences can be hard to overcome."

"We know all about family differences," Lena told her dryly.

"Amen," Jo said. "At least your father is here, Connor. We can't get the General to the dinner table at all."

"Hell, he won't even enter the state. Sorry," Lena

ISSUED TO THE BRIDE ONE AIRMAN | 215

added. Connor was pretty sure Sadie had kicked her under the table.

"Then you know that some fences can't be mended," Sean said gruffly. "No matter what."

"I disagree." Everyone turned to look at Alice, who sat at the foot of the table. "Old hurts can be mended when both parties wish it. Every party at this table wishes it."

Had that been one of her hunches? Connor wondered, taking in the body language around the room. None of his family would look at each other, while the Reeds were examining all of them curiously.

He looked from his parents to his brother. "That true?"

No one answered, but if there was one thing Connor had learned during his time at Two Willows it was that some hunches were to be trusted. If Alice sensed a willingness to mend fences from his family, he was willing to be patient.

"Glad to hear it," he said, as if he'd gotten the answer he wanted. "Because when Sadie and I have kids, they'll need their uncle and grandparents around."

"HE MAY AS well have thrown me to the wolves. He used my future babies as an icebreaker," Sadie complained to Keira later when the men had headed down to the barns with Jo and Lena to check the livestock, Alice had made for her studio in the carriage house and she and Keira were cleaning the kitchen.

"It worked, didn't it?" Keira answered. "I have to

admit I was disappointed to learn you weren't pregnant already, although I suppose I should be happy you two are waiting until you're married. I've wanted a grand-child for years, though, and Dalton isn't in any hurry to settle down."

"I didn't think I was in any hurry, either," Sadie ad-mitted. "But now that I'm marrying Connor, it seems—natural to want a child."

"It is natural," Keira said. "And it's natural for me to want to be part of my grandchild's life. You'll let me be there as much as I can when the time comes, won't you?"

"Of course. Why wouldn't I?" Sadie was shocked her mother-in-law-to-be thought she had to ask.

"Sean might feel he has a better claim."

"Grandparents don't get to make claims," Sadie said tartly. "Babies need all their people around them." She wished she'd had more of her people around her growing up. She wished the General had been close to them—had deemed them worthy of his time and attention. Cass had told her she thought it was his memories of their mother that kept him away—that the past, and her absence, was too hard for him to face.

Sadie thought that was an excuse. They could have mourned together. They could have moved on together as time passed. If the General still hurt so badly he couldn't even set foot on her mother's ranch eleven years on, then he was long past due for the kind of healing time was supposed to afford.

Many people had told her how brave the General

was. Sadie thought he was a coward. He needed to face that fear—bridge that gap.

Come home to them.

Her wedding wasn't enough to bring him home, though. She hated herself for feeling relieved that Cass's hadn't been either. She didn't need to take it personally, although of course she did.

"I'm glad my son is giving marriage a chance. For a long time I thought what his father and I did would keep him from ever considering it. We made so many mistakes. I'm sure Connor has told you." Keira dried another dish. Sadie thought she was a handsome woman. Knowing she'd run a ranch on her own for many years—even a small one—impressed her.

"I don't know that much about your family's history; just that you and Dalton stayed in Ireland and Connor went with his father to Texas. That must have been hard on everyone." Sadie rinsed a pot and added it to the pile Keira was drying.

"You can't even imagine. I hope you can't," Keira said. "Although with the loss of your mother and separation from your father, I suppose you probably can."

Sadie nodded. "What happened to make that… possible? I can't imagine one of my children moving so far away."

"My husband grew far too homesick to stay in Ireland. And I couldn't imagine leaving it. We both dug into our positions. Neither would budge."

"But to split the kids…" Sadie held her breath. Had

she said too much?

"I wonder sometimes if we'll pay for that in the next world," Kiera said bluntly. "We broke our own hearts and our children's hearts. It seemed the fair thing to do, but it was fair to no one. I'd give anything to go back in time and change it."

"What would you do? Keep both boys? Or send them with their father?" Sadie asked.

"Neither." Keira pulled open one drawer after another until she found the one that held the silverware, gave the forks and knives in her hand a final polish and put them away. She shut the drawer with a thump. "I would have done whatever it took to keep my marriage whole. I learned the hard way home is home—but love is far more important."

Sadie's heart ached for all of them, and wondered if that was true. Could she leave Two Willows if Connor ever wanted to move away? Even the thought of it hollowed her out. He could change his mind about making Two Willows his home. What if he wanted to return to Texas?

Or Ireland?

When she glanced at Keira, the woman met her gaze sympathetically. "We were so young when we married. It didn't even occur to us our different countries of origin might cause us hardship. We thought love conquered all."

"But it didn't," Sadie said.

"It should have," Keira said wistfully.

Sadie didn't know what to say.

CASS AND BRIAN came home a week later, and immediately brightened the mood on the ranch. The bustle and conversation that followed their arrival was just what was needed to dispel the awkwardness that had existed since Connor's parents and brother arrived. Connor was sure the Reeds had breathed a sigh of relief each night when he'd taken his family members to the places they were staying. They'd probably braced themselves when he left early each morning to fetch his mother, father and Dalton back in time for breakfast.

At least building the walled garden had given the men something to do, and Sean and Dalton a way to spend time together that didn't require a lot of conversation. Connor was pleased to see his brother and father's relationship improving day by day as the wall grew higher, and he thought Keira and Sadie were bonding, too. Still, his mother and father hadn't reconciled, and he was beginning to suspect he'd been naive to hope they would.

As Cass and Brian passed their phones around the kitchen table at lunchtime to show the photographs they'd taken at the Grand Canyon and elsewhere along their travels, however, Connor noticed his father wasn't following the conversation; he was watching Keira.

Connor stilled. What did it mean? He could barely allow himself to feel any hope as far as his mother and father were concerned.

The ache he felt as he watched his family interact with Sadie's around the table was more for them than for himself, he realized. Because none of them had done this on purpose. None of them deserved this pain. They simply were as influenced by the landscape of their childhoods as anyone would be. That didn't mean they loved each other any less.

Later, he stepped outside for a breath of fresh air and Brian found him there.

"Everything quiet while I was away?"

"Mostly." He filled Brian in on the excitement of the night of the quilting bee, and Steel Cooper's warning. He wished he didn't have to tell the other man about his absence from the ranch or the fact that he hadn't checked in the whole time he was gone, but lying wasn't his way. He told the tale truthfully, and was rewarded by a long, thoughtful look from Brian.

"Were you in town to find information about Grant—or were you trying to decide whether or not you wanted to go through with marrying Sadie?"

Surprised by the question, Connor hesitated and earned another long look.

"It wasn't about Sadie at all," Connor assured him. "You're right; back then I was still figuring out if I was ready to marry her, but that was about me, not her."

"You sure about that?"

"Positive."

After a moment, Brian nodded. "Good."

Connor leaned against the railing that bounded the porch. "This is where I want to be, and Sadie's the woman I want to marry."

"Glad to hear it." Brian braced his forearms on the railing and stared out at Sadie's garden. "I don't think we've seen the last of trouble around here, though."

"Neither do I. Do you have any idea what direction it's going to come from next?"

Brian shook his head. "That first round of trouble-makers—they were all local boys. Seems to me when you're talking about an operation this big, it isn't just local."

"Should we start asking around?"

Brian shrugged. "I think we start by watching and listening. By getting into town more, going to the bars, the restaurants, the grocery stores. Talking to people. Becoming part of the scenery. People need to trust us and feel like we're part of Chance Creek. Then they'll talk to us—give us a head's up when trouble comes calling."

Connor supposed that was the best they could do. "I think the next time I hang out at the Dancing Boot, I better take Sadie along, though."

Brian grinned when Connor explained the comment. "That's right; no more flirting with bartenders. That's gotta be tough on you."

"Fuck you," Connor said companionably. He didn't care if he ever flirted with another woman again. He had Sadie. He'd put her—and her sisters—ahead of such trivial things. They had to act as a unit now—all of them—to look out for trouble. Connor found himself grinning. That's what this was—his new unit. Only this time it included women. Half of its members untrained, half wild and entirely disobedient. A unit of renegades.

This was going to be interesting.

"STAND STILL," ALICE said.

Sadie did as she was told, holding her arms away from her body so Alice could take measurements. She was wearing her mother's wedding gown, as Cass had done before her for her wedding. Cass was taller than Sadie, however. More curvy. Alice was altering the dress to fit better.

"What do you think of Connor?" Sadie asked Cass. She was nervous about her oldest sister's reaction, since her entire romance with Connor had happened while Cass was out of town.

"I think the more important question is, what do you think of Connor?" Cass retorted. "You've only known him a month. Don't you think you're rushing this?"

"That's the pot calling the kettle black," Alice said.

Sadie knew what she meant; Cass had met and married Brian in a pretty short time frame, too.

"I don't think I'm rushing anything," Sadie said, but Cass's words plucked the strings of her own uneasiness. Of course she thought they were rushing it, and if Connor hadn't already invited his family to visit, she would've set their wedding day far in the future. But the invitations had been issued, the tables and chairs, dishes and silverware all ordered. Mia Matheson had handled all the details with a smile and a sigh. "Don't worry about the short notice," she'd said. "Everyone in Chance Creek gets married on short notice."

Sadie had thought about it and realized she was right.

"What is it that made you fall in love with him?" Cass asked more gently.

Sadie found it hard to answer that question. There was Connor's physical attributes, of course. She thought he was incredibly handsome, and his strength and the confident way he conducted himself attracted her. But more than that, she liked his lively sense of humor. His curiosity. The way he'd simply accepted her strange demands when she dragged him around the garden the day she'd realized he could help her listen to the plants. The way he'd held her when she needed to make the tonic for Jean. The way he'd lit up when he'd learned that Halil and his family were safe.

"I like the way he treats me," she said simply. "Like he's all the way here with me. Like he… likes me."

She looked up to see both sisters nodding, and was relieved they understood.

"I think that's what we've all been looking for," Cass said. "It makes sense, given our past."

"I sometimes think it would be easier not to want a husband at all," Alice said. She rushed to add, "But I think Connor's great. I'm so happy for you two."

"I'm sure you'll find someone," Sadie told her. How could Alice not? She was so beautiful, and so kind. Sadie was surprised no one had snapped her up before this.

Alice nodded, but didn't look convinced. "When I try to see my wedding, it's… obscured."

"It's Lena I worry about," Cass said. "She has so much anger in her. She thinks the General wishes we were all boys."

"I think she's right," Sadie said, "but she shouldn't hold off from marriage on that account. She should do what she wants to do."

"We all should," Cass said. "Which is the only reason I'm okay with two of us marrying men the General sent. This trend has to stop, though. So Alice—you, Lena and Jo better start hitting the Dancing Boot every Friday and Saturday night. Find your own guys."

She was teasing, but Alice frowned. "Isn't that how we all got in trouble in the first place?"

Cass's smile faded and Sadie knew she was thinking about the men they'd been dating before Brian came to Two Willows. Men who'd been conspiring together to take their ranch. "I suppose you're right. Well, anyway—I'm glad you found a man you have a connection with, Sadie."

Sadie chuckled. "You have no idea."

Alice looked up. "What do you mean by that?"

Sadie was about to brush off the question when she decided to tell them the truth. It had become apparent during the last few months that the secrets they kept from each other made them more vulnerable.

"When I work in the garden, I've always had this— sense—of what the plants needed. It's as if they're talking to me, although not in words, obviously," she hurried to add. "It's been so strong, it's enabled me to make the garden what it is today, to tend to the hedge maze and to make my herbal cures. But after Mark—it all went away."

Alice touched her arm. "I always felt that you must

have a sense for plants like that, to be able to grow things as beautifully as you do."

"But it went away? What you mean by that?" Cass asked.

"I mean—it was like somebody had flipped the switch. Turned it off. I couldn't feel or hear anything. And the garden started to die."

Alice and Cass exchanged a look. "Now that you say that, you're right; the garden wasn't as green as it should be in summer," Alice said. "But there's been so much else to worry about, I guess I wasn't paying attention."

Sadie rushed to tell her, "It's all right; it came back. But I was getting pretty desperate before it did. I thought—I thought the land was telling me—that I should leave. That I wasn't good enough for it anymore."

"Sadie—" Cass said.

"It's okay," Sadie said again. "Because when Connor came, and he touched me—it all came back."

"Just like that?" Alice asked.

"Just like that," Sadie said, "but at first only when I was touching him. You should've seen me." She laughed. "Dragging him all around the garden, keeping him right by my side as I tended to it." Her voice wavered. "But it's more serious than I'm making out. The hedge was dying, too. It was all dying."

"You said at first that sense you have only came back when you were touching him," Alice pointed out. "What about now?"

"Now I can hear it all the time. He cured me.

Somehow."

Alice went back to her work, but Sadie saw her smile. Had her sister guessed when her abilities had returned fully?

"So Connor restored your ability to hear the plants?" Cass shook her head. "Our family is weird, have you realized that?"

"Are you just realizing that now?" Alice retorted.

"Does that mean he's like you and Alice?" Cass asked. "He can hear things, too?"

Sadie thought she heard wistfulness in her sister's voice, and she felt bad for Cass. It hadn't occurred to her before how it would feel not to have that kind of extra connection to the world. But was that true? Cass was so connected to Two Willows, to their mother—and all of them. She was the glue that held this place together.

"No," Alice answered Cass before Sadie could. "Connor restored your belief in love, didn't he?"

She was right; love was at the heart of it, which was why Sadie thought Cass had more of a connection to Two Willows than she even knew. Cass was the embodiment of love as far as Sadie was concerned.

"He did," she told Alice. "But I think more importantly he restored my belief in myself."

"I'm glad the General sent him, then," Cass said. "Although it's beginning to alarm me how often I've said that lately."

"The General is just trying to harass us," Sadie told her. "We're the ones co-opting his men. Pretty soon we'll have an army."

"I imagine he'll stop sending them," Alice said. "The General isn't a man who likes to lose."

Cass nodded, but Sadie didn't think she was convinced.

Chapter Twelve

"**G**LAD TO HEAR it," Sean was saying when Connor entered the kitchen the following morning, after a quick trip down to the barn to lend Lena, Jo and Brian a hand with the chores. He'd picked up his family earlier and driven them back to the ranch, leaving them with Sadie as she prepared breakfast. Sadie wasn't in the kitchen anymore, and neither was Dalton, but he found both of his parents at the table, his mother picking at the remains of a full breakfast of toast, sausages, eggs and orange slices, his father bent over a bowl of porridge and a cup of black coffee.

"Glad to hear what?" he asked, grateful for the lack of enmity between them for once.

"The Blakes finally tore down their old barn and put up a new one," his mother said.

"That place was an eyesore for years," Sean chimed in.

"Some people think old barns are artistic." Connor couldn't help himself. His father was always going on about eyesores back in Texas.

"The Blake barn wasn't artistic," his father snapped.

"You remember it, don't you? That awful shade of green. Blake got a discount on the paint." His mother laughed, but when Connor shook his head, her laughter died. "You don't remember it?"

"Nope. Who are the Blakes again?" He grabbed a plate from the cupboard and served himself some eggs, but the silence behind him made him turn around in time to see his parents exchange a significant look.

"Margaret Blake used to watch you when I went to appointments in town," Keira told him. "She was our sitter for years."

Connor tried to picture a woman like that, but nothing more came to him than a vague sense of a kind woman. As soon as Dalton was eight or nine, their parents had been comfortable leaving them on their own. "Sorry. Don't remember her."

"You have to remember her. What about the picnic we had? The one where Henry Davies turned the rowboat over and she went right in the pond?" his father asked.

"No." He must have been very young for that.

"Margaret was watching you when you got that awful strep throat. Your dad and I were away overnight. You remember that, don't you?"

He shrugged. "Not really. I remember my pocket-knife, though. The first day I got it I cut down the clothesline. Got yelled at."

"That was in Texas," his father said quietly. "You must remember something from Ireland."

"Sure and of course I do." Connor put on a thick

Irish brogue to lighten the moment. But instead of laughing, both his parents looked dismayed. "What? I remember. Of course I remember—I was ten when we left."

"Name your best mate in school. The boy you walked with the very first day," his father said.

Connor had a flash of being dressed up in new clothes. Walking slowly down the road, excited and anxious all at once. Dalton had told him stories about school. Some good, some terrifying.

"Didn't Dalton walk with me?"

"Hell, no. I didn't want to be seen with the likes of you," Dalton said, coming in and taking a seat at the table. "It was Danny Sullivan. Don't you remember Danny?"

"Yeah. I guess. Red hair. Freckles. In trouble a lot." Connor shrugged. In truth, those first months in Texas, he'd spent so much time trying not to remember his home, he figured he'd erased a bunch of his early years. On his short visits back to Ireland, he'd spent his time with family, not friends.

"He's forgotten it all," Keira said to Sean. "You must have truly hated Ireland to erase its memory from our son." She stood up, scraping her chair over the floor, and strode right out the back door.

Connor set his plate on the counter and moved to follow her, but his father held up a hand. "No, son. I'll go. This is my doing."

Connor watched his parents through the window as his mother strode down the path that bisected Sadie's garden, and his father followed steadily. Dalton came to stand beside him. "They're both getting older."

"Of course they are." Regret made him curt, but Connor wasn't sure what he was regretting. He hadn't been the one who made the decision to leave Ireland. He'd been a kid.

But he should have visited more.

"You really don't remember?" Dalton asked. His gentle accent brought back more memories than Connor wanted to admit.

"I tried to forget," he admitted. "Otherwise I'd have lost my mind."

Dalton sagged a little. "Never thought of it like that. I always assumed you were too busy enjoying Texas."

"Losing you two—losing my home—" He couldn't even put into words how much that had hurt him. How the flat, hot, hard land of Texas seared the soul right out of him. How he'd searched for something familiar and found only strangeness.

How his father had been fair—but as hard as the land around them without his wife to soften his edges.

How it felt to know his mother had let him go.

"It wasn't right, what they did. They made a devil's bargain." Dalton's anger was clear.

"And we're all still paying for it."

"Aye."

Connor took a deep breath. "We can change that." They had to. They all couldn't go on in so much pain.

"We'll still be half a world apart," Dalton pointed out.

"So we video chat. We schedule calls. We email. Text. Distance doesn't matter like it once did."

"Suppose not. You could come home, you know. The property is small, but—"

"If I came home we'd both have to find second jobs," Connor told him. "And I've already promised Sadie I'll make Two Willows my home. You could move here, you know," he added.

Dalton elbowed him. "I can't do that."

"I know." Connor sighed. He did know. "But if I can get on a plane once in a while, so can you."

"Aye, that I can do."

They watched their father finally catch up to their mother in the empty doorway to the walled garden. The stones had almost reached shoulder height.

"What do you suppose he's saying to her?" Dalton asked.

"I have no idea. I'd better get going, though." He checked the clock. "Got a bunch of errands in town. Want to come?"

Dalton waved him off. "I'm for breakfast. I'll keep tabs on Ma and Dad."

Several hours later, Connor had knocked six errands off his list and was just leaving the hardware store when he ran into Grant coming in. The man was walking with a purpose, but he hesitated when he spotted Connor. Connor wished he knew Grant's story. What had brought him to Chance Creek?

"Hey," Grant said when he spotted him. "Congrats. On your wedding. Heard all about it."

"Yeah? From who?" He supposed word was getting around, but Grant didn't run in the same circles he and Sadie did, and he hadn't been to the ranch to bother Jo in days.

"Small town." Grant shrugged. "Everyone knows."

Connor nodded. That could be true.

"Tying on the old ball and chain, huh? Good luck to you." Grant sauntered into the hardware store, leaving Connor to walk slowly to his truck. Why had the short exchange rubbed him so wrong? Grant's gratingly negative attitude toward marriage was part of it. No matter what you thought about the institution, it was bad form to rain on someone else's parade when they were days away from their wedding.

He didn't want Jo anywhere near that surly, cocky idiot. Sadie had told him about the piece of work Jo's last boyfriend had turned out to be. She didn't need any more trouble.

He had just reached his truck and opened the passenger side door to deposit his purchases on the seat when a female voice he recognized spoke behind him.

"Where've you been hiding, cowboy?"

Connor closed his eyes. Tracy. The last person he wanted to run into today. "I'm not hiding."

"You left in an awful hurry the last time you were in the Boot. I was only gone a moment. Seems to me you could have waited to say goodbye."

"Something came up." He placed his bags inside the truck and closed the door, planning to circle around to the driver's side and take off, but Tracy blocked his way.

She placed a hand on his chest, a glint in her eye he didn't like. Something was different about Tracy today. In the bar, she'd been flirtatious, just out to have a good time. Today she looked—

Angry.

"I saw you talking to Grant Kimball just now."

"What of it?"

"He's trouble, you know." She flattened her palm on his chest over his heart. When Connor shifted, she twisted her fingers in his shirt so he couldn't easily pull away.

"What makes you say that?" His uneasiness increased, not the least because he was afraid someone would see them in this awkwardly intimate position. He'd already been warned about her by Steel Cooper—in words very similar to the ones she'd just used to warn him about Grant. She was obviously a woman on a mission—and he wasn't sure what her objective was.

"I know things about him. Come have a cup of coffee with me and I'll tell you everything."

"I don't have time for a cup of coffee." This was a setup. He could smell it a mile away—

"Come on, there aren't any single men worth a damn in this town. You're the most interesting thing to come along in ages. Can you blame a girl for wanting to spend time with you? It's just coffee."

Her flirtatious tone contrasted with that sharp glint in her eye and the tight grip she had on his shirt. He had to get out of here before someone saw them and misunderstood. "I told you, I don't have time. I'm running late as it is."

"Right. You have to run home to Sadie Reed. Yeah; I know you're together. She's got you tied to her apron strings, doesn't she?"

"Look, I—"

Without warning, Tracy pulled him close, went up on tiptoe and kissed him hard on the mouth.

"Hey!" He shoved her away.

Tracy stumbled back, but caught herself, laughing at him. "Give me a break, cowboy. You know you liked it." She shoved something into her pocket as she backed off. What was it? Her phone? Had it been in her other hand?

"I'm getting married in two weeks. You can't just go around kissing me."

Tracy's laughter died and her eyes went hard again. "Yeah, I heard something about that." She took a step closer, her hands balled into fists. "Funny you failed to mention it back at the bar, huh?"

Connor bit back the words he'd meant to say. She had him there. "Look, I—"

"Save the lie, asshole. You deserve everything you've got coming to you." She whirled around and strode away.

"What the hell do you mean by that?" Connor called after her.

She held up her middle finger and kept going.

SADIE WAS BACK in the greenhouse mixing up batches of chamomile tea when her phone buzzed in her pocket.

Figuring it was Connor, she pulled it out. Her heart dropped when she came face to face with a photograph of Connor kissing Tracy Jones. Tracy, the woman who'd flaunted her relationship with Mark while Sadie was dating him.

It couldn't be real. But there it was in color. Not just a little kiss, either; their mouths fused together like they'd rushed together in a fit of passion. The time stamp on the photo said it had been taken just minutes ago. She braced herself against the table and tried to calm down.

It was a trick. A hoax of some kind. Tracy hated her for dating Mark—hated all of them for putting him in the hospital.

Sadie sagged against the potting table, her heart pounding. Connor had said he hadn't done anything with Tracy, but if he was kissing her—today—

She looked at the photo again. That was the hardware store behind them. He was supposed to be picking up more cement to finish the walled garden. He'd said he wanted to get it done before the wedding.

But he was kissing Tracy—

So there wouldn't be any wedding after all.

Sick to her stomach, tears gathering in her eyes, she bent over, still grasping the edge of the table to hold herself up. This was what it felt like when your world crumbled around you a second time in two months. She'd thought Mark had torn her heart apart, but that was nothing compared to the pain of Connor's betrayal.

She held up the phone. Forced herself to look at the

photo again.

This time something caught her eye: Caitlyn Warren, who worked with Ellie Donaldson at her bridal boutique. She was standing behind Connor's truck, looking across its bed at the couple as they snapped the selfie.

Before she could stop herself, Sadie called Ellie's Bridals. She had to learn for sure if what she was seeing was true. Maybe Tracy had manipulated a photo, although Sadie couldn't work out how.

"Ellie here," a cheerful voice answered.

"Ellie, it's... it's Sadie Reed. Is Caitlyn there?" She was afraid the roughness of her voice would give away how close she was to tears, but Ellie didn't seem to notice.

"Just a minute."

Moments later, a younger voice answered, "This is Caitlyn. How can I help you?"

"Caitlyn, it's Sadie Reed," Sadie said again, clearing her throat when the words caught there.

"Hi, Sadie—what's up? I... heard you're getting married."

Was it her imagination or did Caitlyn sound hesitant? "I'm going to cut to the chase. Tracy Jones just sent me a photo of her kissing my fiancé. You're standing in the background. Did you see them?"

There was a long pause. Caitlyn had to have heard the pain in her voice. "Sadie, I don't want to get in the middle of this—"

"Answer me." Sadie wasn't in the mood to safeguard anyone's feelings. Not when hers were shattered.

Caitlyn sighed. "I'd just come out of the store. I was in line after Connor."

Sadie wasn't at all surprised Caitlyn knew Connor's name. In a town as small as Chance Creek, newcomers stood out and people thrived on gossip.

"Did he kiss her?"

Another pause. "Yes, but—"

Sadie had heard enough. "Thank you," she managed, and cut the call. She couldn't breathe. Her throat ached. How could Connor do this? She'd thought he loved her.

But he was a man. And this is what men did. They took what they could get. They lied and cheated. They didn't care.

None of them ever cared.

Suddenly stifled in the close, humid greenhouse, Sadie raced toward the door and pushed it open, stumbled outside and braced her hands on her knees while she sucked in fresh air. Dizzy—nauseous—she sank to her knees in the dirt.

She couldn't marry Connor.

And—Sadie looked around her, horrified—

She couldn't hear—anything.

A wail began deep inside her, but Sadie choked it down when she saw movement—Sean and Keira exiting the walled garden hand in hand. Her own pain magnified as she watched Connor's father tuck a lock of his mother's hair behind her ear. She didn't have to be tuned in to her surroundings to know what they'd just done.

So Connor had gotten what he'd wanted all along, she realized. His parents had flown to Montana for his wedding—for a wedding that turned out to be fake, after all. And they'd fallen back in love.

He would get his family back. While she—

She'd have to leave hers—for good.

"THIS IS GETTING to be a habit," Cab said when he ushered Connor into his office.

"This shouldn't take too long. I'm looking for information about Grant Kimball. Last time I came in, you didn't have anything on him. How about now?" Connor found himself unwilling to head back to Two Willows after that scene in the parking lot. It wasn't his fault Tracy had kissed him—except she was right; he had flirted with her at the Boot. Or at least he hadn't refused the free drinks she'd brought him, which pretty much amounted to the same thing.

She was furious at what she thought was his duplicity, even if he hadn't meant anything by their conversation. He'd managed to burn his bridges with a valuable informant. All he could hope was that Cab knew enough to make up for that.

His phone buzzed and he glanced down at it.

You're a bastard, Lila had texted.

Damn it; he'd thought he'd run her off. This was all he needed today.

Cab waved him into a seat and took his own. "I've found out a few things. Not much. He's new in town.

Related to the Coopers somehow, but I couldn't trace the connection. You got a beef with him?"

"Not yet. But something doesn't sit right." He wasn't ready to repeat what Tracy had said. Cab already thought he was a fool when it came to women.

His phone buzzed again.

You're a real asshole. You know that?

"Why do you say that?" Cab asked.

Connor ignored Lila. He figured Cab was a man who could appreciate a good hunch. "It's a gut reaction. Look, as far as I know he's just a newcomer who met up with Jo and fell for her. But don't you think it's strange that he first came around to try to get one of her puppies, and that's where Jo spotted the intruder a few weeks back—near where the puppies sleep?"

"She said the intruder wasn't Grant."

"Hell of a coincidence, though."

His phone buzzed a third time.

I believed you. You said you wanted me.

Hell. He hadn't really meant it. Connor tried to focus on the sheriff.

"Maybe. Maybe not. With that kind of lineup for the dogs, maybe there's more than one person unwilling to wait," Cab suggested.

"Maybe. They're not that unusual a breed, though. I looked them up online. They're worth a few hundred bucks—not thousands."

"To some hopped-up kid needing a fix, that's

enough if they knew someone willing to buy one."

"Tell me about the Coopers," Connor said. He didn't look down when his phone buzzed again.

Cab laced his hands behind his neck and leaned back in his chair. "Now, there's a story. There've been Coopers here for as long as there've been Reeds, although they left town for a spell before coming back. A rough lot. Clannish. Got a Hatfield and McCoy type thing going with the Turners—another old family."

"Over what? Land?"

Cab scoffed. "Over pride. Someone stood someone else up at the altar—about a hundred years ago. None of them are willing to move on. Get called out there once a month, it feels like."

"How does that fit in with Jo's puppies?"

"I don't see how it does, to be honest. Grant's young. Single. Jo's a good-looking girl. Could be that simple."

"Could be." Something told him it wasn't, though. Connor stood up. "Thanks for the information."

"Hey," Cab called to him when he headed for the door. "You ever go out to the Coopers' place, you take backup, you hear me? In fact, just don't go. We don't need that kind of trouble here."

Connor nodded. Seemed to him trouble was coming whether they needed it or not.

Outside, he looked at the rest of Lila's texts.

Liar.

I waited for you. I thought you loved me.

I thought you cared.

Hell, this was a mess. Connor did the only thing he could. Dialed her number and held his breath.

"I was straight with you that I never wanted something serious," he said when Lila picked up. "I told you I was seeing other women. You said you were seeing other men."

Lila's voice was hoarse with tears. "I lied," she wailed. "I lied so you'd think I was more interesting. I thought you'd come around."

Nothing on the battlefield had ever made him feel so small as Lila's words did. He hadn't meant to hurt her. He'd been careless—

Too careless for far too long.

"I'm sorry." He knew it was inadequate.

"Do you... love her?"

"I do."

Lila's sobs filled his ears. Connor didn't know what to do. Finally, he said, "Lila, you have to find someone who loves you—exactly for who you are. Someone who isn't an ass like me."

"Fuck you!" Lila hung up and Connor could only pocket the phone helplessly. All that time he'd tried to avoid getting hurt—and he only managed to hurt everyone else.

WHEN CONNOR ARRIVED home, Sadie was waiting for him on the back porch, a can of diet soda in her hand. He looked tired. All that kissing must have worn him out.

"No lemonade today?" he said, climbing the stairs and leaning against the railing close to where she sat.

No. No lemonade. Not for what she had to say. Seemed to her a diet drink was more fitting when it came to cutting something out of her life. "There's some inside, though. Help yourself."

His eyes narrowed. "Something wrong?"

"Yeah, something's wrong. I'm calling off the wedding."

"Sadie—"

She swallowed hard. She wouldn't cry. Wouldn't feel a speck of the emotion battering her from inside. Wouldn't back down now even when she thought the pain of moving forward might kill her. "I'm through with you. I'm through with men."

"What—?"

Enough talk. She held out her phone. Showed him the photo Tracy had taken when she kissed him earlier.

"She kissed *me*—"

"You kissed her back. And it doesn't look like it's the first time." If he thought she was fooled, he was gravely mistaken.

"I was only talking to her because I wanted information—" He tried again.

Another lie. Another brick added to the wall she was building around her heart. Sadie stood up. "I'm going to buy that plane ticket. When your parents' visit is over, I expect you gone." She brushed past him, but Connor reached for her. Took hold of her arm.

"You can't just walk away after a bombshell like

that. We have to talk about this—"

Sadie wrenched herself out of his arms. "There's nothing to talk about."

But she only made it another step before a scream tore the air. Sadie froze. Connor whipped around. That sounded like—

Jo screamed again, a bloodcurdling shriek that blasted Connor into action. He dashed past Sadie, who raced after him.

They sped toward the carriage house, past the garden, past the cars and trucks parked in the dirt lot. Jo came around the corner as they approached, her face streaked with tears.

"They're gone! They're all gone!"

Chapter Thirteen

"**A**RE YOU HURT? What happened?" Connor asked Jo, almost grateful for the interruption. Sadie was right behind him, her face no longer the cold, hard mask she'd shown him on the porch. She rushed up to Jo and took her in her arms.

"Are you okay?" she echoed.

That was more like it. When he'd approached Sadie moments ago, her calm had unnerved Connor more than anything else—because behind that blank facade, her fury had been palpable. He'd thought he'd lost the battle before he'd stepped foot into the fray. Sadie wanted to leave him so badly she was willing to leave her home.

He couldn't believe Tracy had photographed that kiss. If she'd wanted to screw up his life, it had worked.

Now he had to focus on the crisis at hand, as much as he wanted to turn to Sadie, take her in his arms and make it clear Tracy had never meant anything to him. "Are you hurt?" he asked Jo again.

She shook her head, but her words came out in gasps between her sobs. "No. I came—I came to check on the dogs and—and—they're not there. None of them are there!"

"What's wrong? What's going on?" Brian raced up from the direction of the barns. Connor's father and brother rushed out from inside the house.

"Someone stole the dogs," Connor told them hurriedly. Max—they'd stolen Max, too. Fury welled up inside him. What kind of coward went after a pack of dogs?

"We've got to find them. Where are they?" Jo wailed.

"We'll find them. I promise," Sadie said. "We'll get them back."

"Grant?" Connor said to Brian. "He's the one who's been bothering Jo."

"He wouldn't steal them." Jo's voice rose higher.

"We don't know that," Sadie told her.

Jo's face crumpled again. "What about—that other guy—the one skulking around?" she demanded through her tears. "It has to be him."

"But no one knows who he is."

"We'll find him—we'll find your dogs," Connor said. He nodded to Brian. "I think I know where to start."

"I'm coming, too," his father rushed to say.

"Me, too," Dalton said.

Connor thought fast. "Dad, you come with us. Dalton, you stay here with the women." He put up a hand to stop his brother's protests. "Keep them safe, okay? Let's go, before whoever it is gets too far away."

He spared one last look for Sadie, wishing he'd had more time to talk to her, but knowing she'd never leave as long as Jo needed her. When he got back he'd have to convince her he'd done nothing wrong.

He couldn't lose Sadie now.

"WE'RE NOT GOING to find dogs at a bar," Brian told him when Connor pulled up in front of the Dancing Boot a short time later.

"We're not looking for dogs. We're looking for Tracy Jones." Without waiting for an answer, he got out and stalked inside, knowing Brian and his father would be on his heels. Inside, he had to wait a moment for his eyes to adjust to the low light. This early in the afternoon, the clientele was sparse, but just as he'd hoped, Tracy was already working the bar, drying glasses and putting them away.

When she spotted him, she threw down the towel. "I don't need what you're selling."

"Well, I need answers." Connor crossed the room, braced his hands on the bar and leaned over it. "Grant Kimball. Start talking."

"Complete asshole," she snapped back, her eyes flashing with fury. Connor wondered if she'd pursued Grant, too. What had she said? She was sick of the men in Chance Creek and wanted someone new? Grant was as new as he was. If Grant had turned her down, too, no wonder she was furious. Especially if she'd heard he was sniffing around Jo. Losing multiple men to the Reed women had to sting.

"I need more than that. Why's he here?"

"Why should I tell you anything?"

"Because someone stole Jo Reed's dogs, and I don't care what you think of me, or Sadie—Jo doesn't deserve to lose the animals she loves."

"I don't know anything about any stupid dogs. And Jo's as much of a Reed as Sadie is. They can all go rot for all I care." Tracy picked up the towel. Another patron, an old man with the ruddy complexion of a lifelong alcoholic, was watching their exchange with interest from a nearby bar stool.

Connor ignored him and stifled the urge to reach across the bar to shake Tracy. "McNab. They're worth a pretty penny. They're almost weaned, which means Jo's just about to be paid for them."

Tracy shrugged. "What's it to me?"

"McNab breed?" the man on the bar stool said. "John Willett's got a litter of them up in Silver Falls. Plenty of people breed those dogs."

"I don't give a damn about who's breeding them," Connor told the man. "What I want to know is—"

His phone buzzed. With a growl of frustration, Connor grabbed it. When he saw Sadie's name he took the call.

"We just found a ransom note. It had fallen down from where they'd left it," Sadie said without preamble. Her voice was shaking. "They want two hundred and fifty thousand dollars for the dogs. Which is totally ridiculous, of course—but it says... it says it's what we *owe them*. This isn't about dogs. This is about the drugs, isn't it? About the fact we're still alive while Bob isn't."

Connor's grip on the phone tightened. "Who is it from?"

"I don't know—there aren't any names, but it says 'we' and 'us.' 'You owe *us* money. Two hundred and fifty thousand dollars. Bring it to the Old Town Mart on High Street.' That's in Silver Falls. 'Two a.m. Bring the cops and we'll skin the puppies alive. We'll send you the film to watch.'"

Connor's gut tightened. "Sadie—"

"Jo's beside herself," Sadie said. "She's absolutely hysterical. If they do it—if they film it—"

"They won't. We won't let them." But Connor thought they'd just gotten a clear message about the kind of men they were dealing with. "You're right; this isn't about dogs. This is about the drugs you blew up."

Was Sadie crying? Connor thought she was, which made him all the more determined to find the men responsible and—

He lowered the phone. Turned to Tracy, who flinched at something she saw in his gaze. "Tell me about Grant Kimball. Now. Or I swear to God—"

After a moment, Tracy dropped her tough girl act. When she spoke again, she sounded defeated. "Like I said, he's a complete asshole. Arrives in town and struts around because he thinks he's hot shit. He's connected, you know. His family's into all kinds of stuff back in Tennessee. Bunch of jailbirds. He's only here because it got too hot for him. Him and his friend."

"Friend?" Connor leaned closer. "What friend?"

"Ron Cooper."

"And they're both staying at the Cooper place?"

"Hell, no." Tracy laughed, but sobered quickly. "Ron Cooper's not welcome there. Gotta be a pretty black sheep if you're the black sheep of the Cooper family, I always say. But that's what he is. They're both staying up in Silver Falls. At the Wild Spring."

Connor looked to Brian.

"Never heard of it."

"Bunch of cabins up on Heckam Ridge. Near the lake." Tracy sighed. "I'll draw you a map."

"You're telling the truth?" He wouldn't put it past her to play another trick.

"I'm telling the truth. Which is more than I can say for you—or Grant." Her bravado slipped again and something shifted in Connor's heart. Life was brutal sometimes, and his gut told him Tracy had seen some of that brutality. "Why don't you put the Willetts' place on there, too." He turned to Brian and his father. "I've got an idea."

WHEN CASS TOOK over Jo's care, wrapping her up in a light blanket despite the day's heat and curling up next to her on the couch in the living room, Sadie joined a white-faced Keira in the kitchen. She'd already brewed an herbal tea for Jo with a strong sedative power. There was nothing more she could do at the moment. Outside, Dalton paced like a caged animal and she knew he was frustrated. He wanted to be where the action was.

"Is this what's it's always like here? Shoot-outs?

Dognappings?" Kiera traced a finger over one of the grooves in the kitchen table. She kept looking out the window, as if the men might return any moment.

Sadie shook her head. "Chance Creek has its problems; all small towns do. But it's hard to hide in a place this small. Someone will see something. It will all turn out okay." She hoped. If Connor couldn't find those puppies, Jo's heart would break.

"Of course, Two Willows is a magic place," Keira said, almost to herself. She caught Sadie's eye and elaborated. "I can feel it. It's like my home; it's more than just a piece of land."

Sadie didn't want to think about that. "It's going to be hard to leave it," she agreed, then bit her lip, wishing she could take the words back.

"Connor said you two would make your home here. Have you changed your minds?" Keira frowned. "Has something happened between you?"

Sadie thought about lying. Decided she couldn't. She was too tired to keep up a charade—too burnt out from everything that had happened these past few months. "There's someone else."

"Someone you love?"

Sadie shook her head. "Someone Connor wants. I don't think he's ready for a commitment like marriage. I don't know why he even proposed." She knew she shouldn't say any of this to Connor's mother. Unfortunately, her own mother wasn't here to spill it to, and Keira was so easy to talk to.

"Because he loves you. Anyone can see that."

"Then why did he kiss another woman this morning?" Suddenly angry, Sadie pulled out her phone and pulled up the photo again, her eye catching a text from Caitlyn that began with the words, URGENT—PLEASE READ. After Keira gasped at the image of her son kissing Tracy, Sadie opened Caitlyn's text. Had she heard about the dogs and—?

What she read stopped her heart in its tracks.

Tracy kissed Connor, not the other way around. She asked him out. When he said no, she kissed him. When he told her he was getting married, she got furious. I think she already knew and set him up. She's a bitch—don't let her ruin everything.

Sadie scanned the text again, and the sinking feeling in her gut grew stronger.

Boy-crazy—that's what they'd called Tracy back in high school. The kind of girl who'd ditch her friends last minute, tell lies about another girl, create drama—whatever it took to get a boy's attention.

Or a man's.

Tracy had slept with Mark knowing all the while he was dating Sadie. She wouldn't put it past the woman to kiss Connor, then put the blame on him.

Keira had obviously seen the text, too. "I can't tell you what to do," she told Sadie. "I have no idea if my son is guilty or innocent in this. Maybe he's turned into a right old bastard. How would I know?" She looked out the window again. "All I can say is don't rush to judgement. Don't rush to leave. Coming back is so hard.

You can waste so much time in stubbornness."

Sadie supposed Keira would know. She wondered where Connor and the others were now. Had they gotten any leads? They were putting themselves in danger to save Jo's dogs. She hugged her arms across her chest, wishing she'd listened to Connor instead of believing Tracy.

Keira turned to study her. "Lass, it's not enough to sit and wait and see. That's what I'm trying to tell you. You need to fight for love."

"How do I do that?"

"Call her. That woman. Find out right from the horse's mouth what happened."

"You think she'll tell me?" Sadie wasn't so sure. Tracy had crossed a lot of lines.

"It's hard not to answer a direct question. Especially when you aren't expecting it. Even when you're a true reprobate."

Why not give it a try? Keira was right; maybe she'd find out something. At any rate, it would give her something to do while they waited to hear from the men.

She dialed the number of the Dancing Boot and was relieved when Tracy herself answered.

"Tracy, it's Sadie Reed. Are you sleeping with my fiancé?"

She held her breath through the long pause that followed her demand.

"No," Tracy said finally. "I should have. If he'd seen me first, he would have wanted me; you know that."

"But you didn't sleep with him."

"Fuck it." Tracy sounded fed up. Spent. "We talked, all right? All he wanted was to know about Grant. I kissed him—to show him what he was missing. That's all there was to it. So you can have him, but I'm warning you. Stop it. Stop taking all the men."

"All the men? Who else have I taken?" Sadie couldn't believe what she was hearing.

"Mark—"

"Mark? The man who tried to kill my sisters? To steal my home? You're actually angry I dated him?"

"Who the hell am I supposed to date?" Tracy exploded. "I've known everyone in town since I was four!"

And hit on most of them by now, Sadie didn't say out loud. She didn't need to.

"I'm not a… whore," Tracy said bitterly.

"I know." Sadie softened; she did know. Tracy was a woman who wanted to be wanted. Who couldn't seem to fill the hole that encompassed her need no matter how many men she was with. "I didn't take Connor on purpose—"

"Whatever. Just stop." Tracy hung up on her. Sadie turned to Keira, but found she couldn't speak. Tears of relief slipped down her cheeks, and when the older woman opened her arms, Sadie fell into her embrace.

"There, there, lass," she said, stroking Sadie's hair as she cried. Sadie hadn't realized how wound up the past weeks' events had left her and she couldn't seem to stop. Keira let her cry, murmuring nonsense words of comfort, and something shifted deep inside Sadie. Some old wound she hadn't even known she still bore.

Her tears changed from ones of relief to ones of a long-held sorrow.

"Cry it out," Keira murmured. "She's with you still, you know."

Sadie stiffened. How had Keira known—?

"Your mother's here. Watching over you."

Sadie's breath hitched and a new outpouring of grief welled up in her. When she'd finally cried herself dry, she pulled back and wiped her eyes with the hem of her T-shirt. "How did you know I was thinking of her?"

"Doesn't take a gift to know a lass needs her mother in times like this. Or that a mother would never truly leave such wonderful daughters."

Sadie smiled and scrubbed a hand across her cheeks. "That's kind."

"I can't fill her shoes, but I hope I can be a friend," Keira said. "And I hope one day soon I'll be able to call you daughter."

Sadie couldn't find an answer, but the possibility didn't seem as far-fetched as it had just minutes ago. Nothing had happened between Connor and Tracy, even though Tracy had wanted it to. Maybe she could trust Connor.

Maybe she could marry him.

But first they had to bring Jo's puppies home.

Her phone buzzed in her pocket and Sadie pulled it out. It was Lena.

"Damn fence is down. I've got cattle going every

which way. I need help."

"Jo can't do it."

"You can."

Sadie made a face. She was as good a horsewoman as any of her sisters, but she wasn't that big on herding cattle.

"What is it?" Keira asked.

Sadie relayed Lena's message and was relieved when Keira brightened. "Leave it to Dalton and me. We've got this."

IT WAS MID-AFTERNOON by the time Connor and the others reached Silver Falls. The stop at the Willetts' place had taken longer than Connor would have liked.

"You lose my dogs, you'll owe me full price for them," Willett said, but he'd heard about all the trouble at Two Willows over the past couple of months, and he was a man who knew right from wrong. "If you ask me, there's too much of those drugs coming through the area these days. I know it'll never go away for good, but it didn't used to be like this. Can't say I'm surprised there's a Cooper behind it."

With Willett's dogs in the back of the truck, and Brian back there to keep them calm, Connor continued on up into the hills to the Wild Spring, driving past the entrance to the *resort*, as it was labeled on the sign, and parking some way down the road. From here it looked like nothing more than a dozen ramshackle summer cottages that at some point had been converted to year-round use. He could tell they'd be cold in winter. Damp, too, most likely. He'd bet anything there was mold in the walls, and when he noticed the chimneys, he doubted the woodstoves attached to them would be anywhere near up to code. He sent his father in to scout the place and locate #11, where Ron Cooper was supposed to be staying. Connor was growing impatient by the time his father returned.

"Checked it out. Hardly looks like anyone's living there. Lady next door told me he spends most of his time up at a drying shed he rents from the park's owner. She's a talkative type. Lonely. She would have given me the pedigree of everyone in the resort if I'd had the time to listen."

"*Resort*," Connor echoed with a shake of his head. "More like *end of the road*. Did she say he's up there now?"

"I took a look. He's there, all right. Got himself a lawn chair and he's all stretched out like he's working on his tan. Didn't want to get too close. Figured if he's got the dogs around they might smell my scent and give me away."

"Good work. What about Grant?" Where was Max? Connor wondered. In that shed? His fists clenched.

"Sounds like he's in and out. Sometimes staying here, sometimes not. She hasn't seen him in a few days. Says his truck hasn't been around at all."

Connor ticked over the information in his head, asked his father a few more questions and made his plan. When he'd filled Brian and his father in, they got Willett's puppies out of the truck, put them on leads and took a long, circular route through the woods that bordered the road to come within striking distance of the drying shed.

It was heavy work. The terrain was nearly vertical in places, the ground uneven. It was hard to keep the puppies in line and Connor was afraid their yipping would give them away too far in advance.

The dogs settled down as they tired out, though, and when Connor emerged on a rise of ground with a line of sight to the drying shed, Sean handed him the binoculars, and he spotted Ron. Just like Sean had said, the man was laid out in his reclining lawn chair like he didn't have a care in the world.

"Is he stupid?" Brian whispered when Connor had passed him the binoculars.

"Confident," Connor corrected him. "He's got the dogs where he wants them. He thinks he's got us over a barrel."

"Think Grant's inside?"

"I think we'd better count on it. Although I don't see him as the type to sit in a shed while his buddy's getting a tan."

"He has to know no one in their right mind would waste a quarter million dollars rescuing puppies," Sean said.

"Maybe. But maybe that's not his game. Think about it; you and the women blew up their drugs. They want money and they want revenge. Either way things go here, they win."

"How do you figure that?"

"If we're crazy enough to give them the money, they get what they want. If we don't and they kill those animals…"

"Jo will lose her mind," Brian said.

"And her sisters will blame us for failing. It's like releasing a snake into paradise. A slow, nasty revenge." Connor didn't think they'd stop with that, though.

"Maybe they're not really after all that much money," Sean said suddenly. "Maybe they've set the bar high to see how much you'll cough up."

"That could be," Brian said. "So, now what?"

"I get as close as I can. You get the dogs into position," Connor said. "Be ready in case Grant's in that shed."

Sean and Brian moved off, leaving Connor to continue a slow, steady advance toward Ron. The cowboy had a lanky build, a sharp nose and straw-colored hair that showed under his hat. Connor made a wide circle slowly around to the back of the shed and scouted every step before he placed his foot down. He couldn't make a single sound. Nothing the dogs inside might hear—

As Connor came around the corner, Sean released the Willett dogs right on cue. They ran barking across the clearing mere feet in front of Ron, who jumped to his feet.

"What the hell?" Ron, momentarily confused at the sight of the puppies—which he must have thought were the ones he'd locked into the drying shed—stopped in his tracks long enough for Connor to cold-cock him with the butt of his pistol. The man dropped like a stone. Connor searched him quickly, removed a Glock from a holster tucked under Ron's armpit and handed it to Brian, who'd looped back to reach his side.

"Tie him up. I'll get Jo's dogs." Careful to make sure first neither Grant nor anyone else was inside, he busted down the door of the shed and rounded up the puppies, taking a moment to give Max a squeeze and whisper to him it would be all right soon while the puppy showed his enthusiasm with a lot of wet kisses.

It took longer for him and Sean to collect the Willett dogs, but they eventually lured them back with treats, and soon the bed of Connor's truck was full of puppies.

"What'll we do with him?" Brian nudged Ron with his foot and the man groaned. Coming around, he thrashed for a moment, but when he realized he was trussed hand and foot, he soon gave up.

"You'll pay. Don't think you won't," he snarled at them.

"Save it for the sheriff."

"Fuck you."

"You're the one who's fucked."

"I wouldn't be too sure about that. I don't think there's a big penalty for stealing a couple of stupid dogs."

Connor lost his patience, grabbed a roll of duct tape, ripped off a length of five inches and slapped it over Ron's mouth. "You bother anyone at Two Willows again, I'll put you in the ground where you belong," Connor snarled at him. Ron was right, and that pissed him off. Plus, he still had no proof Grant was connected to any of this. The thought of him roaming free—hitting on Jo—

"Get him in the truck. Grab the dogs. Let's get out of here."

Brian drove the truck. Sean climbed into the bed with the dogs. Connor sat in back with Ron, who kept writhing and trying to shout against the duct tape over his mouth until Connor wanted to bash him with the butt of his pistol again. He was hot, sweaty and frustrated. After all this, Ron would probably get off with little more than a fine.

If that.

"We'll take him straight to the sheriff's office. I don't know what Cab can do, but it's a start," Brian said.

They were quiet for the rest of the trip back into town, except for Ron, who never stopped trying to talk. They were almost to the Sheriff's Department when a phone buzzed. Connor patted his pockets, but it wasn't his.

"That yours?" he asked Brian.

"Nope."

Sean was in the truck bed, so it couldn't be his.

Ron's words were garbled against the duct tape, but Connor finally figured out he was trying to say the cell phone was his. Connor yanked him forward, spotted a rectangular shape in his back pocket and fished it out. It was Grant video-calling him.

"Your friend's a little busy," Connor told Grant when he accepted the call.

"Oh, yeah? Well, I've been busy, too." Grant's face

filled the phone, but then the image tilted, and a moment later, Jo came into view. "Say hello, honey."

Connor's chest tightened.

Hell.

"Connor?" Jo's voice was slurred and her eyes were unfocused. "Connor—they've got—" Grant yanked her away and the next moment, all Connor could see was his face.

"Got your attention now? You know what we want. You know when and where we want it. You don't get another chance. Fuck this up, and Jo's dead."

He hung up, leaving Connor speechless.

Ron said something against the duct tape that sounded cocky as hell.

Connor whirled around and slammed a fist into his face. "Go!" he yelled at Brian, who had already slammed his foot down on the gas. "I'll call Cab and tell him what's going down."

"ALL RIGHT, LADIES. Thank you for your hospitality, but your sister and I should be on our way," Grant said. He hoisted Jo up over his shoulder.

Sadie could kick herself for giving her sister a sedative tea. Jo dangled as limply as a rag doll. She must have overdone it with the herbs; that's what she got for tampering with them when her connection to them was cut.

"You can't take her," Cass cried, but like Sadie, her hands were tied behind her back. Both of them seated in kitchen chairs, trussed up like turkeys. Sadie had never felt so helpless. When Grant had come in waving a gun, there was nothing they could do. Thank goodness Alice was in town and wasn't due back for several hours, and Keira and Dalton were off rounding up cattle with Lena. She, Cass and Jo had been the only ones in the house when Grant burst through the back door.

"I can do whatever I want. When I'm gone, you two had better rustle up some cash. Two hundred and fifty grand. Got it?"

"Don't you hurt her," Sadie said. "If you do, I'll kill you."

"Yeah, yeah." When he turned, Jo flopped against his back, and Grant craned his neck to try to get a better look at her. He nearly rammed Jo into the kitchen counter and Sadie flinched. "What the hell did you do to your sister?" he demanded of them.

She must be out cold, Sadie thought. "She was upset. She needed to sleep. I gave her a—" Sadie shrieked when Jo reared up suddenly, grabbed a knife from the carving block on the counter and stabbed it into Grant's back with all her strength.

Grant roared, dropped Jo to the ground and turned a circle, clutching at his back. Jo scrambled to her feet, grabbed another knife from the butcher's block and ran to her sisters. First she cut Cass free, then Sadie, sawing through the plastic ties on their hands with a strength Sadie hadn't known she possessed. Once free, Jo shoved both of them toward the living room.

"Get outside! Now!"

"Dammit!" Grant grappled with the knife in his back and finally pulled it free with another roar of pain. He charged after them, and Sadie increased her speed, tugging Jo after her.

They nearly made it to the front door before he rounded the corner and took a shot. The bullet whizzed by Sadie's head and buried itself in the thick, wooden front door. She grabbed a vase from the delicate table that stood in the entryway and chucked it at him.

He twisted sharply to dodge it, exposing the still-growing blossom of blood across the back of his white shirt. "Fuck!" he yelled. "You fucking whore—I'll—"

Cass yanked open the front door. Sadie pushed Jo out of it. "Go!"

"—kill you!" Grant pulled the trigger on the pistol again, as Cass dashed after Jo.

Sadie didn't wait to see where the bullet hit. She leaped out the door, yanked it closed behind her and ran like her life depended on it.

It did.

There was no cover on this side of the house. They had to get around back—get her car—no, she realized as she skidded around the corner. She didn't have her keys. Hide in the carriage house maybe, or keep running—

"Sadie!"

Cass and Jo had made it to the carriage house. Sadie raced their way.

"Run!" Jo cried, as awake as if she'd never been dosed. Sadie realized belatedly she probably never was.

How many times had Jo spit out one of her mixtures the moment she turned her back? Thank goodness she'd done it again.

Sadie reached the carriage house and Cass pulled her inside. Jo slammed shut the door and locked it.

"Phone—phone!" Cass cried.

Sadie patted her pocket, but Grant had taken hers.

"He's got mine," Jo said.

"Mine, too." Cass scanned the room. "We need weapons."

"Connor and Brian know what happened. They must be on their way," Sadie reminded her.

"From Silver Falls," Cass retorted. "We don't have that kind of time."

She was right. Grant might be injured, but he had a pistol and they didn't. "Let's get upstairs."

Alice's workshop was full of costumes, and Sadie realized it could buy them time. "We can hide," she said, keeping her voice low as they darted up the old wooden stairs. She wondered where Grant was now. Back at the house? Or right outside?

"That's not good enough," Cass hissed.

"He's got to get up the stairs before he can get us."

As if he'd heard their words, Grant called out from the front of the carriage house, "I know you're in there. You can't get away from me!"

"How is he still moving?" Jo said. "I got him good!"

"Not good enough," Cass said. "Look at him!"

Alice's second-story workshop was lined with large arched windows, and Cass had crossed to stand beside one, her back pressed to the wall to stay out of sight.

Windows, Sadie thought, a memory coming back to her. "Window seats."

"What?" Cass asked.

"Check the window seats. Alice saves everything!"

Jo understood first. She fell to her knees, scrambled across the wooden floor to the closest window and propped open the seat cushion. Beneath it was a capacious storage space. Jo began to rustle through it. Sadie did the same with another one. "Hurry," she hissed at Cass. "He'll find a way in."

Her window seat was filled with toys from their childhoods, back when they'd shared the space as more of a playroom than anything else. During rainy days, and in the winter, they'd turn on the radiators, heat it up until it was cozy and romp around in the large open space when their mother had had enough of them inside.

A chess set, decks of cards, board games, pads of drawing paper, scribbled over with their childish drawings—Sadie chucked them over her shoulder to see what was underneath.

"There's nothing in here." Jo scrambled to the next window.

"Nothing here, either," Cass said. "Nothing good. Why does she keep this stuff?"

Sadie ignored her. The storage space in front of her was nearly empty, but she ran her hand around the base of it one last time—

—and pulled out a slingshot.

"What's that?" Cass called.

Sadie held it up.

"Fat lot of good that'll do against a pistol."

She was right. And still—

"So far it's the best we've got." She jammed it in her back pocket and moved to another window, stopping on the way to scoop up a hard rubber ball. She jammed that in her pocket, too.

Cass pulled held up a bottle. "Jesus—she's got lamp oil in here. That's dangerous."

Lamp oil? Sadie rushed to her side. "Find cloth—tear it into strips. Lots of them. Find small heavy things to wrap them around." She held up the hard rubber ball as an example, and grabbed a swath of fabric from where it lay on Alice's worktable. With shaking hands, she tore off strips, wrapped them around the ball and tied them in place until she'd mummified it—leaving a tail of cloth dangling from it. She doused the tail with lamp oil. "That's one."

"Sadie—"

"Got a better idea?" she said as a thump downstairs announced Grant had stopped circling the building and was getting serious about getting in. "We set them on fire and nail him with them when he tries to come in."

"And set the carriage house on fire around us!"

"There's a fire extinguisher." Sadie pointed to it. "Another one downstairs. Besides, the bottom floor is concrete and so is the pony wall." She spotted a bottle of water, tore another long strip of fabric and wet it thoroughly. She wrapped that around the rubber tubing, hope it would help prevent it from burning. She tested the rubber and breathed a sigh of relief when it stretched but didn't snap. Age hadn't hurt it.

"That's crazy," Cass said.

"I don't know what else to do," Sadie told her. The pony wall extended four feet up from the cement floor downstairs. All she could do was hope the missiles wouldn't find anything to burn when they landed. And that they kept Grant at bay until the men reached them.

All three of them spread out to find cores for their fabric-covered missiles. Sadie found some batteries, a small glass votive candlestick and a paperweight. She wrapped them up as fast as she could and doused them, too. Cass and Jo handed her more missiles, but they'd only constructed seven of them when another crash downstairs told them Grant had made it inside.

"The stairs. Now!" Sadie scooped up one of the missiles. Her sisters grabbed the other ones. Cass snatched a pack of matches off Alice's worktable.

At the top of the stairs, Sadie got in position, fetched the slingshot from her pocket and positioned the first of the missiles against the rubber strap. Cass held out the missile's tail. Jo readied a match.

They all held their breath.

"Fucking whores," Grant bellowed.

Suddenly, he was on the stairs. Jo lit a match, nearly dropped it, caught it and held it to the missile's tail. It caught more quickly than Sadie expected, and when the flame whooshed up to engulf the ball, she dropped it with a shriek and watched it roll down the steps harmlessly and land at Grant's feet. Grant kicked it out of the stairwell down to the first floor.

"Going to take a lot more than that!"

Thank God for that concrete floor, Sadie thought wildly as he stormed up the stairs two at a time. Cass handed Sadie the next missile and she held it firm. Jo lit a match. The cloth lit, but this time Sadie was ready for it. She let go the rubber and it snapped forward, propelling the fiery missile straight at Grant. It hit him square in the chest and he batted at it, dropping his pistol and slapping out the flames that caught fire to his shirt. He stumbled down several steps, caught himself with a hand on the railing and kicked the flaming missile down the stairs.

Cass handed her a third missile, Sadie positioned it and Jo lit the tail. As Grant turned around, Sadie nailed him in the face and he bellowed, flailed his arms, and slid and tripped most of the way down the stairs before he caught himself. With a roar of rage, he scooped up the fallen pistol on his way back up and fired off two shots. They buried themselves in the walls before Sadie took another shot and hit him again.

"Fuck!"

This time he charged them. Sadie couldn't get off another shot. Jo lit the tail of the fourth missile, and it roared to life between Sadie and Grant as he flung himself at her and knocked her down at the top of the stairs.

The slingshot went flying. The burning ball of cloth singed them both and they scrambled apart, kicking and yelling on the small landing, while Cass and Jo jumped out of the way back into the workshop. The missile, still burning, fell down several steps and stopped. Sadie slapped the flames from her shirt, singeing her hands, but hardly feeling it.

Cass lunged between them for the pistol Grant had dropped again. So did Grant, his shirt still on fire. He knocked her off her feet and got there first, but Sadie scrambled to grab the pistol, too, just as Jo chucked one of the remaining missiles—unlit—at Grant and struck him on the cheek. He huffed out a breath as Sadie tried to twist the pistol out of his hand. Cass reached to help. Sadie dug her fingernails into Grant's hand, drawing blood.

"Fuck… you." His grip on the gun was loosening, but before she cold yank it away, he backhanded Sadie with his free hand, wrapped his fingers in her hair and lifted the pistol to her head.

"Sadie!"

It was Connor at the base of the stairs, a gun in his hand.

Too late, Sadie thought. Too late to save her. Too late for her to tell him she'd been wrong.

"Say goodbye," Grant snarled, pressing the gun's barrel against her cheek. "Fuck!"

Sadie fell back when he suddenly let go. Caught a glimpse of the gun inexplicably in Jo's hand. Heard the deafening double crack of two shots exploding in the close quarters. Struck her head against the wall so hard she saw stars.

Grant staggered against her. Sadie drew back. Missed a step—

And tumbled down the flight of stairs.

"I HEAR GUNSHOTS," Brian yelled, leaping from the truck the moment Connor hit the brakes.

Connor followed seconds later, not bothering to turn off the vehicle. Both of them raced into the carriage house, Sean at their heels, and Brian swore when he saw the flames licking up the walls that encompassed the stairwell to Alice's loft. The shrill barks and yips of the puppies followed them, along with Ron's muted shouts, but the dogs were leashed and couldn't get out of the truck bed, and, bound hand and foot, Ron couldn't get away, either.

Connor leaped for the opening to the stairs in time to see Grant grab Sadie and put a gun to her head. He cried her name, aimed and fired—just as another shot rang out. When Sadie pitched down the stairs, he thought he'd hit her. He raced to catch her, pulled her into his arms. Felt her all over, looking for blood.

There was none. Connor knelt on the stairs, cradling Sadie. The woman he loved.

"Cass? You okay?" Brian shouted, passing him on the stairs.

"We're—we're okay." Cass's voice came from the upper landing.

"Connor?"

He bent over Sadie, kissing her forehead in relief. She was alive. She was okay. So were Cass and Jo. But who had shot Grant at the same time he had? Two bullets had buckled him. His prone form still lay at the top of the stairs.

"You're okay," he told Sadie. "Everyone's okay."

Sadie sat up slowly, a hand pressed to her forehead. Connor followed her gaze to where Cass cradled Jo on the upper landing. Brian was bent over Grant's still form beside them.

"He's dead," Brian called down.

Sadie let out a breath as if she'd been holding it. "You got him."

"I got him," Connor agreed. "But I wasn't the only one."

At the top of the stairs, Jo sobbed in Cass's arms as Cass stroked her hair.

Connor met Sadie's wide-eyed gaze. Nodded. "Jo got him, too, I think."

When Sadie buried her head against his chest, he held her as if he'd never let go.

IT WAS EVENING by the time Cab and his deputies left Two Willows. Grant's body had been removed, the scene of his death blocked off with police tape. Jo and Sadie had been treated and released at the hospital, both of them bruised but otherwise unhurt, although Jo had already agreed to see a counselor the following day.

Connor knew their real wounds were inside. Sadie was tearful. Jo withdrawn so deep inside herself it worried him. He'd always considered her the gentlest of the Reed sisters. She'd been afraid for her life—her sisters' lives—when she'd helped kill Grant. It was impossible to know whose bullet had ended his life, of course. Probably either shot would have done him in.

Still, he'd served in the military for years. This wasn't the first time he'd ended a life.

It would be a lot harder for Jo to get past what had happened today.

Lena had been furious to find out what had happened while she'd been out on the range with Keira and Dalton. "I can't believe I didn't hear anything. How could I have not known?" she kept saying. Connor worried about her, too. Grant must have pulled down the fence to distract as many of them as possible; he'd only needed to grab one sister to be able to negotiate for what he wanted.

Lena blamed herself for not guessing it was all a ruse—and of course Dalton felt he was to blame—but neither of them could have known. Lena had positioned herself on the back porch again, and Brian knew she was keeping watch because there wasn't anything else she could do to make things better.

When Cass, Alice and Jo went to curl up on the couch in the living room, the television on for company, Sadie hung back with Connor. His family had already left the ranch, to give the rest of them space and time to recover. There were sheriff's deputies positioned in the driveway again. Nothing more would happen tonight.

"Cab locked Ron Cooper up? For what—puppy theft? Or did he have enough proof he and Grant were working together?" Sadie asked.

"Ron had outstanding warrants back in Tennessee. He's being extradited. He'll be escorted back where he came from, and according to Cab, he'll definitely see some jail time." Connor was more grateful than he could say Ron's past had caught up to him. He wouldn't have been able to stand it if the man had gone free.

"And Grant's dead, so that's that. Cab said the case is obviously self-defense. Jo won't be prosecuted. Neither will you."

Connor tried to hide his reaction. Must have failed.

"What?" Sadie asked.

"I hope that's that."

"But you don't believe it?"

"We won't be prosecuted, but I think we need to be careful. I think you all started a fight and it's not over yet."

Sadie's shoulders sagged. "At least Jo's dogs are back. She would have been devastated if they'd been killed." He knew Sadie was worried about her sister, too. Jo hadn't been in love with Grant—not yet—but she'd been well on her way toward falling for him.

And she'd shot him.

She'd need looking after. She'd need peace and quiet. Connor wondered if that was possible here at Two Willows.

Hadn't they had enough trouble?

"Will you step outside with me?" Connor snagged two beers out of the refrigerator and led the way. They passed Lena on the porch and walked into the garden. He popped the top off one and handed it to Sadie, taking heart from the fact she still wore her engagement ring. "How about us?" he asked quietly. "Are we going to survive this?"

SADIE SIGHED AND took a long drag on her bottle, then wished she had something warm to drink instead. Despite the heat of the day, she felt cold. "I want to. I love you," she said simply. It was true, and there wasn't anything more to add to that statement.

"You sound hesitant."

She thought that over. "I'm... afraid. When I love people—they don't always stick around."

Connor nodded. "I know what you mean."

She knew he did, but... "Your parents seemed pretty cozy earlier."

"I'm afraid to hope that's true," he admitted. "I want it to be."

"I think it is. I think they're going to try for a second chance."

"I'd like a second chance," Connor said. "Sadie, I never want to hurt you."

"I know that. I really do." She met his gaze. "But if I let myself love you—really love you—things can happen outside our control. What if Grant had killed you?"

"What if he'd killed you?" Connor countered. "I couldn't stand it, lass. I couldn't. But I wouldn't give up loving you all the same, just to keep my heart safe. Life is... hard. Love is risky. It means taking a chance. But the rewards—" He took her beer, set it down. "The rewards make up for everything."

"Do you believe that?" she asked as he pulled her into an embrace. In answer, he kissed her, and the world switched back on with a blare of a radio turned up loud. This time the feeling was almost too much. Her nerves had been stretched past their limits these past twenty-four hours. Still, she couldn't turn her back on the connection she had to this ranch.

And she couldn't turn her back on Connor, either. For better or for worse, she loved him. Truly loved him. And he loved her, too. When she'd needed him most, he'd come for her.

There was no going back now.

"I believe in us," Connor said, and kissed her again. "I believe in our future together."

Sadie leaned against him. Felt his strength. His love.

"I believe in that, too."

Chapter Fourteen

"SO HERE WE are again," Cab said, sitting across the battered kitchen table from Connor and Brian the following morning.

"Here we are again," Brian agreed.

"I've talked to the women. I've talked to your family, Connor. Now I want to hear what you two have to say. Two Willows draws its fair share of trouble, doesn't it? You beginning to rethink your methods for getting rid of those drug dealers?" the sheriff asked Brian.

Connor was glad he'd commissioned Dalton to take his parents away again for the day. He'd loaned them his truck, given them a list and sent them to Billings to pick up the things for the wedding that were difficult to find in town. Max was patrolling the kitchen, sniffing in every corner. He didn't seem to want to let Connor out of his sight. Connor was okay with that.

Brian shrugged. "Seems to me our only other choice was to roll over."

"That may be, but what I want to know is how come I never get called until it's too late to do anything about the trouble?"

"Honestly?" Brian said.

"No, keep lying to me." Cab shook his head in disgust.

"We didn't think you'd take puppy theft all that seriously," Brian went on. "It didn't seem like a number one priority for the County Sheriff's office. But it's the kind of thing that could rip this family apart."

Cab considered this. "Yeah, I can see that," he said. "But here's what I want you to see. This is bigger than you think. So far you've dealt with a few two-bit local boys, and a couple more two-bit out-of-town boys. That doesn't mean they won't send in the big guns sooner or later."

"I think we've made our position clear. We're not going to back down if they do," Brian said.

"Maybe so," Cab said. "That doesn't mean they'll quit coming."

Connor leaned in closer. "We've got more men on the way."

"I'm glad to hear that," Cab said. "You might need them."

EVERY TIME SADIE moved, she ached. If there was a part of her body that had been left unscathed by her tumble down the carriage house stairs, she hadn't found it. Even her fingers hurt, which made cleaning the upstairs bathroom difficult.

But for some reason she needed to clean the upstairs bathroom. Needed to clean every room in the house. Only motion could stop the delayed reaction of fear and shock that brought her screaming out of a nightmare before the sun rose.

She had spent the evening close to Connor, touching him often to remind herself he was really there. They'd agreed to go forward with the wedding as planned, even though they were all thoroughly shaken by Grant's attack.

Sadie had thought she was all right, but when she'd woken this morning, shaken and terrified, she'd known she needed to do something tangible to clear Grant's influence out of the house.

Cass had found her scrubbing the kitchen floor at 5:00 a.m., opened her mouth to ask why, then shook her head, grabbed the broom and began to sweep the rest of the rooms on the first floor.

Alice joined them soon after, and had taken on the job of dusting all the knickknacks in the house, picking them up, wiping down the shelves and mantelpiece and everywhere else they sat, before cleaning them and replacing them.

When they had finished their morning chores down in the barns, Jo and Lena came back and pitched in. Lena was still pale, her lips set in a tight line. Sadie knew she was furious with herself for not being there when Grant had struck. Nothing any of them said could calm her down. She had grabbed rags and a bottle of cleaner, and was currently cleaning every window in the house.

Jo was...a shadow of herself. So insubstantial Sadie was afraid if she didn't keep watch on her, she'd disappear for good. Already she ached to dose Jo with tinctures and healing teas, but she knew what her sister needed most was time. In theory, her sister was cleaning, too, but for Jo that consisted of spending the whole morning in front of the linen closet, taking out the sheets and blankets and towels, unfolding them, refolding them and putting them back again, until Cass finally drove her to town to the meet the counselor, and brought her back to rest on the couch for the remainder of the afternoon.

When Connor and Brian finished with the sheriff, they came to seek the women, but when they took in the industry with which the sisters were cleaning, Connor grabbed Max's collar, held up a hand to stop Brian, and both men and dog backed out the room, out of the house, and disappeared.

By dinnertime, Sadie was as sore as she'd ever been in her life. Her back, which had already ached from her fall, now ached from bending over and scrubbing just about every floor in the house. Her knees could barely straighten when she stood up. Her wrists hurt from the pressure she'd exerted on the scrub brush.

When she went out to the greenhouse, fetched a thick bunch of dried white sage and lit it in the kitchen, her sisters appeared as if she'd summoned them—even Jo—and together they started in the basement and wound through the house, making sure the cleansing smoke blew into every corner, cupboard and closet.

When it was done they returned to the kitchen, where Sadie blew out the sage and tapped it against the damp sink to put out the flames. She felt lighter. More hopeful.

Grant was gone, and he'd never bother them again.

"I don't want to cook," Cass said in a brisk voice, as if to bring them back to normal life. "Because if we messed up the kitchen again now, I think I'd cry."

"We have to feed Connor's family," Alice said as Connor's truck pulled in to park near the carriage house, and the O'Rileys began to get out. Dalton had kept his parents away from the ranch the whole day. Sadie figured they'd be hungry and tired by now, too.

"At least the house is clean for your wedding, Sadie," Jo said quietly.

"You know what?" Alice asked. "Maybe it's time for another movie night."

No one answered her for a moment. Then Cass said, a little uncertainly, "Popcorn and margaritas?"

"Don't forget the pizza first," Lena said as her stomach growled.

Sadie's shoulders relaxed a fraction of an inch. If her sisters were well enough to want a movie night, maybe everything would be okay after all.

"I'd better check on the animals first, though," Lena said. She paused, and Sadie knew why: it was Jo's cue to say she'd come, too.

But Jo didn't say anything.

Sadie's heart sank.

Cass pulled her phone out of her pocket when it buzzed. "Brian and Connor already took care of the evening chores. They're on their way back to the house. Brian and I will take care of everything for our movie night," she said, texting him back.

Jo trailed after Cass, Alice and Lena when they went outside to greet the O'Rileys and wait for Brian and Connor. Sadie followed, eager to see Connor again.

Cass intercepted Brian when he came, while Alice explained to the O'Rileys their plans for the evening.

"Why don't you go inside and relax?" Sadie told them. "Jo, would you get them some lemonade? Lena, can you come with me a second?" She'd had an idea. When Jo disappeared with Connor's family inside, Max following the crowd, his tail wagging, she whispered it into Lena's ear.

"It's worth trying," Lena said and headed for the carriage house.

CONNOR WAITED FOR the back door to close before he reached for Sadie's hand. He'd worried about her all day. He knew the violence that had happened at Two Willows affected the women deeply. Last night she'd assured him she was ready to go through with the wedding, but when he'd come across her scrubbing the floor this morning, he'd been afraid she'd changed her mind. Women cleaned like that when their hearts were in turmoil.

It had been a struggle to back off and give her space, but he thought now he'd done the right thing. When he looked at Sadie he could see her turmoil was gone.

"Are we still good?" he asked, just to be sure.

"We're still good."

"Walk with me?" He led her toward the maze, not knowing why but feeling like he should. This was a time for clarity. When they reached the center, he led her to the stone.

"After everything that's happened, I want you to know you can be one hundred percent sure of me," he told her. "I love you. I don't want any other woman. I don't want any other home. I want to be here with you—forever."

"I know—"

He put one hand on the flank of the stone. Kept hold of Sadie's hand with the other. "I want the stone to tell you."

Connor bent down and kissed her.

THE FLASH OF intuition, the brightening she always felt when they touched, flared up stronger than she'd ever felt it, immediately wrapping her in a Technicolor swoop of sound.

Her heart felt so ragged—so tender—she wasn't sure she could stand the love in Connor's eyes when he pulled back again.

"You're all I want, lass. Forever."

"Connor, I know—"

After all, hadn't he proven what he'd do to be with her? He'd followed her all around her garden, held her while she brewed tonics, made love to her in the maze, went off to save Jo's puppies without hesitation—

And then charged back here to save her the moment he knew she was in danger.

He loved her.

Connor loved her.

It was love, Sadie knew, that turned on her abilities. Love that connected her to Two Willows.

And for better or for worse, Connor defined love for her. Had since the day she first saw him and fell for him before he even opened his mouth to speak.

"Where's my answer?" Connor asked the sky.

"Right here." She wrapped her arms around Connor's neck, and gave into the beauty and mystery of pledging her heart to another human being. No one could know the future. No one could ever be perfectly sure of another human being—or of themselves. All they could do was take the leap and trust that love wouldn't let them down. She wanted to make that leap with Connor.

"I want to make love to you," he whispered against her neck. "But you've been through too much and they're waiting for us."

"Let them wait," she whispered, twining her arms around his neck even more tightly.

When Connor began to undress her, she sighed in contentment, knowing she was exactly where she was supposed to be.

This time, instead of pressing her up against the stone, he laid her down on the grass and made love to her sweetly and slowly, teasing, tormenting her and coaxing her until her pleasure was complete. It was nearly an hour before they pulled apart, and drew their clothes back on. Sadie, fastening her bra, stopped and pointed. "What's that?"

Connor turned to see something glinting among the branches of the hedge. He reached for it just as Sadie did, and together they lifted a locket free from where it was caught.

Sadie's eyes filled with tears when she recognized it. "It was my mother's," she explained to Connor. "She lost it just a week before died. She was so sad—she wore it all the time. The General gave it to her when they were married."

"Like the one he gave to Cass."

"That's right." Sadie could barely keep her voice even. She opened the clasp and showed Connor the photo inside. "That's my father."

Connor glanced at her sharply and Sadie realized why. "The General," she corrected herself. He was still the General. Still the man who wouldn't come home—no matter how much she needed him.

"What does it mean, lass? Is it an answer?"

Sadie nodded, her heart full. No matter how angry she was with the General, her mother had loved him—deeply and always, until she drew her last breath.

"She's telling us—she's saying she's happy," Sadie managed to say. "She's saying love can last."

"Aye, lass. I believe that."

Sadie believed it, too. She allowed Connor to fasten the locket around her neck, and touched it reverently. She could almost feel her mother's presence nearby—

Suddenly she was in a hurry to finish dressing.

Connor followed her example and soon they were

heading back through the maze.

"Do you think they're halfway through the movie?" he asked.

"Probably halfway through the pizza at least." It was strange to talk of such normal things after what had just happened, but by the time they'd reached the house, slipped upstairs to clean up, and come back down again, she'd regained her composure. She'd tucked the locket under her shirt to show her sisters later.

They found everyone in the front room, sitting on the floor, with Jo in the center, the puppies frisking and playing among them. Jo was petting Max, still wan and pale, but not as lost as she had been earlier. When Max reached up to lick her chin, she even smiled.

"Puppies. That your idea?" Connor asked in an undertone.

Sadie nodded. "I figured they'd help."

"YOU'RE MAKING A big mistake," Connor told the General that evening. "Sadie's only going to get married once. You should be here." He pet Max, who'd followed him into his room. He was beginning to think he'd have a constant companion from now on.

"Don't tell me what I should or shouldn't do." The General bent close to the screen, until his face filled it. "If I came home now, Two Willows would be in an uproar. Lena would haul out the cannons. The others would take to the hills. It'll be Sadie's day; keep it about her."

"You're going to have to repair your relationship

with your daughters someday." His conversation with Sadie earlier made that clear. She loved her father. Missed him desperately, despite her anger. He had to try to get the General to the wedding.

"I know what I have to do, and you know what your orders are. Focus on that."

"My orders are to marry your daughter, which I'm doing, and which means I have to keep her happy. It would make her happy to have her father walk her down the aisle."

The General glanced away from the screen, and for a moment Connor saw vulnerability in the set of his jaw, but when he turned back, it was gone. "I'm coordinating missions all over the world; yours is just a side note. A way to get rid of a handful of troublesome men who overstepped their orders. End of story."

Connor leaned forward, gripping the edge of the table. "I'm not the one who chose this mission, and I didn't leave the Air Force voluntarily. You want to pull me back in, say the word. I'll be there, ready to fight."

"Like hell you will." The General's voice rose. "My daughters' husbands are going to stay right there at Two Willows in Montana. They are not going to serve in Florida, they are not going to serve overseas. That's not the life my daughters deserve!"

So the General understood what he'd done when he'd left his wife alone for so many years, Connor thought. And maybe—just maybe—he understood what he'd done to his daughters.

"Point taken, sir. But with all due respect, there's

still time for you to—"

"You take care of Sadie. Don't let her down."

The General signed off and the screen went blank.

"IT's BEAUTIFUL," KEIRA said as she walked through the finished walled garden with Sadie ten days later. They'd first checked Sadie's market stand to make sure all was well, and collected the honor system cash that had been left by purchasers. On their way to the garden, they'd passed Jo, who was handing over the last of the puppies to their delighted new owners. Sadie was glad to see that Jo already seemed more like herself. Her voice was confident when she spoke to her customers, and she wasn't overly sad at letting the puppies go. But then her sister always felt it was her duty to spread the joy of animals in the world. "People are better when they go through life with animals," she always said.

"It is beautiful," Sadie told Keira. Connor, Sean, Brian and Dalton had worked together every day to get it done before the wedding. Their work was impeccable, the capstones giving the rough walls an orderly appearance. She could imagine the enclosed space filled with pathways, flowerbeds, fruit trees and climbing vines. One day her children would play in here, and feel as if they'd stepped into a fairy tale. All that was missing were the gates.

"Do you know what you'll plant here?"

"I have some ideas." She'd begun to sketch out plans for the garden, realizing how much she loved to design the shape of the paths and the beds, and what plant should go where.

"Everything seems ready for the wedding."

Sadie read the unasked question in her voice. "I'm ready, too." She was. She would step into her marriage with more assurance than most women, she thought. She and Connor had already been through the wringer. They'd seen what the worst could bring out in each other, and they'd come back together again, stronger and wiser. She wore her mother's locket every day as a talisman. She'd shown it to her sisters who'd all been touched to see it, and they'd agreed that after the wedding they'd take turns keeping possession of it. None of them mentioned that the General was the enemy. It was their mother's locket—which made it beyond reproach.

"What about you? You'll be going home soon." She wondered what would happen then. Connor's parents had gotten very chummy these past few weeks.

"Yes, I'll be going home soon." Keira smiled. "Sean will join me in about a month." She held up her hand, where a beautiful ring sparkled on her fourth finger.

Sadie gasped. "You're getting remarried?"

Keira nodded. "We'll set the ceremony far enough in the future when you two can come and join us. I want my whole family there when I walk down the aisle to marry the man I love."

Sadie embraced her. "I'm so happy for you. I think Connor will be thrilled. But where are you going to live?"

"Half the year in Ireland, and half the year here. We

want to travel, too. After all, that's how we met in the first place. Sean plans to retire. Dalton will run my family's ranch, and I'll step back and give him the room he needs. I hope he finds a wife soon, too."

As they walked back to the house, Two Willows glowed in the strong summer sunshine, and Sadie's heart was full. "This is where I belong."

"This is where you belong," Keira agreed. "With my son." She smiled at something over Cass's shoulder. "Speaking of the devil…"

Sadie turned to see Connor striding toward them, Max at his heels like usual these days.

"I'll give you two lovebirds some privacy," Keira said. "See you back at the house." She gave Connor a peck on his cheek as she passed him. "I'm so happy for both of you," she told him.

"I'm happy, too," he said, taking Sadie's hand and kissing her. Max danced off to explore this new area. "So, is it everything you hoped for?" Connor asked, turning in a circle to indicate the garden. "We still need some plants in here, but otherwise—"

"Otherwise, it's perfect," she told him. "I can't wait to get some trees in the ground."

Connor smiled. "I'm glad to hear it. I was hanging out in your garden last night and your plants told me a secret."

"Oh, yeah? What did they say?"

"That a walled garden was useless without a garden gate to shut out the world."

"We'll have to get on that."

"Be right back."

Sadie looked forward to designing the perfect gate for the garden and wondered if Connor and the other men could build it, or if they'd need—

Sadie gasped as Connor and Brian lugged a heavy wooden door into view. Her eyes filled as she took in the beautiful craftsmanship. Unable to speak, she could only stand while the men maneuvered it into place. Made of solid vertical planks, it was arched, with a circular portal and a wrought-iron handle.

"This is what it'll look like when it's hung. What do you think?"

"I think it's going to make this look like a fairy garden. Connor, it's wonderful. Where did you find it?"

The smile that spread across her fiancé's face made Sadie's heart contract. "I had it custom made. I designed it the first night we talked, and found a local man who could do the work."

"The first night?" He'd known all along what would please her? He'd ordered the gate before they'd even begun the work? How had he seen the vision in her head?

If she'd had any remaining doubts about Connor, that would have put all of them to rest. But Sadie didn't have any remaining doubts. Not about him—

Not about her love for him.

Brian steadied the door while Connor came to join her. "It fits, doesn't it?"

"Absolutely. This garden will be everything I could have dreamed of. More, even."

"I've got one more gift for you, lass." Connor rejoined Brian and they lifted the gate to one side and leaned it against the wall. Connor disappeared around the wall and came back a moment later, struggling to carry something wrapped in burlap. When he set it down, Sadie realized what it was.

"A tree!"

"Two trees actually. Apple trees—a male and a female, so they'll pollinate and thrive. It seemed right, somehow."

Sadie listened to the garden for a moment and realized it was right; she didn't have any apple trees and the ranch needed some.

"Where do you want them?"

She listened again. Pointed. "One there. The other there."

Brian brought them a shovel. Connor dug the holes. When they'd managed to plant the small trees, Sadie couldn't stop smiling. Someday their children would play under them. Someday they'd all eat their fruit.

Connor took her hand and stood beside her. "I see our kids. Two boys and a girl," he said. When he bent to kiss her, she was already rising up on tiptoe to meet him.

"Two girls and a boy, you mean. I love you," she added.

"I love you, too."

Chapter Fifteen

W HEN THE MORNING of his wedding dawned cloudy, Connor wondered if it was a sign, and doubt momentarily pierced all his resolve. What if he couldn't be a good husband to Sadie? What if somebody else could have made her far happier? He was grateful when he went downstairs, Max at his heels, that Brian was the only one else awake so early.

"I already checked the weather report," Brian said without even looking up from his eggs. "The sun will come out at about ten, and by the time you're standing at the altar, you'll be sweating."

He shoved his phone across the table, and Connor picked it up, looked at the weather report as Max went to inspect his food dish, and his heart eased.

"Just want Sadie to be happy on her wedding day."

"Bullshit. You thought you were doomed."

Connor laughed heartily, and it was just what he needed to loosen up. The rest of the morning flew by, helping to set up for the wedding, playing with Max, getting gussied up for the ceremony and making sure he had the wedding bands he'd purchased at Thayer's.

Sooner than he thought possible, he was making his way to the temporary altar set up outside, where Reverend Halpern stood already.

"Fine day for a wedding," Halpern said.

"Fine day, indeed," Dalton said, coming to stand by Connor's side. "Hot, though."

Connor relished the heat. He relished the murmur of voices of their guests chattering in their folding seats placed out on the lawn. This was his wedding day, and he wasn't running away. He was taking his stand here at the altar, waiting for his bride.

He didn't know how many minutes passed until the music struck up, and Jo appeared in the doorway, wearing the same spring-green colored bridesmaid gown she'd worn for Cass's wedding. She looked far older than she had the day he'd first come to Two Willows, but Connor thought she was already on the mend. He saw something steely in her eyes these days. For the first time he thought she might be a match for Hunter, after all.

The assembled crowd sighed in pleasure as first Jo, then Lena, then Alice, then Cass began to walk up the aisle, but Connor had eyes only for Sadie, and when she stepped out of the house in her mother's wedding gown, his heart stopped for a beat before picking up again with a fast thump, thump, thump. The long aisle gave him plenty of time to gaze at the woman who'd stolen his heart as she walked toward him. In the front row of the audience, happy tears streaked down his mother's face, and she dabbed at them with a cloth handkerchief, his father holding her hand.

So much love filled this assembly, Connor could barely take it in. He hadn't felt this way since he was a child, back in the small house in Ireland where his family used to live. His heart swelled and broke through the hard shell he'd protected it with all these years. Feeling free for the first time since he set foot in this country with his father, Connor realized there was plenty of time left in his life to heal all the wounds that had come before. His wife would help him. So would his family. And he found himself thanking God the General had given him this mission. But it went back even earlier than that, didn't it? It was Halil and Fatima he really needed to thank, with their example of what true love could look like. He would always hold them up as a beacon in his marriage; something to strive for.

As Sadie joined him, and her sisters took their places, he realized he knew what true happiness was. He took Sadie's hand, only then noticing the faded ribbon she'd tied around her wrist. The red, white and blue stripes seemed like a promise to Connor—that fate was on their side. That they were meant to be together.

That his family would be whole again.

He turned to face the reverend, his heart full, ready for everything—ready for the rest of his life.

MANY HOURS LATER, hoarse from talking and laughing, her feet aching from dancing in her high-heeled shoes, face sore from smiling so much, Sadie entered the house to take a moment to herself. She was crossing the kitchen when Jean Finney came out of the hall, from the direction of the bathroom. She rushed forward to take Sadie's hand.

"Congratulations! I'm so happy for you, Sadie. I cried through the whole ceremony, it was so beautiful."

"How are you doing? Don't overdo it today, okay?" Sadie led her to the table and tugged her to sit down in a chair. She sat, too, in order to make sure Jean stayed there for a minute.

"I'm doing great," Jean said with a wide smile. "I went to the doctor yesterday. Had an ultrasound. The baby is doing fine. The heartbeat is strong. The doctor says I should be out of trouble, and I should carry the baby to term."

Sadie threw her arms around her friend, overjoyed. She would never take her gift for granted again. Jean was doing so well and she wasn't the only one. Ellie had come to see her the other day. Sadie had been thrilled to hand her the tonic she needed, but even more thrilled to hear Caitlyn had agreed to a fifty-fifty partnership.

"I feel as if a weight is off my shoulders," Ellie had confessed. "I didn't realize I needed a break until you told me to take one!"

Thank God Connor had come and restored her belief in love in time so that she could help Jean. Her healing legacy was restored. Sadie didn't know what she'd have done if the General hadn't sent him. The walled garden would be a legacy that lasted long after she was gone, but her healing was far more important to her.

Sadie asked Jean question after question, until Jean asked a question of her own.

"Where are you going for your honeymoon?"

"India," Sadie confessed. She hadn't even thought about a honeymoon until Connor had showed her the tickets last night. "Can you believe it? I've hardly ever been off the ranch!"

"You'll have a marvelous time. What will we do without you, though?"

Sadie understood her concern. "I've left plenty of tonics of all kinds in the greenhouse. Come find Alice whenever you need something. I've left her a million instructions. It's only for two weeks; I'll be back before you notice I'm gone."

"Good. I want you to have fun, but I need you, Sadie. We all do. Don't ever leave."

"I won't." She knew that in her heart. Two Willows was her home, for now and for always. Her family was here. Her connection to the land was back as strong as ever.

And she was happy.

Connor found them like that ten minutes later. "It's time to cut the cake," he told Sadie. "Is something wrong?"

Sadie realized her cheeks were damp. "No, everything's right." She shared Jean's news. "You have to take some of the credit; you helped me make the crucial batch of tonic."

Jean thanked both of them again, and left to rejoin the party. Connor kissed Sadie.

"Didn't you say we have to go cut the cake?" she asked.

"In a minute," he said. "I want to be alone with my wife."

"Your wife," she echoed. "That sounds so strange. But right, too, you know I mean?"

He tightened his arms around her. "I know exactly what you mean. Sadie O'Riley, I've spent a lifetime looking for you, and never even realized it. Now you're mine."

"Now I'm yours," she agreed and stood on tiptoe to meet his kiss. "Forever."

JO WAS STACKING dirty dishes near the sink in the kitchen when she heard a knock on the front door. She should have been out mingling with the guests, but while she was thrilled for the happiness Sadie had found with Connor, she found it hard to feel much enthusiasm about anything these days. The counselor she was seeing twice a week said that was to be expected, and that it would pass. She recommended lots of time being active. "Get out in the sun, work with your animals. The heart has a tremendous capacity to heal."

Jo rinsed her hands, dried them on a tea towel and headed toward the door. People needed to go home, not keep arriving, she thought dispiritedly. No matter what the counselor said, she wasn't ready to be among company.

Twice she'd ignored her instincts. Twice she'd been burned. First by Sean Pittson, who'd twisted her around his little finger and nearly helped to yank her ranch right out from under her feet, and then by Grant, who'd held her puppies ransom, then tried to kidnap her at gunpoint.

She still couldn't believe she'd stabbed him.

And shot him.

Helped kill him.

After spending her life dedicated to helping living things.

Never again, she promised herself for the hundredth time that day. She'd learned her lesson: animals were to be trusted. People weren't—especially men. She was done with them.

Forever.

So when she pulled the door open and took in the stranger on the other side, she stopped in her tracks. He was tall, muscular, with a sharp gaze that seemed to take in everything about her at once. Older than her by at least a decade, he was dressed for the wedding in clean dark jeans, a crisp white shirt, a dark blazer and a black cowboy hat. He was handsome—oh, so handsome—but there was something haunted about him.

This was a man who'd seen war, Jo realized.

A man who'd seen death.

Which meant the General had sent him.

"Howdy." His Southern drawl was thick as molasses, and his voice threaded through her, waking places she'd sworn to herself were asleep for good. "Name's Hunter. Hunter Powell. You must be Jo."

"I'm not marrying you," she blurted. Best to get it

out there right now. His gaze had fixed on hers like an eagle spotting its prey. The General had sent Brian, and Cass had married him. He'd sent Connor, and Sadie stood out back in her wedding dress right now, cutting her cake. There was no way—no way—she'd fall for this trap.

A slow grin spread over Hunter's face, tangling Jo's emotions into a breathless knot.

"We'll see about that."

Other books in the Brides of Chance Creek Series:

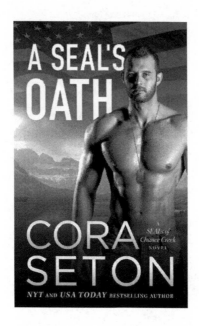

Read on for an excerpt of Volume 1 of **The SEALs of Chance Creek** series – *A SEAL's Oath*.

NAVY SEAL BOONE Rudman should have been concentrating on the pile of paperwork in front of him. Instead he was brooding over a woman he hadn't seen in thirteen years. If he'd been alone, he would have pulled up Riley Eaton's photograph on his laptop, but three other men ringed the table in the small office he occupied at the Naval Amphibious Base at Little Creek, Virginia, so instead he mentally ran over the information he'd found out about her on the Internet. Riley lived in Boston, where she'd gone to school. She'd graduated with a fine arts degree, something which confused

Boone; she'd never talked about wanting to study art when they were young. She worked at a vitamin manufacturer, which made no sense at all. And why was she living in a city, when Riley had only ever come alive when she'd visited Chance Creek, Montana, every summer as a child?

Too many questions. Questions he should know the answer to, since Riley had once been such an integral part of his life. If only he hadn't been such a fool, Boone knew she still would be. Still a friend at least, or maybe much, much more. Pride had kept him from finding out.

He was done with pride.

He reached for his laptop, ready to pull up her photograph, whether he was alone or not, but stopped when it chimed to announce a video call. For one crazy second, Boone wondered if his thoughts had conjured Riley up, but he quickly shook away that ridiculous notion.

Probably his parents wondering once again why he wasn't coming home when he left the Navy. He'd explained time and again the plans he'd made, but they couldn't comprehend why he wouldn't take the job his father had found him at a local ranch.

"Working with horses," his dad had said the last time they talked. "What more do you want?"

It was tempting. Boone had always loved horses. But he had something else in mind. Something his parents found difficult to comprehend. The laptop chimed again.

"You going to get that?" Jericho Cook said, looking up from his work. Blond, blue-eyed, and six-foot-one inches of muscle, he looked out of place hunched over his paperwork. He and the other two men sitting at the table were three of Boone's most trusted buddies and members of his strike team. Like him, they were far more at home jumping out of airplanes, infiltrating terrorist organizations and negotiating their way through disaster areas than sitting on their asses filling out forms. But paperwork caught up to everyone at some point.

He wouldn't have to do it much longer, though. Boone was due to separate from the Navy in less than a month. The others were due to leave soon after. They'd joined up together—egging each other on when they turned eighteen over their parents' objections. They'd survived the brutal process of becoming Navy SEALs together, too, adamant that they'd never leave each other behind. They'd served together whenever they could. Now, thirteen years later, they'd transition back to civilian life together as well.

The computer chimed a third time and his mind finally registered the name on the screen. Boone slapped a hand on the table to get the others' attention.

"It's him!"

"Him, who?" Jericho asked.

"Martin Fulsom, from the Fulsom Foundation. He's calling me!"

"Are you sure?" Clay Pickett shifted his chair over to where he could see. He was an inch or two shorter than Jericho, with dark hair and a wiry build that concealed a perpetual source of energy. Even now Clay's foot was tapping as he worked.

Boone understood his confusion. Why would Martin Fulsom, who must have a legion of secretaries and assistants at his command, call him personally?

"It says Martin Fulsom."

"Holy shit. Answer it," Jericho said. He shifted his chair over, too. Walker Norton, the final member of their little group, stood up silently and moved behind the others. Walker had dark hair and dark eyes that hinted at his Native American ancestry. Unlike the others, he'd taken the time to get his schooling and become an officer. As Lieutenant, he was the highest ranked. He was also the tallest of the group, with a heavy muscular frame that could move faster than most gave him credit for. He was quiet, though. So quiet that those who didn't know him tended to write him off. They did so at their own peril.

Boone stifled an oath at the tremor that ran through him as he reached out to accept the call, but it wasn't every day you got to meet your hero face to face. Martin Fulsom wasn't a Navy SEAL. He wasn't in the military at all. He'd once been an oil man, and had amassed a fortune in the industry before he'd learned about global warming and had a change of heart. For the last decade he'd spearheaded a movement to prevent carbon dioxide particulates from exceeding the disastrous level of 450 ppm. He'd backed his foundation with his entire fortune, invested it in green technology and used his earnings to fund projects around the world aimed at helping him reach his goal. Fulsom was a force of nature, with an oversized personality to match his incredible wealth. Boone liked his can-do attitude and his refusal to mince words when the situation called for plain speaking.

Boone clicked *Accept* and his screen resolved into an image of a man seated at a large wooden desk. He was gray-haired but virile, with large hands and an impressively large watch. Beside him stood a middle aged woman in a severely tailored black suit, who handed him pieces of paper one at a time, waited for him to sign them and took them back, placing them in various folders she cradled in her arm.

"Boone!" The man's hearty voice was almost too much for the laptop's speakers. "Good to finally meet you. This is an impressive proposal you have here."

Boone swallowed. It was true. Martin Fulsom—one of the greatest innovators of their time—had actually called *him*. "It's good to meet you, too, Mr. Fulsom," he managed to say.

"Call me Martin," Fulsom boomed. "Everybody does. Like I said, it's a hell of a proposal. To build a fully operational sustainable community in less than six months? That take guts. Can you deliver?"

"Yes, sir." Boone was confident he could. He'd studied this stuff for years. Dreamed about it, debated it, played with the numbers and particulars until he could speak with confidence about every aspect of the community he wanted to build. He and his friends had gained a greater working knowledge of the fallout from climate change than any of them had gone looking for when they joined the Navy SEALs. They'd realized most of the conflicts that spawned the missions they took on were caused in one way or the other by struggles over resources, usually exacerbated by climate conditions. When rains didn't come and crops failed, unrest was sure to follow. Next came partisan politics, rebellions, coups and more. It didn't take a genius to see that climate change and scarcity of resources would be two prongs spearheading trouble around the world for decades to come.

"And you'll start with four families, building up to ten within that time frame?"

Boone blinked. Families? "Actually, sir…" He'd said nothing about families. Four *men*, building up to ten. That's what he had written in his proposal.

"This is brilliant. Too brilliant." Fulsom's direct gaze caught his own. "You see, we were going to launch a community of our own, but when I saw your proposal, I said, 'This man has already done the hard work; why reinvent the wheel? I can't think of anyone better to lead such a project than someone like Boone Rudman.'"

Boone stifled a grin. This was going better than he could have dreamed. "Thank you, sir."

Fulsom leaned forward. "The thing is, Boone, you have to do it right."

"Of course, sir, but about—"

"It has to be airtight. You have to prove you're sustainable. You have to prove your food systems are self-perpetuating, that you have a strategy to deal with waste, that you have contingency plans. What you've written here?" He held up Boone's proposal package. "It's genius. Genius. But the real question is—who's going to give a shit about it?"

"Well, hell—" Fulsom's abrupt change of tone startled Boone into defensiveness. He knew about the man's legendary high-octane personality, but he hadn't been prepared for this kind of bait and switch. "You yourself just said—"

Fulsom waved the application at him. "I love this stuff. It makes me hard. But the American public? That's a totally different matter. They don't find this shit sexy. It's not enough to jerk me off, Boone. We're trying to turn on the whole world."

"O-okay." Shit. Fulsom was going to turn him down after all. Boone gripped the arms of his chair, waiting for the axe to fall.

"So the question is, how do we make the world care about your community? And not just care about it—be so damn obsessed with it they can't think about anything else?" He didn't wait for an answer. "I'll tell you how. We're going to give you your own reality television show. Think of it. The whole world watching you go from ground zero to full-on sustainable community. Rooting for you. Cheering when you triumph. Crying when you fail. A worldwide audience fully engaged with you and your followers."

"That's an interesting idea," Boone said slowly. It was an insane idea. There was no way anyone would spend their time watching him dig garden beds and install photovoltaic panels. He couldn't think of anything less exciting to watch on television. And he didn't have followers. He had three like-minded friends who'd signed on to work with him. Friends who even now were bristling at this characterization of their roles. "Like I said, Mr. Fulsom, each of the *equal* participants in the community have pledged to document our progress. We'll take lots of photos and post them with our entries on a daily blog."

"Blogs are for losers." Fulsom leaned forward. "Come on, Boone. Don't you want to change the world?"

"Yes, I do." Anger curled within him. He was serious about these issues. Deadly serious. Why was Fulsom making a mockery of him? You couldn't win any kind of war with reality television, and Boone approached his sustainable community as if he was waging a war—a war on waste, a war on the future pain and suffering of the entire planet.

"I get it. You think I'm nuts," Fulsom said. "You think I've finally blown my lid. Well, I haven't. I'm a free-thinker, Boone, not a crazy man. I know how to get the message across to the masses. Always have. And I've always been criticized for it, too. Who cares? You know what I care about? This world. The people on it. The plants and animals and atmosphere. The whole grand, beautiful spectacle that we're currently dragging down into the muck of overconsumption. That's what I care about. What about you?"

"I care about it, too, but I don't want—"

"You don't want to be made a fool of. Fair enough. You're afraid of exposing yourself to scrutiny. You're afraid you'll fuck up on television. Well guess what? You're right; you will fuck up. But the audience is going to love you so much by that time, that if you cry, they'll cry with you. And when you triumph—and you *will* triumph—they'll feel as ecstatic as if they'd done it all themselves. Along the way they'll learn more about solar power, wind power, sustainable agriculture and all the rest of it than we could ever force-feed them through documentaries or classes. You watch, Boone. We're going to do something magical."

Boone stared at him. Fulsom was persuasive, he'd give him that. "About the families, sir."

"Families are non-negotiable." Fulsom set the application down and gazed at Boone, then each of his friends in turn. "You men are pioneers, but pioneers are a yawn-fest until they bring their wives to the frontier. Throw in women, and goddamn, that's interesting! Women talk. They complain. They'll take your plans for sustainability and kick them to the curb unless you make them easy to use and satisfying. What's more, women are a hell of lot more interesting than men. Sex, Boone. Sex sells cars and we're going to use it to sell sustainability, too. Are you with me?"

"I…" Boone didn't know what to say. Use sex to sell sustainability? "I don't think—"

"Of course you're with me. A handsome Navy SEAL like you has to have a girl. You do, don't you? Have a girl?"

"A girl?" Had he been reduced to parroting everything Fulsom said? Boone tried to pull himself together. He definitely did not have a *girl*. He dated when he had time, but he kept things light. He'd never felt it was fair to enter a more serious relationship as long as he was throwing himself into danger on a daily basis. He'd always figured he'd settle down when he left the service and he was looking forward to finally having the time to meet a potential mate. God knew his parents were all too ready for grandkids. They talked about it all the time.

"A woman, a fiancée. Maybe you already have a wife?" Fulsom looked hopeful and his secretary nodded at Boone, as if telling him to say yes.

"Well...."

He was about to say no, but the secretary shook her head rapidly and made a slicing motion across her neck. Since she hadn't engaged in the conversation at all previously, Boone decided he'd better take her signals seriously. He'd gotten some of his best intel in the field just this way. A subtle nod from a veiled woman, or a pointed finger just protruding from a burka had saved his neck more than once. Women were crafty when it counted.

"I'm almost married," he blurted. His grip on the arms of his chair tightened. None of this was going like he'd planned. Jericho and Clay turned to stare at him like he'd lost his mind. Behind him Walker chuckled. "I mean—"

"Excellent! Can't wait to meet your better half.

What about the rest of you?" Fulsom waved them off before anyone else could speak. "Never mind. Julie here will get all that information from you later. As long as you've got a girl, Boone, everything's going to be all right. The fearless leader has to have a woman by his side. It gives him that sense of humanity our viewers crave." Julie nodded like she'd heard this many times before.

Boone's heart sunk even further. Fearless leader? Fulsom didn't understand his relationship with the others at all. Walker was his superior officer, for God's sake. Still, Fulsom was waiting for his answer, with a shrewd look in his eyes that told Boone he wasn't fooled at all by his hasty words. Their funding would slip away unless he convinced Fulsom that he was dedicated to the project—as Fulsom wanted it to be done.

"I understand completely," Boone said, although he didn't understand at all. His project was about sustainability. It wasn't some human-interest story. "I'm with you one hundred percent."

"Then I've got a shitload of cash to send your way. Don't let me down."

"I won't." He felt rather than heard the others shifting, biting back their protests.

Fulsom leaned so close his head nearly filled the screen. "We'll start filming June first and I look forward to meeting your fiancée when I arrive. Understand? Not a girlfriend, not a weekend fling—a fiancée. I want weddings, Boone." He looked over the four of them again. "Four weddings. Yours will kick off the series. I can see it now; an empty stretch of land. Two modern pioneers in love. A country parson performing the ceremony. The bride holding a bouquet of wildflowers the groom picked just minutes before. Their first night together in a lonely tent. Magic, Boone. That's prime time magic. *Surviving on the Land* meets *The First Six Months.*"

Boone nodded, swallowing hard. He'd seen those television shows. The first tracked modern-day mountain men as they pitted themselves against crazy weather conditions in extreme locations. The second followed two newlyweds for six months, and documented their every move, embrace, and lovers' quarrel as they settled into married life. He didn't relish the idea of starring in any show remotely like those.

Besides, June first was barely two months away. He'd only get out of the Navy at the end of April. They hadn't even found a property to build on yet.

"There'll be four of you men to start," Fulsom went on. "That means we need four women for episode one; your fiancée and three other hopeful single ladies. Let the viewers do the math, am I right? They'll start pairing you off even before we do. We'll add other community members as we go. Six more men and six more women ought to do it, don't you think?"

"Yes, sir." This was getting worse by the minute.

"Now, I've given you a hell of a shock today. I get that. So let me throw you a bone. I've just closed on the perfect piece of property for your community. Fifteen hundred acres of usable land with creeks, forest, pasture and several buildings. I'm going to give it to you free and clear to use for the duration of the series. If—and only if—you meet your goals, I'll sign it over to you lock, stock and barrel at the end of the last show."

Boone sat up. That was a hell of a bone. "Where is it?"

"Little town called Chance Creek, Montana. I believe you've heard of it?" Fulsom laughed at his reaction. Even Walker was startled. Chance Creek? They'd grown up there. Their families still lived there.

They were going home.

Chills marched up and down his spine and Boone wondered if his friends felt the same way. He'd hardly even let himself dream about that possibility. None of them came from wealthy families and none of them would inherit land. He'd figured they'd go where it was cheapest, and ranches around Chance Creek didn't come cheap. Not these days. Like everywhere else, the town had seen a slump during the last recession, but now prices were up again and he'd heard from his folks that developers were circling, talking about expanding the town. Boone couldn't picture that.

"Let me see here. I believe it's called... Westfield," Fulsom said. Julie nodded, confirming his words. "Hasn't been inhabited for over a decade. A local caretaker has been keeping an eye on it, but there hasn't been cattle on it for at least that long. The heir to the property lives in Europe now. Must have finally decided he wasn't ever going to take up ranching. When he put it on the market, I snapped it up real quick."

Westfield.

Boone sat back even as his friends shifted behind him again. Westfield was a hell of a property—owned by the Eaton family for as long as anyone could remember. He couldn't believe it wasn't a working ranch anymore. But if the old folks were gone, he guessed that made sense. They must have passed away not long after he had left Chance Creek. They wouldn't have broken up the property, so Russ Eaton would have inherited and Russ wasn't much for ranching. Neither was his younger brother, Michael. As far as Boone knew, Russ hadn't married, which left Michael's daughter the only possible candidate to run the place.

Riley Eaton.

Was it a coincidence that had brought her to mind just moments before Fulsom's call, or something more?

Coincidence, Boone decided, even as the more impulsive side of him declared it Fate.

A grin tugged at his mouth as he remembered Riley as she used to be, the tomboy who tagged along after him every summer when they were kids. Riley lived for vacations on her grandparents' ranch. Her mother would send her off each year dressed up for the journey, and the minute Riley reached Chance Creek she'd wad up those fancy clothes and spend the rest of the summer in jeans, boots and an old Stetson passed down from her grandma. Boone and his friends hired on at Westfield most summers to earn some spending money. Riley stuck to them like glue, learning as much as she could about riding and ranching from them. When she was little, she used to cry when August ended and she had to go back home. As she grew older, she hid her feelings better, but Boone knew she'd always adored the ranch. It wasn't surprising, given her home life. Even when he was young, he'd heard the gossip and knew things were rough back in Chicago.

As much as he and the others had complained about being saddled with a follower like Riley, she'd earned their grudging respect as the years went on. Riley never complained, never wavered in her loyalty to them, and as many times as they left her behind, she was always ready to try again to convince them to let her join them in their exploits.

"It's a crime," he'd once heard his mother say to a friend on the phone. "Neither mother nor father has any time for her at all. No wonder she'll put up with anything those boys dish out. I worry for her."

Boone understood now what his mother was afraid of, but at the time he'd shrugged it off and over the years Riley had become a good friend. Sometimes when they were alone fishing, or riding, or just hanging out on her grandparents' porch, Boone would find himself telling her things he'd never told anyone else. As far as he knew, she'd never betrayed a confidence.

Riley was the one who dubbed Boone, Clay, Jericho and Walker the Four Horsemen of the Apocalypse, a nickname that had stuck all these years. When they'd become obsessed with the idea of being Navy SEALs, Riley had even tried to keep up with the same training regimen they'd adopted.

Boone wished he could say they'd always treated Riley as well as she treated them, but that wasn't the truth of it. One of his most shameful memories centered around the slim girl with the long brown braids. Things had become complicated once he and his friends began to date. They had far less time for Riley, who was two years younger and still a kid in their eyes, and she'd withdrawn when she realized their girlfriends didn't want her around. She still hung out when they worked at Westfield, though, and was old enough to be a real help with the work. Some of Boone's best memories were of early mornings mucking out stables with Riley. They didn't talk much, just worked side by side until the job was done. From time to time they walked out to a spot on the ranch where the land fell away and they could see the mountains in the distance. Boone had never quantified how he felt during those times. Now he realized what a fool he'd been.

He hadn't given a thought to how his girlfriends affected her or what it would be like for Riley when they left for the Navy. He'd been too young. Too utterly self-absorbed.

That same year he'd had his first serious relationship, with a girl named Melissa Resnick. Curvy, flirty and oh-so-feminine, she'd slipped into his heart by slipping into his bed on Valentine's Day. By the time Riley came to town again that last summer, he and Melissa were seldom apart. Of all the girls the Horsemen had dated, Melissa was the least tolerant of Riley's presence, and one day when they'd all gone to a local swimming hole, she'd huffed in exasperation when the younger girl came along.

"It's like you've got a sidekick," she told Boone in everyone's hearing. "Good ol' Tagalong Riley."

Clay, Jericho, and Walker, who'd always treated Riley like a little sister, thought it was funny. They had their own girlfriends to impress, and the name had stuck. Boone knew he should put a stop to it, but the lure of Melissa's body was still too strong and he knew if he took Riley's side he'd lose his access to it.

Riley had held her head up high that day and she'd stayed at the swimming hole, a move that Boone knew must have cost her, but each repetition of the nickname that summer seemed to heap pain onto her shoulders, until she caved in on herself and walked with her head down.

The worst was the night before he and the Horsemen left to join the Navy. He hadn't seen Riley for several days, whereas he couldn't seem to shake Melissa for a minute. He should have felt flattered, but instead it had irritated him. More and more often, he had found himself wishing for Riley's calm company, but she'd stopped coming to help him.

Because everyone else seemed to expect it, he'd attended the hoe-down in town sponsored by the rodeo that last night. Melissa clung to him like a burr. Riley was nowhere to be found. Boone accepted every drink he was offered and was well on his way to being three sheets to the wind when Melissa excused herself to the ladies' room at about ten. Boone remained with the other Horsemen and their dates, and he could only stare when Riley appeared in front of him. For once she'd left her Stetson at home, her hair was loose from its braids, and she wore makeup and a mini skirt that left miles of leg between its hem and her dress cowboy boots.

Every nerve in his body had come to full alert and Boone had understood in that moment what he'd failed to realize all that summer. Riley had grown up. At sixteen, she was a woman. A beautiful woman who understood him far better than Melissa could hope to. He'd had a fleeting sense of lost time and missed opportunities before Clay had whistled. "Hell, Tagalong, you've gone and gotten yourself a pair of breasts."

"You better watch out dressed up like that; some guy will think you want more than you bargained for," Jericho said.

Walker's normally grave expression had grown even more grim.

Riley had ignored them all. She'd squared her shoulders, looked Boone in the eye and said, "Will you dance with me?"

Shame flooded Boone every time he thought back to that moment.

Riley had paid him a thousand kindnesses over the years, listened to some of his most intimate thoughts and fears, never judged him, made fun of him or cut him down the way his other friends sometimes did. She'd always been there for him, and all she'd asked for was one dance.

He should have said yes.

It wasn't the shake of Walker's head, or Clay and Jericho's laughter that stopped him. It was Melissa, who had returned in time to hear Riley's question, and answered for him.

"No one wants to dance with a Tagalong. Go on home."

Riley had waited one more moment—then fled.

Boone rarely thought about Melissa after he'd left Chance Creek and when he did it was to wonder what he'd ever found compelling in her. He thought about Riley far too often. He tried to remember the good times—teaching her to ride, shoot, trap and fish. The conversations and lazy days in the sun when they were kids. The intimacy that had grown up between them without him ever realizing it.

Instead, he thought of that moment—that awful, shameful moment when she'd begged him with her eyes to say yes, to throw her pride that single bone.

And he'd kept silent.

"Have you heard of the place?" Fulsom broke into his thoughts and Boone blinked. He'd been so far away it took a moment to come back. Finally, he nodded.

"I have." He cleared his throat to get the huskiness out of it. "Mighty fine ranch." He couldn't fathom why it hadn't passed down to Riley. Losing it must have broken her heart.

Again.

"So my people tell me. Heck of a fight to get it, too. Had a competitor, a rabid developer named Montague."

Fulsom shook his head. "But that gave me a perfect setup."

"What do you mean?" Boone's thoughts were still with the girl he'd once known. The woman who'd haunted him all these years. He forced himself to pay attention to Fulsom instead.

Fulsom clicked his keyboard and an image sprung up onscreen. "Take a look."

Letting his memories go, Boone tried to make sense of what he was seeing. Some kind of map—an architect's rendering of a planned development.

"What is that?" Clay demanded.

"Wait—that's Westfield." Jericho leaned over Boone's shoulder to get a better look.

"Almost right." Fulsom nodded. "Those are the plans for Westfield Commons, a community of seventy luxury homes."

Blood ran cold in Boone's veins as Walker elbowed his way between them and peered at the screen. "Luxury homes? On Westfield? You can't do that!"

"I don't want to. But Montague does. He's frothing at the mouth to bulldoze that ranch and sell it piece by piece. The big, bad developer versus the environmentalists. This show is going to write itself." He fixed his gaze on Boone. "And if you fail, the last episode will show his bulldozers closing in."

"But it's our land; you just said so," Boone protested.

"As long as you meet your goals by December first. Ten committed couples—every couple married by the time the show ends. Ten homes whose energy require-ments are one-tenth the normal usage for an American home. Six months' worth of food produced on site stockpiled to last the inhabitants through the winter. And three children."

"Children? Where do we get those?" Boone couldn't keep up. He hadn't promised anything like that. All he'd said in his proposal was that they'd build a community.

"The old-fashioned way. You make them. No cheat-ing; children conceived before the show starts don't count."

"Jesus." Fulsom had lost his mind. He was taking the stakes and raising them to outrageous heights… which was exactly the way to create a prime-time hit, Boone realized.

"It takes nine months to have a child," Jericho pointed out dryly.

"I didn't say they needed to be born. Pregnant bel-lies are better than squalling babies. Like I said, sex sells, boys. Let's give our viewers proof you and your wives are getting it on."

Boone had had enough. "That's ridiculous, Fulsom. You're—"

"You know what's ridiculous?" Fulsom leaned for-ward again, suddenly grim. "Famine. Poverty. Violence. War. And yet it never stops, does it? You said you wanted to do something about it. Here's your chance. You're leaving the Navy, for God's sake. Don't tell me you didn't plan to meet a woman, settle down and raise some kids. So I've put a rush on the matter. Sue me."

He had a point. But still—

"I could sell the land to Montague today," Fulsom said. "Pocket the money and get back to sorting out hydrogen fuel cells." He waited a beat. When Boone shook his head, Fulsom smiled in triumph. "Gotta go, boys. Julie, here, will get you all sorted out. Good luck to you on this fabulous venture. Remember—we're going to change the world together."

"Wait—"

Fulsom stood up and walked off screen.

Boone stared as Julie sat down in his place. By the time she had walked them through the particulars of the funding process, and when and how to take possession of the land, Boone's temples were throbbing. He cut the call after Julie promised to send a packet of information, reluctantly pushed his chair back from the table and faced the three men who were to be his partners in this venture.

"Married?" Clay demanded. "No one said anything about getting married!"

"I know."

"And kids? Three out of ten of us men will have to get their wives pregnant. That means all of us will have to be trying just to beat the odds," Jericho said.

"I know."

Walker just looked at him and shook his head.

"I get it! None of us planned for anything like this." Boone stood up. "But none of us thought we had a shot of moving back to Chance Creek, either—or getting our message out to the whole country." When no one answered, he went on. "Are you saying you're out?"

"Hell, I don't know," Jericho said, pacing around the room. "I could stomach anything except that marriage part. I've never seen myself as a family man."

"I don't mind getting hitched," Clay said. "And I want kids. But I want to choose where and when to do it. And Fulsom's setting us up to fail in front of a national audience. If that Montague guy gets the ranch and builds a subdivision on it, everyone in town is going to hate us—and our families."

"So what do we do?" Boone challenged him.

"Not much choice," Walker said. "If we don't sign on, Fulsom will sell to Montague anyway."

"Exactly. The only shot we have of saving that ranch is to agree to his demands," Boone said. He shoved his hands in his pockets, unsure what to do. He couldn't see himself married in two months, let alone trying to have a child with a woman he hadn't even met yet, but giving up—Boone hated to think about it. After all, it wouldn't be the first time they'd done unexpected things to accomplish a mission.

Jericho paced back. "But his demands are—"

"Insane. I know that." Boone knew he was losing them. "He's right, though; a sustainable community made only of men doesn't mean shit. A community that's actually going to sustain itself—to carry on into the future, generation after generation—has to include women and eventually kids. Otherwise we're just playing."

"Fulsom's the one who's playing. Playing with our

lives. He can't demand we marry someone for the sake of his ratings," Jericho said.

"Actually, he can," Clay said. "He's the one with the cash."

"We'll find cash somewhere else—"

"It's more than cash," Boone reminded Jericho. "It's publicity. If we build a community and no one knows about it, what good is it? We went to Fulsom because we wanted him to do just what he's done—find a way to make everyone talk about sustainability."

"By marrying us off one by one?" Jericho stared at each of them in turn. "Are you serious? We just spent the last thirteen years of our lives fighting for our country—"

"And now we're going to fight for it in a whole new way. By getting married. On television. And knocking up our wives—while the whole damn world watches," Boone said.

No one spoke for a minute.

"I sure as hell hope they won't film that part, Chief," Clay said with a quick grin, using the moniker Boone had gained in the SEALs as second in command of his platoon.

"They wouldn't want to film your hairy ass, anyway," Jericho said.

Clay shoved him. Jericho elbowed him away.

"Enough." Walker's single word settled all of them down. They were used to listening to their lieutenant. Walker turned to Boone. "You think this will actually do any good?"

Boone shrugged. "Remember Yemen. Remember what's coming. We swore we'd do what it takes to make a difference." It was a low blow bringing up that disaster, but it was what had gotten them started down this path and he wanted to remind them of it.

"I remember Yemen every day," Jericho said, all trace of clowning around gone.

"So do I." Clay sighed. "Hell, I'm ready for a family anyway. I'm in. I don't know how I'll find a wife, though. Ain't had any luck so far."

"I'll find you one," Boone told him.

"Thanks, Chief." Clay gave him an ironic salute.

Jericho walked away. Came back again. "Damn it. I'm in, too. Under protest, though. Something this serious shouldn't be a game. You find me a wife, too, Chief, but I'll divorce her when the six months are up if I don't like her."

"Wait until Fulsom's given us the deed to the ranch, then do what you like," Boone said. "But if I'm picking your bride, give her a chance."

"Sure, Chief."

Boone didn't trust that answer, but Jericho had agreed to Fulsom's terms and that's all that mattered for now. He looked to Walker. It was crucial that the man get on board. Walker stared back at him, his gaze unfathomable. Boone knew there was trouble in his past. Lots of trouble. The man avoided women whenever he could.

Finally Walker gave him a curt nod. "Find me one, too. Don't screw it up."

Boone let out the breath he was holding. Despite the events of the past hour, a surge of anticipation warmed him from within.

They were going to do it.

And he was going to get hitched.

Was Riley the marrying kind?

RILEY EATON TOOK a sip of her green tea and summoned a smile for the friends who'd gathered on the tiny balcony of her apartment in Boston. Her thoughts were far away, though, tangled in a memory of a hot Montana afternoon when she was only ten. She'd crouched on the bank of Pittance Creek watching Boone Rudman wade through the knee-deep waters, fishing for minnows with a net. Riley had followed Boone everywhere back then, but she knew to stay out of the water and not scare his bait away.

"Mom said marriage is a trap set by men for unsuspecting women," she'd told him, quoting what she'd heard her mother say to a friend over the phone.

"You'd better watch out then," he'd said, poised to scoop up a handful of little fish.

"I won't get caught. Someone's got to want to catch you before that happens."

Boone had straightened, his net trailing in the water. She'd never forgotten the way he'd looked at her—all earnest concern.

"Maybe I'll catch you."

"Why?" She'd been genuinely curious. Getting overlooked was something she'd already grown used to.

"For my wife. If I ever want one. You'll never see me coming." He'd lifted his chin as if she'd argue the point. But Riley had thought it over and knew he was right.

She'd nodded. "You are pretty sneaky."

Riley had never forgotten that conversation, but Boone had and like everyone else he'd overlooked her when the time counted.

Story of her life.

Riley shook off the maudlin thoughts. She couldn't be a good hostess if she was wrapped up in her troubles. Time enough for them when her friends had gone.

She took another sip of her tea and hoped they wouldn't notice the tremor in her hands. She couldn't believe seven years had passed since she'd graduated from Boston College with the women who relaxed on the cheap folding chairs around her. Back then she'd thought she'd always have these women by her side, but now these yearly reunions were the only time she saw them. They were all firmly ensconced in careers that consumed their time and energy. It was hard enough to stay afloat these days, let alone get ahead in the world—or have time to take a break.

Gone were the carefree years when they thought nothing of losing whole weekends to trying out a new art medium, or picking up a new instrument. Once she'd been fearless, throwing paint on the canvas, guided only by her moods. She'd experimented day after day, laughed at the disasters and gloried in the triumphs that took shape under her brushes from time to time. Now she rarely even sketched, and what she produced seemed inane. If she wanted to express the truth of her situation through her art, she'd paint pigeons and gum stuck to the sidewalk. But she wasn't honest anymore.

For much of the past five years she'd been married to her job as a commercial artist at a vitamin distributor, joined to it twenty-four seven through her cell phone and Internet connection. Those years studying art seemed like a dream now; the one time in her life she'd felt like she'd truly belonged somewhere. She had no idea how she'd thought she'd earn a living with a fine arts degree, though. She supposed she'd hadn't thought much about the future back then. Now she felt trapped by it.

Especially after the week she'd had.

She set her cup down and twisted her hands together, trying to stop the shaking. It had started on Wednesday when she'd been called into her boss's office and handed a pink slip and a box in which to pack up her things.

"Downsizing. It's nothing personal," he'd told her.

She didn't know how she'd kept her feet as she'd made her way out of the building. She wasn't the only one riding the elevator down to street level with her belongings in her hands, but that was cold comfort. It had been hard enough to find this job. She had no idea where to start looking for another.

She'd held in her shock and panic that night and all the next day until Nadia from the adoption agency knocked on her door for their scheduled home visit at precisely two pm. She'd managed to answer Nadia's questions calmly and carefully, until the woman put down her pen.

"Tell me about your job, Riley. How will you as a single mother balance work and home life with a child?"

Riley had opened her mouth to speak, but no answer had come out. She'd reached for her cup of tea, but only managed to spill it on the cream colored skirt she'd chosen carefully for the occasion. As Nadia rushed to help her mop up, the truth had spilled from Riley's lips.

"I've just been downsized. I'm sorry; I'll get a new job right away. This doesn't have to change anything, does it?"

Nadia had been sympathetic but firm. "This is why we hesitate to place children with single parents, Riley. Children require stability. We can continue the interview and I'll weigh all the information in our judgement, but until you can prove you have a stable job, I'm afraid you won't qualify for a child."

"That will take years," Riley had almost cried, but she'd bitten back the words. What good would it do to say them aloud? As a girl, she'd dreamed she'd have children with Boone someday. When she'd grown up, she'd thought she'd find someone else. Hadn't she waited long enough to start her family?

"Riley? Are you all right?" Savannah Edwards asked, bringing her back to the present.

"Of course." She had to be. There was no other option but to soldier on. She needed to get a new job. A better job. She needed to excel at it and put the time in to make herself indispensable. Then, in a few years, she could try again to adopt.

"Are you sure?" A tall blonde with hazel eyes, Savannah had been Riley's best friend back in school, and Riley had always had a hard time fooling her. Savannah had been a music major and Riley could have listened to her play forever. She was the first person Riley had met since her grandparents passed away who seemed to care about her wholeheartedly. Riley's parents had been too busy arguing with each other all through her childhood to have much time left over to think about her. They split up within weeks after she left for college. Each remarried before the year was out and both started new families soon after. Riley felt like the odd man out when she visited them on holidays. More than eighteen years older than her half-siblings, she didn't seem to belong anywhere now.

"I'm great now that you three are here." She wouldn't confess the setback that had just befallen her. It was still too raw to process and she didn't want to bring the others down when they'd only just arrived. She wasn't the only one who had it tough. Savannah should have been a concert pianist, but when she broke her wrist in a car accident several years after graduation, she had to give up her aspirations. Instead, she had gone to work as an assistant at a prominent tech company in Silicon Valley and was still there.

"What's on tap for the weekend?" Nora Ridgeway asked as she scooped her long, wavy, light brown hair into a messy updo and secured it with a clip. She'd flown in from Baltimore where she taught English in an inner-city high school. Riley had been shocked to see the dark smudges under her eyes. Nora looked thin. Too thin. Riley wondered what secrets she was hiding behind her upbeat tone.

"I hope it's a whole lot of nothing," Avery Lightfoot said, her auburn curls glinting in the sun. Avery lived in Nashville and worked in the marketing department of one of the largest food distribution companies in North America. She'd studied acting in school, but she'd never been discovered the way she'd once hoped to be. For a brief time she'd created an original video series that she'd posted online, but the advertising revenue she'd generated hadn't added up to much and soon her money had run out. Now she created short videos to market low-carb products to yoga moms. Riley's heart ached for her friend. She sounded as tired as Nora looked.

In fact, everyone looked like they needed a pick-me-up after dealing with flights and taxis, and Riley headed inside to get refreshments. She wished she'd been able to drive to the airport and pick them up. Who could afford a car, though? Even when she'd had a job, Riley found it hard to keep up with her rent, medical insurance and monthly bills, and budget enough for the childcare she'd need when she adopted. Thank God it had been her turn to host their gathering this year. She couldn't have gotten on a plane after the news she'd just received.

When she thought back to her college days she realized her belief in a golden future had really been a pipe dream. Some of her classmates were doing fine. But most of them were struggling to keep their heads above water, just like her. A few had given up and moved back in with their parents.

When she got back to the balcony with a tray of snacks, she saw Savannah pluck a dog-eared copy of *Pride and Prejudice* out of a small basket that sat next to the door. Riley had been reading it in the mornings before work this week as she drank her coffee—until she'd been let go. A little escapism helped start her day off on the right foot.

"Am I the only one who'd trade my life for one of Austen's characters' in a heartbeat?" Savannah asked, flipping through the pages.

"You want to live in Regency England? And be some man's property?" Nora asked sharply.

"Of course not. I don't want the class conflict or the snobbery or the outdated rules. But I want the beauty of their lives. I want the music and the literature. I want afternoon visits and balls that last all night. Why don't we do those things anymore?"

"Who has time for that?" Riley certainly hadn't when she was working. Now she'd have to spend every waking moment finding a new job.

"I haven't played the piano in ages," Savannah went on. "I mean, it's not like I'm all that good anymore—"

"Are you kidding? You've always been fantastic," Nora said.

"What about romance? I'd kill for a real romance. One that means something," Avery said.

"What about Dan?" Savannah asked.

"I broke up with him three weeks ago. He told me he wasn't ready for a serious relationship. The man's thirty-one. If he's not ready now, when will he be?"

"That's tough." Riley understood what Avery meant. She hadn't had a date in a year; not since Marc Hepstein had told her he didn't consider her marriage material. She should have dumped him long before.

It wasn't like she hadn't been warned. His older sister had taken her aside once and spelled it out for her:

"Every boy needs to sow his wild oats. You're his shiksa fling. You'll see; you won't get a wedding ring from him. Marc will marry a nice Jewish girl in the end."

Riley wished she'd paid attention to the warning, but of course she hadn't. She had a history of dangling after men who were unavailable.

Shiksa fling.

Just a step up from Tagalong Riley.

Riley pushed down the old insecurities that threatened to take hold of her and tried not to give in to her pain over her lost chance to adopt. When Marc had broken up with her, it had been a wake-up call. She'd realized if she waited for a man to love her, she might never experience the joy of raising a child. She'd also realized she hadn't loved Marc enough to spend a life with him. She'd been settling, and she was better than that.

She'd started the adoption process.

Now she'd have to start all over again.

"It wasn't as hard to leave him as you might think." Avery took a sip of her tea. "It's not just Dan. I feel like breaking up with my life. I had a heart once. I know I did. I used to feel—alive."

"Me, too," Nora said softly.

"I thought I'd be married by now," Savannah said, "but I haven't had a boyfriend in months. And I hate my job. I mean, I really hate it!" Riley couldn't remember ever seeing calm, poised Savannah like this.

"So do I," Avery said, her words gushing forth as if a dam had broken. "Especially since I have two of them now. I got back in debt when my car broke down and I needed to buy a new one. Now I can't seem to get ahead."

"I don't have any job at all," Riley confessed. "I've been downsized." She closed her eyes. She hadn't meant to say that.

"Oh my goodness, Riley," Avery said. "What are you going to do?"

"I don't know. Paint?" She laughed dully. She couldn't tell them the worst of it. She was afraid if she talked about her failed attempt to adopt she'd lose control of her emotions altogether. "Can you imagine a life in which we could actually pursue our dreams?"

"No," Avery said flatly. "After what happened last time, I'm so afraid if I try to act again, I'll just make a fool of myself."

Savannah nodded vigorously, tears glinting in her eyes. "I'm afraid to play," she confessed. "I sit down at my piano and then I get up again without touching the keys. What if my talent was all a dream? What if I was fooling myself and I was never anything special at all? My wrist healed years ago, but I can't make myself go for it like I once did. I'm too scared."

"What about you, Nora? Do you ever write these days?" Riley asked gently when Nora remained quiet. When they were younger, Nora talked all the time about wanting to write a novel, but she hadn't mentioned it in ages. Riley had assumed it was because she loved teaching, but she looked as burnt out as the rest of them. Riley knew she worked in an area of Baltimore that resembled a war zone.

Her friend didn't answer, but a tear traced down her cheek.

"Nora, what is it?" Savannah dropped the book and came to crouch by her chair.

"It's one of my students." Nora kept her voice steady even as another tear followed the tracks of the first. "At least I think it is."

"What do you mean?" Riley realized they'd all pulled closer to each other, leaning forward in mutual support and feeling. Dread crept into her throat at Nora's words. She'd known instinctively something was wrong in her friend's life for quite some time, but despite her questions, Nora's e-mails and texts never revealed a thing.

"I've been getting threats. On my phone," Nora said, plucking at a piece of lint on her skirt.

"Someone's texting threats?" Savannah sounded aghast.

"And calling. He has my home number, too."

"What did he say?" Avery asked.

"Did he threaten to hurt you?" Riley demanded. After a moment, Nora nodded.

"To kill you?" Avery whispered.

Nora nodded again. "And more."

Savannah's expression hardened. "More?"

Nora looked up. "He threatened to rape me. He said I'd like it. He got... really graphic."

The four of them stared at each other in shocked silence.

"You can't go back," Savannah said. "Nora, you can't go back there. I don't care how important your work is, that's too much."

"What did the police say?" Riley's hands were shaking again. Rage and shock battled inside of her, but anger won out. Who would dare threaten her friend?

"What did the school's administration say?" Avery demanded.

"That threats happen all the time. That I should change my phone numbers. That the people who make the threats usually don't act on them."

"Usually?" Riley was horrified.

"What are you going to do?" Savannah said.

"What am I supposed to do? I can't quit." Nora seemed to sink into herself. "I changed my number, but it's happening again. I've got nothing saved. I managed to pay off my student loans, but then my mom got sick... I'm broke."

No one answered. They knew Nora's family hadn't

had much money, and she'd taken on debt to get her degree. Riley figured she'd probably used every penny she might have saved to pay it off again. Then her mother had contracted cancer and had gone through several expensive procedures before she passed away.

"Is this really what it's come to?" Avery asked finally. "Our work consumes us, or it overwhelms us, or it threatens us with bodily harm and we just keep going?"

"And what happened to love? True love?" Savannah's voice was raw. "Look at us! We're intelligent, caring, attractive women. And we're all single! None of us even dating. What about kids? I thought I'd be a mother."

"So did I," Riley whispered.

"Who can afford children?" Nora said fiercely. "I thought teaching would be enough. I thought my students would care—" She broke off and Riley's heart squeezed at Nora's misery.

"I've got some savings, but I'll eat through them fast if I don't get another job," Riley said slowly. "I want to leave Boston so badly. I want fresh air and a big, blue sky. But there aren't any jobs in the country." Memories of just such a sky flooded her mind. What she'd give for a vacation at her uncle's ranch in Chance Creek, Montana. In fact, she'd love to go there and never come back. It had been so long since she'd managed to stop by and spend a weekend at Westfield, it made her ache to think of the carefree weeks she spent there every summer as a child. The smell of hay and horses and sunshine on old buildings, the way her grandparents used to let her loose on the ranch to run and play and ride as hard as she wanted to. Their unconditional love. There were few rules at Westfield and those existed purely for the sake of practicality and safety. *Don't spook the horses. Clean and put away tools after you use them. Be home at mealtimes and help with the dishes.*

Away from her parents' arguing, Riley had blossomed, and the skills she'd learned from the other kids in town—especially the Four Horsemen of the Apocalypse—had taught her pride and self-confidence. They were rough and tumble boys and they rarely slowed down to her speed, but as long as she kept up to them, they included her in their fun.

Clay Pickett, Jericho Cook, Walker Norton—they'd treated her like a sister. For an only child, it was a dream come true. But it was Boone who'd become a true friend, and her first crush.

And then had broken her heart.

"I keep wondering if it will always be like this," Avery said, interrupting her thoughts. "If I'll always have to struggle to get by. If I'll never have a house of my own—or a husband or family."

"You'll have a family," Riley assured her, then bit her lip. Who was she to reassure Avery? She could never seem to shake her bad luck—with men, with work, with anything. But out of all the things that had happened to her, nothing left her cringing with humiliation like the memory of the time she'd asked Boone to dance.

She'd been such a child. No one like Boone would have looked twice at her, no matter how friendly he'd been over the years. She could still hear Melissa's sneering words—*No one wants to dance with a Tagalong. Go on home*—and the laughter that followed her when she fled the dance.

She'd returned to Chicago that last summer thinking her heart would never mend, and time had just begun to heal it when her grandparents passed away one after the other in quick succession that winter. Riley had been devastated; doubly so when she left for college the following year and her parents split. It was as if a tidal wave had washed away her childhood in one blow. After that, her parents sold their home and caretakers watched over the ranch. Uncle Russ, who'd inherited it, had found he made a better financier than a cowboy. With his career taking off, he'd moved to Europe soon after.

At his farewell dinner, one of the few occasions she'd seen her parents in the same room since they'd divorced, he'd stood up and raised a glass. "To Riley. You're the only one who loves Westfield now, and I want you to think of it as yours. One day in the future it will be, you know. While I'm away, I hope you'll treat it as your own home. Visit as long as you like. Bring your friends. Enjoy the ranch. My parents would have wanted that." He'd taken her aside later and presented her with a key. His trust in her and his promises had warmed her heart. If she'd own Westfield one day she could stand anything, she'd told herself that night. It was the one thing that had sustained her through life's repeated blows.

"I wish I could run away from my life, even for a little while. Six months would do it," Savannah said, breaking into her thoughts. "If I could clear my mind of everything that has happened in the past few years I know I could make a fresh start."

Riley knew just what she meant. She'd often wished the same thing, but she didn't only want to run away from her life; she wanted to run straight back into her past to a time when her grandparents were still alive. Things had been so simple then.

Until she'd fallen for Boone.

She hadn't seen Uncle Russ since he'd moved away, although she wrote to him a couple of times a year, and received polite, if remote, answers in turn. She had the feeling Russ had found the home of his heart in Munich. She wondered if he'd ever come back to Montana.

In the intervening years she'd visited Westfield whenever she could, more frequently as the sting of Boone's betrayal faded, although in reality that meant a long weekend every three or four months, rather than the expansive summer vacations she'd imagined when she'd received the key. It wasn't quite the same without her grandparents and her old friends, without Boone and the Horsemen, but she still loved the country, and Westfield Manor was the stuff of dreams. Even the name evoked happy memories and she blessed the ancestor whose flight of fancy had bestowed such a distinguished title on a Montana ranch house. She'd always wondered if she'd stumble across Boone someday, home for leave, but their visits had never coincided.

Still, whenever she drove into Chance Creek, her heart rate kicked up a notch and she couldn't help scanning the streets for his familiar face.

"I wish I could run away from my dirty dishes and laundry," Avery said. Riley knew she was attempting to lighten the mood. "I spend my weekends taking care of all my possessions. I bet Jane Austen didn't do laundry."

"In those days servants did it," Nora said, swiping her arm over her cheek to wipe away the traces of her tears. "Maybe we should get servants, too, while we're dreaming."

"Maybe we should, if it means we could concentrate on the things we love," Savannah said.

"Like that's possible. Look at us—we're stuck, all of us. There's no way out." The waver in Nora's voice betrayed her fierceness.

"There has to be," Avery exclaimed.

"How?"

Riley wished she had the answer. She hated seeing the pain and disillusionment on her friends' faces. And she was terrified of having to start over herself.

"What if... what if we lived together?" Savannah said slowly. "I mean, wouldn't that be better than how things are now? If we pooled our resources and figured out how to make them stretch? None of us would have to work so hard."

"I thought you had a good job," Nora said, a little bitterly.

"On paper. The cost of living in Silicon Valley is outrageous, though. You'd be surprised how little is left over when I pay my bills. And inside, I feel… like I'm dying."

A silence stretched out between them. Riley knew just what Savannah meant. At first grown-up life had seemed exciting. Now it felt like she was slipping into a pool of quicksand that she'd never be able to escape. Maybe it would be different if they joined forces. If they pooled their money, they could do all kinds of things.

For the first time in months she felt a hint of possibility.

"We could move where the cost of living is cheaper and get a house together." Savannah warmed to her theme. "With a garden, maybe. We could work part time and share the bills."

"For six months? What good would that do? We'd run through what little money we have and be harder to employ afterward," Nora said.

"How much longer are you willing to wait before you try for the life you actually want, rather than the life that keeps you afloat one more day?" Savannah asked her. "I have to try to be a real pianist. Life isn't worth living if I don't give it a shot. That means practicing for hours every day. I can't do that and work a regular job, too."

"I've had an idea for a screenplay," Avery confessed. "I think it's really good. Six months would be plenty of time for me to write it. Then I could go back to work while I shop it around."

"If I had six months I would paint all day until I had enough canvasses to put on a show. Maybe that would be the start and end of my career as an artist, but at least I'd have done it once," Riley said.

"A house costs money," Nora said.

"Not always," Riley said slowly as an idea took hold in her head. "What about Westfield?" After all, it hadn't been inhabited in years. "Uncle Russ always said I should bring my friends and stay there."

"Long term?" Avery asked.

"Six months would be fine. Russ hasn't set foot in it in over a decade."

"You want us to move to Montana and freeload for six months?" Nora asked.

"I want us to move to Montana and take six months to jumpstart our lives. We'll practice following our passions. We'll brainstorm ideas together for how to make money from them. Who knows? Maybe together we'll come up with a plan that will work."

"Sounds good to me," Avery said.

"I don't know," Nora said. "Do you really think it's work that's kept you from writing or playing or painting? Because if you can't do it now, chances are you won't be able to do it at Westfield either. You'll busy up your days with errands and visits and sightseeing and all that. Wait and see."

"Not if we swore an oath to work on our projects every day," Savannah said.

"Like the oaths you used to swear to do your homework on time? Or not to drink on Saturday night? Or to stop crank-calling the guy who dumped you junior year?"

Savannah flushed. "I was a child back then—"

"I just feel that if we take six months off, we'll end up worse off than when we started."

Savannah leaned forward. "Come on. Six whole months to write. Aren't you dying to try it?" When Nora hesitated, Savannah pounced on her. "I knew it! You want to as badly as we do."

"Of course I want to," Nora said. "But it won't work. None of you will stay at home and hone your craft."

A smile tugged at Savannah's lips. "What if we couldn't leave?"

"Are you going to chain us to the house?"

"No. I'm going to take away your clothes. Your modern clothes," she clarified when the others stared at her. "You're right; we could easily be tempted to treat the time like a vacation, especially with us all together. But if we only have Regency clothes to wear, we'll be stuck because we'll be too embarrassed to go into town. We'll take a six-month long Jane Austen vacation from our lives." She sat back and folded her arms over her chest.

"I love it," Riley said. "Keep talking."

"We'll create a Regency life, as if we'd stepped into one of her novels. A beautiful life, with time for music and literature and poetry and walks. Westfield is rural, right? No one will be there to see us. If we pattern our days after the way Jane's characters spent theirs, we'd have plenty of time for creative pursuits."

Nora rolled her eyes. "What about the neighbors?

What about groceries and dental appointments?"

"Westfield is set back from the road." Riley thought it through. "Savannah's right; we could go for long stretches without seeing anyone. We could have things delivered, probably."

"I'm in," Avery said. "I'll swear to live a Regency life for six months. I'll swear it on penalty of... death."

"The penalty is embarrassment," Savannah said. "If we leave early, we have to travel home in our Regency clothes. I know I'm in. I'd gladly live a Jane Austen life for six months."

"If I get to wear Regency dresses and bonnets, I'm in too," Riley said. What was the alternative? Stay here and mourn the child she'd never have?

"Are you serious?" Nora asked. "Where do we even get those things?"

"We have a seamstress make them, or we sew them ourselves," Avery said. "Come on, Nora. Don't pretend you haven't always wanted to."

The others nodded. After all, it was their mutual love of Jane Austen movies that had brought them together in the first place. Two days into their freshman year at Boston College, Savannah had marched through the halls of their dorm announcing a Jane Austen film festival in her room that night. Riley, Nora and Avery had shown up for it, and the rest was history.

"It'll force us to carry out our plan the way we intend to," Savannah told her. "If we can't leave the ranch, there will be no distractions. Every morning when we put on our clothes we'll be recommitting to our vow to devote six months to our creative pursuits. Think about it, Nora. Six whole months to write."

"Besides, we were so good together back in college," Riley said. "We inspired each other. Why couldn't we do that again?"

"But what will we live on?"

"We'll each liquidate our possessions," Savannah said. "Think about how little most people had in Jane Austen's time. It'll be like when Eleanor and Marianne have to move to a cottage in *Sense and Sensibility* with their mother and little sister. We'll make a shoestring budget and stick to it for food and supplies. If we don't go anywhere, we won't spend any money, right?"

"That's right," Avery said. "Remember what Mrs. John Dashwood said in that novel. 'What on earth can four women want for more than that?—They will live so cheap! Their housekeeping will be nothing at all. They will have no carriage, no horses, and hardly any servants; they will keep no company, and can have no expenses of any kind! Only conceive how comfortable they will be!'"

"We certainly won't have any horses or carriages." Savannah laughed.

"But we will be comfortable, and during the time we're together we can brainstorm what to do next," Riley said. "No one leaves Westfield until we all have a working plan."

"With four of us to split the chores of running the house, it'll be easy," Avery said. "We'll have hours and hours to devote to our craft every day."

Nora hesitated. "You know this is crazy, right?"

"But it's exactly the right kind of crazy," Riley said. "You have to join us, Nora."

Nora shook her head, but just when Riley thought she'd refuse, she shrugged. "Oh, okay. What the hell? I'll do it." Riley's heart soared. "But when our six months are up, I'll be broke," Nora went on. "I'll be homeless, too. I don't see how anything will have improved."

"Everything will have improved," Savannah told her. "I promise. Together we can do anything."

Riley smiled at their old rallying-cry from college. "So, we're going to do it? You'll all come to Westfield with me? And wear funny dresses?"

"And bonnets," Avery said. "Don't forget the bonnets."

"I'm in," Savannah said, sticking out her hand.

"I'm in," Avery said, putting hers down on top of it.

"I guess I'm in," Nora said, and added hers to the pile.

"Well, I'm definitely in." Riley slapped hers down on top of the rest.

Westfield. She was going back to Westfield.

Things were looking up.

End of Excerpt

The Cowboys of Chance Creek Series:

The Cowboy Inherits a Bride (Volume 0)
The Cowboy's E-Mail Order Bride (Volume 1)
The Cowboy Wins a Bride (Volume 2)
The Cowboy Imports a Bride (Volume 3)
The Cowgirl Ropes a Billionaire (Volume 4)
The Sheriff Catches a Bride (Volume 5)
The Cowboy Lassos a Bride (Volume 6)
The Cowboy Rescues a Bride (Volume 7)
The Cowboy Earns a Bride (Volume 8)
The Cowboy's Christmas Bride (Volume 9)

The Heroes of Chance Creek Series:

The Navy SEAL's E-Mail Order Bride (Volume 1)
The Soldier's E-Mail Order Bride (Volume 2)
The Marine's E-Mail Order Bride (Volume 3)
The Navy SEAL's Christmas Bride (Volume 4)
The Airman's E-Mail Order Bride (Volume 5)

The SEALs of Chance Creek Series:

A SEAL's Oath
A SEAL's Vow
A SEAL's Pledge
A SEAL's Consent
A SEAL's Purpose
A SEAL's Resolve
A SEAL's Devotion
A SEAL's Desire
A SEAL's Struggle
A SEAL's Triumph

Brides of Chance Creek Series:

Issued to the Bride One Navy SEAL
Issued to the Bride One Airman
Issued to the Bride One Marine
Issued to the Bride One Sniper
Issued to the Bride One Soldier

About the Author

NYT and USA Today bestselling author Cora Seton loves cowboys, hiking, gardening, bike-riding, and lazing around with a good book. Mother of four, wife to a computer programmer/backyard farmer, she recently moved to Victoria and looks forward to a brand new chapter in her life. Like the characters in her Chance Creek series, Cora enjoys old-fashioned pursuits and modern technology, spending mornings in her garden, and afternoons writing the latest Chance Creek romance novel. Visit **www.coraseton.com** to read about new releases, contests and other cool events!

Blog:

www.coraseton.com

Facebook:

www.facebook.com/coraseton

Twitter:

www.twitter.com/coraseton

Newsletter:

www.coraseton.com/sign-up-for-my-newsletter